CW00552227

Editing: Alison Greene and Tarian P.S.
Book & Page Formatting: TPS Publishing
Cover Art: TPS Publishing

"Fall in love with a man who, when your last threads come unraveled, will catch you— and fall in love with you all over again,"

~ Pyotr Laszkovi

A Place for Cliff

THE DOMINION OF BROTHERS SERIES: BOOK 3

TALON P.S.

BESTSELLING BDSM EROTIC ROMANCE

BESTSELLING EROTIC SERIES

RAINBOW AWARDS 2nd PLACE FOR BEST MM EROTIC
ROMANCE OF THE YEAR

THE DOMINION OF BROTHERS SERIES

WRITTEN BY TALON P.S. & TARIAN P.S.

Five Brothers at Arms share a lust for control and bondage; now they are living the BDSM lifestyle openly, and they are the very Masters who can provide satisfaction to the world of Taboo.

Plenty of people love their kink, but when the Dominion of Brothers arrive in New York, the Lifestyle gets an empowering supporter; with not only a boost in stimulation, their fellow Lifestylers also get a guardian. As it just so happens, the Brothers will stop at nothing to protect their friends, loved ones, and those who look to them for the freedom of consensual sexual expression.

BECOMING HIS SLAVE

DOMMING THE HEIRESS

A PLACE FOR CLIFF

ROUGH ATTRACTION

TAKING OVER TROFIM

RIGHT ONE 4 DIESEL

TOUCHING VIDA~VINCE

SEDUCING HIS THIEF

UNSUSPECTING SAVING

MASTERS' GOLDEN DARK SIDE

Submit your desires within the Dominion of Brothers and submerge yourself into a world of Dominance and Bliss, but get ready~

A Place for Cliff

THE DOMINION OF BROTHERS SERIES: BOOK 3

Abandoned by his parents and left to tend to his sick sister since he was nineteen, Cliff has done little more than wander through his existence. That is until the Patronus Diesel Gentry sends him to meet Pyotr Laszkovi. A man twice his age except his impeccable looks and debonair sexuality has Cliff falling like a love-sick puppy for the man. Problem is, Cliff is about two threads from coming completely undone as a human being.

Despite this, Pyotr sees in him an irresistible young man who satisfies his needs like no other and is willing to be there to catch Cliff when he unravels and stay at his side during the hardest goodbye of all.

(•ᴗ•)

Gay-MM Romance/ Erotic-Romance / Dominance/surrender / Pain Therapy / Age Gap / Deboniar Meets Cute / Family Drama / Family Bonding / Voyeurism / Sexy Regatta Races /

A Place for Cliff

THE DOMINION OF BROTHERS SERIES: BOOK 3
WRITTEN BY TALON P.S.

DEDICATION

To my Twin,

I know you didn't want to finish this one with me but thank you for being with me to the end.

~ Talon

TRADEMARK ACKNOWLEDGEMENT

The author acknowledges the trademarked status and trademark owners of the following wordmarks mentioned in this work of fiction:

Print Book Publications:

P. L. Kerr, J. J. Muehlenkamp, and J. M. Turner
Nonsuicidal Self-Injury: A Review of Current Research for Family Medicine and Primary Care Physicians

P. A. Adler and P. Adler
The Demedicalization of Self-Injury: From Psychopathology to Sociological Deviance

Film Mention:
Grumpy Old Men

Vehicles:
Ford F-150 Raptor Pickup Truck
Berkly Ford Excursion
Audi Quattro
Norton Motorcycle

Alcohol Brands:
Tragos Silver Tequila
Gromoff Premium Vodka

Colognes:
Davidoff Fragrances for Men
English Laundry 3in1 Shower Gel
L'eau De Tarocco by Diptyque
Aqva Pour Homme Marine Toniq
Nautica Oceans
Light Blue Living Stromboli by Dolce & Gabbana
Light Blue pour Homme by Dolce & Gabbana

TABLE OF CONTENTS

A Place for Cliff

CHAPTER ONE

Cliff looked at the piece of paper in his hand for the twentieth time as he stood outside the VA boarding house, then back at the bronze plaque on the brick wall next to the door. He was at the right place, but damned if he knew why. Why hell, he was still floored that Diesel had taken it upon himself to become Kimmi's Guardian Angel at the treatment center. Not only paying off the outstanding medical bills, but also sponsoring the new biological therapy for her, for that alone, Cliff was forever grateful. But, it didn't make any sense why Diesel wanted him to come here. He wasn't a veteran, he'd never even gotten the chance to consider enlisting, after his parents vanished, leaving him to care for Kimmi on his own.

Hope they're rotting away somewhere— the anguished thought he was always harboring, surfaced in his head.

When he realized what the place was Diesel was sending him to, Cliff had figured it must have been a mistake.

So when he saw Diesel at the club again over the weekend, he chased him down to ask why—

~~Did you go?— —It's a boarding house for Veterans back from the Middle East. What was I supposed to do there?— —Did you meet with him? — —No, I never went inside—

Diesel had just looked at him for a long moment then finally spoke again, "Go, meet with him, I think he can help you find exactly what you need."— and with that, the man also known by the title Patronus, walked away before Cliff could question him further.~~

Cliff glanced up the side of the building at the several stories stacked over his head. What the hell was he supposed to be finding here?

Footsteps coming up the sidewalk stirred him from his thoughts and he turned just as a tall, heavily shouldered man with a casual gate walked past him and into the building, with hardly a glance his way. Still, Cliff didn't miss the clear blue eyes shaded by predominant brows of dark brown hair on the man. *Cerulean blue.*

Cliff shook his head. It was unnatural that he should know the name for the particular shade of blue. He owed that much to his little sister. When Kimmi was feeling well enough, she used her innate talent for color to paint. Stained glass mostly, but she'd recently gotten into watercolors which had him forever making stops at the local art supply store to find the exact shade and hue of tinctures she wanted. After several retries, he learned to pay closer attention to the specific shade she was asking for and accepted the fact that there was a much bigger difference between Mediterranean blue, turquoise, and blue-green algae then he'd previously cared to know and each was important.

"Can I help you with something?"

Once more Cliff found himself pulled out of his wandering thoughts. He blinked, looking up to find the man who'd just walked inside, standing at the door, holding it open. The tall cerulean blue-eyed man had popped his head back out to look at him and it took Cliff's breath away.

Some men you could say were sexy, some were handsome or even pretty. This man was all of the above *and* he was beautiful. Cool blues on a warm European face, topped with thick dark, wavy hair the color of coffee— black, no sugar. A strong jawline fringed with a smoothly trimmed beard that hadn't been trimmed in a few days. The man shifted, resting his forearm on the door jamb, taking a notion that he might be standing there awhile, waiting for the answer. *Oh yeah, he asked something.*

"Is this 1638 Old Country Road?"

The man turned his head slightly, glancing at the bronze plate on the side of the building with the beveled letters that said as much, then back at Cliff with an amused smile on his face, "This is the place."

Cliff scowled as he realized just how stupid he just made himself look. Okay, so that was dumb question number-one. *It's best to space them out a little.* "Can you tell me where I can find a Pyotr Laszkovi?"

The smile that had been dancing in the man's eyes arrived on his face and lined his lips as they stretched out into a dashing grin, "You found me. You must be my next session?"

Session?

Cliff thrust his hand out at him. Perhaps too quickly, but since it was already out there, there was nothing he could do but actually follow through and shake the man's hand. "I'm Cliff— Cliff Patterson."

Pyotr's eyes dropped to his hand as if almost surprised by the gesture, then shifted his weight off his arm and brought it down to take Cliff's proffered hand, but he didn't actually shake it— just held it. "You ready to come in?"

"I— *uh*—" Cliff glanced around once more reminding himself he had no idea why he was here. He felt his hand drop and turned back to the man still looking at him through the propped door.

His smile kinked up to one side like a friendly smirk. "When you are ready then. First hall on your right, second office on the right. I'll leave the door open." And just like that, the blue-eyed Pyotr disappeared inside, leaving Cliff standing out there like some lost dim-wit.

It might have helped if he knew why he was here. Patronus hadn't even give him a hint. What would it hurt to go inside? At the very least, maybe the man inside could explain to him why he was sent here, and if not, then at least another chance to look at those soul dipping eyes.

Cliff followed the simple directions and just as the gentleman said, the door was open. Cliff bent across the doorway, peeking in and there he was— sitting behind a cozy wooden desk, reclined back in his chair. Feet propped on the desk and hands clasped over his lap, sitting there patiently, as if the man had known all along Cliff would eventually come in.

"Well, that didn't take long at all." Pyotr glanced at him with a warm, welcoming expression, nothing more, as if he'd known all along but waited for Cliff to enter on his own terms.

Cliff stopped at the doorway, just taking it all in. The room was too small for all the things the man had tried to cram into it— a modest attempt to have all the comforts he wanted at his finger tips in a VA budget-sized room. A large bookcase behind him was stuffed to the gills with books, magazines, old newspapers, and other sundries; some neatly stacked, some not so much. Cliff rand his fingers along them, enjoying the ticked of cures edges flip against his skin.

Another bookcase sat catty-corner and mirrored the likes of the first with the addition of medical reference sets. The rest of the room was consumed with two comfy chairs and a small narrow lounger, the kind you'd expect to find in a psychologist's office. However, these were positioned so close you could sit in one and prop your feet up on another.

A fresh newspaper was laid out on the small table to one side of a chair. Cliff went to it and looked over the headlines, but it wasn't in English. Not even an English alphabet.

"What language is this?" Cliff used the question like one might comment on the weather to break the ice.

"Serbian."

"Really? One of the guys I work with is from Serbia, but I don't think he speaks it," Cliff rattle off as he continued to browse over every small detail around the room, looking for something else to comment on.

The man stayed quiet just watching and waiting patiently.

"Should I close the door?"

Pyotr folded his hands over his lap, his feet still propped on his desk like it was a Sunday afternoon. "If it makes you comfortable," the answer was mild, but didn't hint of whether Cliff should actually close it or not.

Cliff didn't move but glanced down at the rather worn brown tweed sofa lounger pushed back against the wall. It took up the whole space from the door to the corner. "Should I be sitting on this?" He glanced down his shoulder, then up to look at the man who still sat behind his desk in the same relaxed position he was in when Cliff first came in. But, Cliff watched for any change in the man's expression.

"Only if you'd like to lie down."

Cliff twisted rather suddenly to look squarely in his direction. "Why am I here?"

"I'm not sure yet." There was a slight gesture of his hands like a shrug.

"What?"

"I said, I'm not sure." This time Pyotr shook his head when he spoke, but only once.

"Why would you say that?"

"Because you haven't told me what you need from me yet. When you tell me, then I will know. From there, I will help you find what you need and we will accomplish it together."

Cliff stilled. He had half a mind to tell Pyotr to piss off and just march right out of there, but nothing in the man's tone indicated any form of mockery or suggested some game. Rather, every time Pyotr spoke, it sounded like an invitation to stay and talk awhile longer; even though he wasn't striking up the conversation himself.

"How did you know I was coming?" Cliff dropped his gaze as he asked the next question in mind.

"Patronus called to say you might need my help."

Patronus. Pyotr Laszkovi called Diesel by title— and not just any title, but one that clearly defined Diesel's status within the B/D community.

Cliff contemplated what Pyotr said. The response told him something— he just wasn't sure what. "Did he say what kind of help I'm to get?"

"No one knows that but you."

Cliff drew in his focus to gather all the tiny details about the man before him, like he would just looking over other patients sitting in the waiting room of a doctor's office. Pyotr's thumbs stayed perfectly relaxed over his lap; he didn't tap his thumbs, there was no foot tapping or glance at his watch to record the passing of time. The man seemed perfectly content to just sit quietly and wait him out.

Cliff let out a heavy sigh and dropped into the chair closest to him and dropped his face in his hands. This was too frustrating. He didn't know why Diesel would send him here. Yet, he couldn't bring himself to leave—because he did need help. He just didn't know what kind or what part this man was supposed to play. "I don't know what I need."

"Yet, you are here. So perhaps there is something I can do for you. We just need to figure that part out."

Cliff peeked up through his fingers. "How?"

The man shrugged ever so gently. "We can talk. Sometimes it helps to just talk. Next thing you know, it all comes out, and then you'll know."

It sounded like the best damn plan Cliff had ever heard, though he had no idea why because he hated talking. "What am I supposed to call you?"

That smile crept back to the man's face and there was something about it. Though Cliff didn't know what that something was any more than he knew why he was here, but at least that smile didn't fill him with dread.

"My name works. Pyotr, it's almost like Peter."

"Peter— only with an accent," Cliff added the additional perspective.

Pyotr chuckled then. "Yes, only with an accent— and not spelled the same."

Cliff sat back in the chair, letting his head fall back and he turned to look at *Peter-only-not-spelled-the-same.* "Is here something in particular we talk about?"

"Anything you like—" Pyotr dropped his feet to the floor, pushed up, and walked around his desk to the chair across from Cliff and sat down. Letting his forearm rest easily on the armrests. "As long as it is about *you*," he added.

Cliff glanced at his own hands in his lap; they still looked chaffed from wearing the dusted nitrile gloves all day. He didn't even know where to start really. "My sister—"

"Like I said—" Pyotr interrupted gently, "as long as it's about *you*."

It was only a reminder— or perhaps, strange as it seemed, permission. Permission to think about his own feelings or just his own thoughts, and not about what he had to go through to take care of Kimmi.

Cliff sucked in a deep, slow breath and let it out nice and easy with willed determination, to give it a try and see what that was like. "I don't get a lot of time for myself—" he started off. How weird was that? Getting to talk about just himself and he couldn't help but want to continue. "But when I do, I like to go to this club down town—"

Pyotr shifted in the chair and propped his elbow up on the arm, his fingers strumming across his chin. Back and forth they moved, like a violin bow drawn slowly across the instrument's strings, as he listened to the young man talk. First, just surface stories, the shell we all tell others and ourselves of who or what we want others to see us as— *all lies.* Mostly harmless, but we never tell ourselves the truth really.

One thing told, led to another and as Cliff burned up an hour hopping from topic to topic with as much depth as a kid with ADD, Pyotr remained quiet as the young man continued. While Cliff's words seemed inconsequential, the young man's body started to say something completely different. *He was barely holding himself together.* Thread bare at nearly every seam. It wasn't going to be long before the lad came apart and the real insides would come pouring out. When they did, there would be no preventing it. No stitching him back together until after he spilled the entire emotional trauma that lurked inside him. Then it would take some time to sift through the young lad's innards, take what was good and what was necessary and toss the rest. Thread up a new length of good sturdy cord and put Cliff back together. *That's why the young man was here in front of him, Pyotr evaluated. To catch him when he went crashing, insides and all, to the floor.*

Obviously, something took place that the Patronus saw as a sign and, with Cliff being active in the BDSM community at least in some small part circling around the city's prime fetish club, Diesel likely felt it was best to refer him to someone inside the realm. Because somewhere among all the talk, *sex* was going to come up, perhaps even an identity switch. Any average-joe-doctor would likely pull out some Freudian nonsense and send Cliff up river from where he naturally needed to be. There was also that added detail when Diesel used his title when he called. That opened the notion that perhaps Cliff here was in need of some *scene* therapy as well.

Still listening, both with his ears and his eyes, Pyotr did a little more observational work. Taking in the young man— tall and slender, he could see some muscle tone in his arms, though he couldn't say about the rest of his body through the loose t-shirt and relaxed-fitting jeans. Grey-blue eyes like the color of rain clouds moving in.

Dirty blond, choppy hair trimmed short around the neck and ears. The top front of his hair was longer and at the moment was flipped up. Either it was meant to be that way as some youthful hairstyle or the young man spent a lot of nervous moments, raking though it with a tendency to pull it straight up. Whatever the cause, it gave him a frumpy bratty-cute look and Pyotr was instantly taking a liking to him.

Around the lad's neck hung a simple brown heishi necklace with intermittent white shell disks. Nothing special at first glance— the kind you normally found in a beach tourist shop. If could have easily been dismissed as nothing relevant. Only—

Hanging from its center was an orange awareness ribbon charm. The only other jewelry visible was another orange awareness band, sharing space with his watch on one wrist.

Someone in his life was fighting leukemia.

VISIT #2

Pyotr had given Cliff directions to his home in the district of Astoria for their session this time. Foremost, he wanted Cliff out of his office and away from the clinic so as to remove any notion that what they were doing was strictly a doctor/patient arrangement. Rather, they had been brought together to share an experience. And if they were to get involved in a few therapeutic scene's, they needed to be in a more private and personal atmosphere. There was also a personal matter yet to be confessed; Pyotr had found the young man to be irresistibly attractive from their first encounter.

Pyotr was running late getting there himself, and he called ahead to suggest Cliff wait in the park a block over. He found himself looking forward to their visit and when he arrived, he didn't bother to pull his car into the gated courtyard of his home; thankful no one was occupying his curb space. So he parked along the sidewalk and briskly walked the single block to reach Astoria Park.

He found Cliff sitting on a bench under one of the large maples. His arrival went unnoticed so he held back a moment just to watch the young man, to gain some further perspective. He leaned up against a tree and just watched. And it didn't take long to realize there was little to watch, at least of a physical nature, and that in itself led to a deeper insight on Cliff Patterson.

Behind them, a dog barked down the street. Cliff turned, glancing around and spotted Pyotr just a few feet away. His brow furrowed a bit. "How long have you been standing there?"

Pyotr pushed off the tree and walked over. "Not long." He stopped at the bench and looked down at Cliff, enjoying how the sunlight breaking through the leaves flickered over Cliff's face and hair. Pyotr was further amused that, while aware of how imposing he could seem standing over someone at his height, the young man didn't flinch a muscle. "It was interesting to watch you though," Pyotr finally offered.

Cliff's brow lines deepened even more with a twisted crinkle. "How's that?"

Pyotr pushed his hands into the pockets of his slacks to soften his stance. "Watching you, I noticed you don't fidget or shift about impatiently. That's unusual for most young people."

The lines on Cliff's face faded and the expression grew muted. "I've spent a lot of time in waiting rooms: doctors' visits, CT scans, surgeries, financial aid— they all take time." Cliff remembered to make it about him, which wasn't really true. It was always about Kimmi.

"Do you feel up for a walk?" Pyotr motioned toward the trail path.

Cliff shrugged silently and without any further prompting got up, and started walking with an instant quick pace like he had some place to go. Though, it was soon apparent, Pyotr, for all his long legs was taking a much slower stride with no particular place go. Cliff dropped back, waiting for him to catch up, and then adjusted his pace to stay at his side.

They walked in silence for a long while, Pyotr simply waiting for the young man to start up just as he had before. Humorous, he should have expected it. Just like his own ability to wait patiently on his patients, Cliff apparently was equally capable of doing so *quietly*. "You have a sister." It was more an observation than a question, but also a means to get Cliff talking, but only nodded his confirmation. "And she is the one with leukemia?" Again, Cliff nodded. "Must be hard, parents always focused on her. You must feel left out sometimes."

This time Cliff didn't nod. "No. They pretty much left us both a long time ago," he muttered.

Pyotr came to an abrupt stop, catching the young man under his gaze. Twenty-six years of practice, Pyotr had heard them all, every sad story a person could tell and he'd always been able to hide a strong reaction to any of them. However, this time it got away from him.

He'd raised every one of his siblings by himself, but there was a damn good reason why he had. Nevertheless, how did a parent walk out on a sick child? Pyotr swallowed his admonishment and began to stride again. "How long ago?"

"Five years." There was a deep breath that contained an edge of gruff tension, "I had just turned 19 not a week before. I came home after pre-op for a marrow transplant for Kimmi and they were gone. Their things, some of the house furnishings, all gone, and their bank accounts— all closed. Not even a fuckin' letter," Cliff growled the last part, "Kimmi had already undergone a full treatment of high dose chemo with myelosuppression radiation therapy for Bone Marrow Depression. Her condition in mid treatment was registered critical, so she didn't have any time left for them to get through hospital red-tape policies."

Red tape?" he asked knowing it could man a number of things.

"Can't treat a minor without guardian or parent custody."

"How old was she then?"

"Fourteen."

Pyotr sucked in a a deep breath for the sole purpose of ebbing away the climbing tension and let it out as he picked back up their stroll along the trees. "So what happened?"

Cliff stuffed his hands in his jeans, watching his feet more than anything else, paced his steps around alongside him. "One of the in-center aids pushed paperwork straight to a judge's office to make it all legit, making me Kimmi's guardian. I hadn't even left the courthouse when the doctors proceeded with her surgery and the marrow supply treatments."

They walked further while Cliff went on about the last five years and what it was like to find himself trying to take care of his baby sister who suffered from a serious and costly illness. Pyotr kept quiet, giving only the occasional reminder that this was about him and he should talk about his perspective, not his sister's, as they walked along the paved trail.

As they reached the far end of the park to the running track, they climbed up the bleachers, and sat to watch the college athletes at practice.

(•ω•)

Cliff noticed the way Pyotr's eyes followed a few of the trim men as they sprinted down the track, and then shifted to the center field where a small group of men were warming up. He suddenly felt the urge to gain the man's attention back, wanting Pyotr to be looking at him, rather than the others. "Do you—" he paused not certain if the question was allowed, but then he wanted to know or rather his body wanted to know. "Are you by chance, gay?"

Pyotr turned and looked at him, a contented gleam in his eyes, not at all offended by the suggestion. "I am. But not by chance."

Cliff chewed at the inside of his lip. He'd seen another man leave Pyotr's home just as he was walking up the sidewalk earlier. Hell, the home was big enough to house a whole bunch of lovers. "Won't your lover be upset you're out here? With me, that is?"

☙🐛❧

Pyotr never once looked away, now that the topic had been struck. "I'd have to have one first and then there would need to be an understanding that this is what I do for a living. Though, I don't bring clients to my home as I have in your case." While the focus had shifted from Cliff to himself, Pyotr allowed it. Sometimes that was a good way to get the deeper parts out and he was certain the lad had run out of surface details.

☙🐛❧

Cliff looked the man over several times, his eyes roving over the details of his body and those domineering blue eyes shimmering in the sunlight. It didn't make sense. Pyotr was astounding to look at.

He must have taken a thousand mental pictures of the man home with him last week, and stared at them all whenever he had time to close his eyes and think of him. "Why don't you?" Cliff fidgeted for the first time. The question was too personal, but already spoken, so he might as well press on. "I mean you're good looking. Why wouldn't you have someone? And the man I saw?"

Pyotr made a slight chuckling sound, not once losing the amused expression that Cliff liked seeing in his eyes. "The man you saw was most likely Pavle, one of many brothers I have. Pavle has just recently gone through a divorce and now resides at home with me. As for the rest of your question, I'm a very dominant man. I tend to be overly controlling in my relations, but that I don't practice kink can be disappointing for the submissive type that would pursue such control."

Pyotr observed how Cliff's gaze shifted away from him. Perhaps the young man was a little perplexed as to how to file the new information away. While Cliff's reason for asking could have been any number of things, Pyotr had to wonder if there was an unconscious effort to measure any availability from him. A common thing to do when wrapping the mind in a private and unspoken fantasy. "I also tend to have a voraciously demanding sexual appetite once I've chosen to become involved with someone. That too can be an issue for my lover."

A ruddy color came over the top of Cliff's cheeks and he glanced away.

Pyotr loved the color on the young man. As a matter of fact, he was beginning to like a number of things about him and could not deny that had the young man already been given up to him, he would drag Cliff onto his lap and fuck him that very moment. "Does that answer your question?" Pyotr shifted the turn to talk back to Cliff, mostly just to stall what he already considered inevitable between the two of them.

Cliff shrugged then, his eyes looking down at the ground at nothing in particular. "I don't mind that so much," the words almost mumbled, but his thoughts were somewhere else.

"Mind?"

Cliff glanced at him then. "Not having kink. I don't mind not having it." He couldn't say about the rest, as he'd never been with anyone with an insatiable appetite. He had never felt the bliss of being completely spent. Usually, he was left feeling like he could go another round.

"You are a submissive than." Again, it was more a statement then a question.

"Wha—" Cliff's mouth popped open like a carp, then clamped back shut, and his brow furrowed suddenly, "Ah, no." Cliff shook his head, rejecting the observation as not being his own idea of who or what he was. He'd always sought to be recognized as a Dom.

Yet, he wasn't totally thrown that Pyotr might suggest otherwise.

Pyotr strummed at his lip in thought. Cliff's self-perceptions coming off as completely off track didn't come as a surprise— he wasn't the first young man to deny his true submissive nature— thought it was interesting how he didn't throw a fit of hard denial at the suggestion either. "Do you like to Dom over women or men?" he tossed the question out to lure Cliff to self-evaluate his self-proposed role.

(•ω•)

Cliff's eyes dropped to his hands, clasped over the space between his legs, with his elbows parked on his knees. His response stalled. The truth was, he didn't Dom anyone really. Or hadn't yet. Not in the true sense of the word. He'd had sex with both. He didn't consider himself bi-sexual but more like just an opportunist. A curse of living life outside the hospital waiting room fragmented. As for dating, he'd only dated girls, but given the right opportunity, he probably wouldn't mind dating a dude— he just never pursued one before.

(•ω•)

"It helps if you say all those thoughts out loud," Pyotr suggested with a gentle playfulness. He waited, but Cliff never spoke up. Though, even no answer was an answer for Pyotr and only required one more to confirm his building hypothesis. "Have you ever been with a man before?"

Cliff's eyes flickered toward him. The question didn't offend him either, but then he knew it shouldn't, a lot of people in B/d played both sides. "Once or twice."

"And what was it like for you?"

(•ω•)

Cliff's kept his gaze on his hands, eyes open, not allowing himself to fall into a state of fantasy over the man while he sat right next to him. Without even thinking about what he should say, his answer slipped out like a soft breeze. "I really got off on it." *And probably more then he should*, but that was where Cliff's secret laid. He'd played with one of the subs from the club off and on for some time. She had a kink for using a strap on and he'd discovered that he not only enjoyed being on the receiving end, he preferred it. That led to him messing around with some of the dudes. And when he lost the wrestling match against the sexy slave, the Patronus was training, it had been pure bliss— feeling the hot warmth of a real cock deep inside him. When he should have felt humility for losing the challenge, he instead had zoned from it.

It tugged at his mind, vexed him at night as he lay in his bed alone that he'd rather receive, over having his own cock submerged in someone's body— *how twisted was that?* What guy doesn't like fucking someone else?

Pyotr could see there was something else lingering just under the surface, but this wasn't the sort of thing to push. In fact, it was best to end the day at this point. Let that last thought sink in, and the rest would surface soon enough.

VISIT #3

"How do you feel about our sessions so far, Cliff?" Pyotr glanced over at the young man still hovering at the edge of the room, suffering against the wall rather than taking a seat to be comfortable.

Cliff looked tense, uncertain about something, yet there was some deep-rooted yearning to enter that seemed to prick at the young man. It showed in his eyes and the sneakered feet, still pointing in the direction of the room. His eyes stared down at his fingers, clasped in front of him. "I still don't know why I'm here."

"Don't you?" Pyotr got up, crossing the room and passing where Cliff stood. He took a position on the wall just opposite him. It was a deliberate position— using his body language to tell the young man he was not to leave. Today, Cliff would stay and be introduced to his demons.

Cliff's eyes followed the man's every step, feeling the gates close around him as Pyotr came into the hallway and leaned back against the wall. He wasn't actually blocking the hall that led out of the room, but the insinuation of preventing Cliff's plausible escape path was there, nonetheless.

Pyotr continued his observation. For all the lack of moment, there was an incredible amount of body language taking place. And for the first time, the young man appeared annoyed, yet reluctant to comment further.

Pyotr crossed his muscular arms over his midsection, sending off some body vibes of his own. "I believe your purpose for being here is to set you into the proper role you were meant to play."

"I told you before, I'm a Dom," Cliff persisted as though they'd been debating this for some time already.

Pyotr didn't miss the mental foot stomping tone. "You believe that because you were forced into caring for your sister under intense conditions and had to be the person in charge in your home life. You misplaced your sexual needs in the same role, which is why you have not been able to find satisfaction."

Cliff's expression and refusal to look him in the eyes said everything. Pyotr kicked off the wall, one hand scooping over Cliff's shoulder, and eased him toward the center of the room, allowing the younger man to face off with him when they stopped. "Give me your hands."

"Why?" Cliff retorted.

"Do as I say," Pyotr replied with a command that came across as nonnegotiable.

Cliff held out his arms, and just as Pyotr took hold of his wrists, he witnessed the flash of panic flare up in his eyes. As if something would go wrong because he wasn't able to escape.

Pyotr watched the emotional conundrum develop in the young man, but what he hadn't expected was how quickly the mental panic became physical.

Without any form of warning, Cliff jerked and kicked off with all his body weight at once, sending them both off balance. Pyotr had two choices— let go, which would have been counterproductive or go down with him. He quickly chose the latter, coming down on knees, straddled over Cliff's body, where a whole new storm of emotions went into play in the surprised young man.

Cliff's arms thrashed about and still Pyotr held his wrists. The physical tussle sparking something within himself feeding his drive for competition to kick in and with a surging burst of energy, he slammed Cliff's wrists to the floor on either side of his head, and firmly pinned him there. He held him there, his legs straddled over his hips.

Cliff's struggles shifted gears, pitching about his body in a defiantly, bratty manner that was turning Pyotr on. Only right now, this wasn't foreplay for sex. This was about Cliff giving up his control and feeling the release of letting go. Tying Cliff up would be easier, no doubt, but Cliff didn't need control swiped from him. He needed to give it over. Growing up, there was no one to take over, to take care of things for him or his sister and provide for them when there should have been. It all weighed down on the young man. That was the part Cliff needed most to let go of, but only to someone who was going to be there for him when he did. But among all the struggling and squirming, Cliff never uttered a command to unhand him.

"Did anyone ever tell you, you're such a *shejtan*?" Pyotr continued to ride out the young man's writhing body, bucking underneath him, despite the erection he was quickly developing.

Cliff bowed up, continuing to test the hold on his pinned arms. "What is that?"

"Means brat." Pyotr shifted his weight forward to press harder while leaning over him, with a wicked glint in his eyes.

Cliff's lip pushed out in a defiant grimace. "Once or twice, maybe."

Pyotr chuckled. He was sure somebody did. But, did they find it as sexy on the young man as he did?

(ꞏᵕꞏ)

Cliff bucked up against him. But the imposing weight of the man stayed put and he only succeeded in grinding his growing hard-on against the even harder muscles of Pyotr's body again. Each time the contact sent jolts of elicit currents through his balls and up his tail bone. Cliff continued to struggle and buck with a lazy like motion, wanting to cheat out more contact with the bulge in Pyotr's pants that seemed to quickly be turning rock-hard, but not so much, he'd might actually risk breaking free. "Get off me," he finally barked.

(ꞏᵕꞏ)

"But this is where you brought us," Pyotr felt it pertinent to point out the obvious.

"I didn't want this." More squirming, more deliberately accidental contact.

"Then perhaps you should hand control over to someone who does know what you want."

Cliff stilled finally, gaping up at Pyotr. "What is that supposed to mean?"

"It means, when you are trying to control things, you don't succeed very well in getting what you say you want, or what you actually need. So perhaps you should hand the controls over to someone who can bring you there. Perhaps then, you will succeed at receiving your hidden desires."

(•ш•)

Cliff's movements ebbed. "Is that someone you?" he asked, finding himself suddenly panting as if he'd just run around the block. He'd just asked the question he carried with him for the last two weeks. And just knowing the answer was about to come, scared the hell out of him, regardless of the outcome.

"It can be— you need only say you want me, and I will do the rest." Pyotr sat back on his heels, pulling Cliff's hands up, pressed his wrists together, and held them level to his mid-section. He kept them there and waited.

Cliff lay there, watching Pyotr watch *him*. He became increasingly aware of how close his hands were to the other man's crotch and the erection that had stirred such an exquisite friction with his. It stole his breath away. He'd never felt such want in his life and it was almost painful that it had stopped. He was a kid with a raging hard-on and not a clue what to do with it.

Heat brandished his fingertips, filling with the desire to touch Pyotr and the cock that clearly strained against the worn denim. Cliff need only stretch out his fingers and he'd be able to feel the other man's crotch and discover if Pyotr's bulge was straining with the same arousal as his was. Just then he shot a gaze up to inspect Pyotr's, fearful that his thoughts were easily readable.

(•ш•)

As Pyotr remained over the young man, enjoying watching Cliff's eyes drift down his body only to snap back up over and over like a kid trying to snatch a cookie out from under watchful eyes. Cliff had ceased all his bucking underneath him, remaining still— all but his fingers. They were another story. Rather than seemingly trying to avoid any embarrassing contact, they were purposely attempting to find that accidental touch.

"What do you need?" Pyotr asked of the subdued man under him, not at all restraining the amusement he felt.

Cliff's attention came to a sudden focus, directed straight up at him with hopeful silvery blue eyes. "Can I come back? I mean, in a few days instead of waiting a week?"

Pyotr had to take a deep breath just to keep himself from tearing into the young man's lips that very moment. *Come Back?* As far as he was concerned, Cliff could come back every day or better yet, just stay. *Strides,* he reminded himself. He took another deep breath to steady the excitement he felt threatening to throw him out of his usual languorous pace. *In strides.*

"Only if you admit your visits here are beneficial to you."

Cliff stuttered, trying to come up with an answer. Hell, he hadn't even gotten his head wrapped around why he was here and he wasn't so sure about being labeled a submissive at all. How was he to know if coming here was beneficial? All he really knew was that he didn't want to wait another seven days to see Pyotr again. "Is saying I *want* to be here beneficial enough?"

Pyotr rocked up to get to his feet, purposely perpetuating the accident Cliff's fingers sought by pressing his growing arousal against the young man's palms just seconds before letting his wrists go free and pushed up off the floor.

"When did you have in mind?" Pyotr opened the floor for discussion. After all, he had told Cliff he need only say he wanted him and he would do the rest. Cliff wasn't just a *shejtan*, he was a sly one at that. Pyotr grinned to himself.

Cliff sat up, finally free of the body he hadn't wanted to lose just yet and he wrapped his arms around his knees as he watched the incredibly sexy man stroll to the desk in the far corner. Pyotr flipped open an appointment book and glanced over it, waiting for further input from him. Cliff tried to calculate what would be considered acceptable. Three days seemed right, any longer and he might go out of his mind, anything sooner and the man might think he was just some crazy, love sick school boy.

"Three days, Sir."

Pyotr stilled, his eyes flickered up. The nuances so evident it was almost like a hiccup in his smooth movements but gone just as quickly. "Three it is."

VISIT #4

Once again, Pyotr had Cliff by his wrists, and even standing up, Cliff discovered there was little he could do to break free from the older man's strong grip that held him firmly but without bruising.

"Do you use the universal safewords from the club?"

Cliff nodded.

"You know better than that. A nod is not an answer. You must repeat them to me," Pyotr corrected him.

Cliff gulped down a breath and swallowed hard, while still testing the hold on his wrists, but finally gave up the answer as directed, "Red, yellow, and green."

Pyotr had his arms stretched out awkwardly to each side like wings and his eyes flickered to the wall behind him. Like the flip of a switch that glinted in those blues eyes, Cliff saw the decision made. He glanced over his shoulder, twisting his neck to a painful bend to see what it was on the wall that had been a part of the flickering thoughts. It took a moment for it to register in his head what he was looking at, but once it did, there was no mistaking the stainless steel snap-lock shackles bolted into the wall. It was decidedly clear that was where Pyotr wanted him.

Cliff didn't move as Pyotr pressed into him, no more fleeting connection but making the connection between their bodies a solid contact. Another step into him and Pyotr was pushing his body backwards; one step after another, until his back hit the wall. Like it or not, Cliff's arms were lifted until just over the level of his head, then one wrist was pressed into one of the clamps.

The pressure from his wrist activated a spring plate and the shackles snapped shut around his arm. Cliff's thoughts were drifting south at the moment, even as Pyotr repeated the capture of his other wrist then stepped away. Cliff pushed his hips out in a feeble attempt to keep the contact with Pyotr's body, a movement that didn't go unnoticed. Nor did Pyotr's eyes fail to register Cliff's cock pressing against his jeans. But, had the man caught onto how quickly Cliff had gone hard against him? Like a Porsche taking off across the finish line before the race had officially started. That's how quickly his body reacted.

⊙ω☉

Pyotr eased around silently, turning his back to the now shackled young man and pressed the heel of his hand against his own erection through his pants and made a slight adjustment to regain some comfort in the area before turning back around to face his new captive.

Since they had begun their sessions, Cliff had watched him almost as acutely as Pyotr watched him, but unlike himself, the young lad wasn't sure what he wanted to do about it. Pyotr knew exactly what he wanted to do with the young man— *in due time.* For now, he decided a little show of eye candy might help Cliff along with his own decision making.

He dropped down in the comfy chair across from the wall that held Cliff restrained and casually began to press along the hard ridge of flesh that bulged under his jeans with the heel of his hand again. He shifted further down in the chair, legs stretched out, tan feet peeking out from the legs of faded denim. He dropped his head half back against the chair, eyes locked on his reluctant surrendered subject.

"What are you doing?" Cliff questioned him with some surprise.

"Enjoying you." Pyotr slowly unzipped his pants, slipping his fingers under the fabric to tease his erection some more.

"And you're going to do it in front of me?" Cliff dropped his gaze unsure if he could or should watch.

"Precisely."

"Why?"

"Because I don't want you doing anything. I want you to surrender your self-control for just a moment. Trust that I will keep you safe and make the right decisions for you while you are here under my care."

Somewhere in there, Pyotr discovered existed a trigger word and Cliff was quickly thrashing against the shackles, but they didn't budge.

"And I have to be chained to the wall for that?"

Pyotr pushed up from his chair, dragging his briefs down with a thumb until they tucked under the tight sacks under his cock. He stepped up and leaned in until his lips were just a breath away from Cliff's ear. "Yes." He moved to Cliff's other side, doing the same to other ear, teasing him with the warmth of his breath, "And as you watch me pleasure myself, you're going to tell me what turns you on. As well as what it is you want."

Cliff rolled his head to catch a touch of Pyotr's. "What does it matter what I want? I can't have it anyways."

There it was. One of the threads that needed to be done away with— Cliff's belief that he could not have what he wanted.

"Because this is about you. Even when—" he paused a moment then decided to rephrase that, "*Especially* when you are surrendered to me, it is about you. A Master gets his pleasure from seeing to yours."

"Are you saying you're my Master?" Cliff's stormy grey eyes floated up to find his.

"Right now, while you are a captive on my wall? Yes, decidedly so." Pyotr glided his hand softly over his shaft, not actually gripping it, just enjoying the feathery touch for the moment. He was certain the *scene* would take some time; so, he was prepared to stretch this out as long as he needed to. "What is it you want the most right now, Cliff?"

Cliff swallowed hard; he could feel the hammering of his Adam's apple in his throat. What he wanted was standing dangerously close to him right now. What he wanted was to be pressed up against him and not the wall. What he didn't want, was to be rejected. And right now, that far outweighed what he wanted. He kept silent and glanced away.

"Perhaps something smaller then. Something far easier to grant," Pyotr offered, still standing so close Cliff could feel the heat of Pyotr's body radiating against him.

Cliff shook his head trying to interpret what the man had just said to him, like he was a mind reader or something.

"Such as what you need," Pyotr turned to him and spoke.

This time it was a command, rather than a request, and Cliff's answer came stumbling out, "A kiss."

He no sooner said it, he looked away. Not wanting to see the mockery that would inevitably be on the other man's face. He knew it was stupid of him to even suggest that the handsome and intelligent Dr. Pyotr Laszkovi might kiss him, but he hadn't actually meant to say it out loud either. He flexed his arms and hands curling them into fists as he silently reprimanded himself for it, not fully understanding why he needed the kiss or had given in to the command so willingly.

Pyotr was taken by surprise by the request. It had come sooner than he expected, but who was he to deny the young man at the price of such a luxury as tasting those lips. And Cliff certainly had kissable lips.

Pyotr caught Cliff's jaw in the palm of his hand, pulled him around and rushed in to kiss him. Two sets of soft pliable lips crushed together. He tilted his head, twisting the moist embrace between them. Then Pyotr opened his mouth and sucked on the young man's lips to lure him to give in to his own request.

Time froze for what might have been eons in Cliff's head before he realized Pyotr was actually kissing him. But once reality set in, he couldn't ignore how wonderful it felt. The wet warmth of Pyotr's lips sucking on his sent a shivering wave of something all the way down his body and fired off a pulse of something else in his cock. He tilted up to offer more of himself to the man and before he knew it, he was craning his neck forward to get his tongue inside Pyotr's mouth before he lost the chance to taste him.

Pyotr responded, but it wasn't to pull away. The alpha male sensed his needs and was instantly taking over again. Pyotr's hand slipped behind Cliff's head, lifting him further and his tongue dove inside.

Hunger let loose in Cliff's mouth, eating him alive, and he was swimming in it. He let out a moan before he knew it was happening and then another. It was like some dream he'd fallen into, floating in this new swirl of flavors that licked at the inside of his mouth and across his palate. It felt like nothing he'd ever had, and he hoped like hell it never ended. *Fuck breathing.* Even when Pyotr allowed Cliff to catch a lung full of air with a gasp, his lips returned to consume the boy's breath. What Pyotr delivered was anything but subtle or gradual. Once he asked, he got the full flavor of his request and when Pyotr finally released his mouth, Cliff's entire body went up in flames to have more. His eyes fell down to the erection that pointed up at him, caught up in the sight of clear fluids coming from the slit.

"What's on your mind?" Pyotr asked.

Without looking, he knew from the tone Pyotr wanted him to say what he saw. "How do you know this is right for me?" Cliff dodged the answer that was expected of him.

"You are, after all, taking this rather well. You're quite calm. You have your safeword if you need to use it."

"Can I have my hands back then?" Cliff dodged any discussion about using a safeword.

"Why? Do you want to touch me?"

Cliff couldn't think of anything else but. But it was more than a touch he wanted, he wanted to experience the other man. "I don't know— yes—maybe," he shied away. He couldn't let himself admit to what he wanted. It was still too new. Yet he felt like a kid with his hand already in the cookie jar. You just don't take your hand out without retrieving one for the effort.

"You need to be certain." Pyotr's hand hovered over the shaft of red flesh standing up out of his jeans, brushing against it lightly with the heel of his palm. Letting Cliff watch. Letting him adjust to the view.

Cliff closed his eyes, fighting what he wanted. It would be so much easier if he could just surrender in the heat of the moment. "Why can't I just let things happen?"

"Because letting things happen usually begets the panicking thoughts of— *how did I let this happen*— which later turns to regret."

☾☽

Pyotr could see the quivering movement in the young man's mouth, as the gears in his head shifted about, trying to formulate a response that would both get him what he desired and do so without having to face it head-on. A matter Pyotr had no intention of allowing Cliff to do. He took the choice away from him. "Tonight, you'll settle for watching. You've had your kiss; the rest will come later." He took Cliff's jaw in his hand and turned him to look into his face. "When you are ready."

Had it not been for Pyotr's hand on Cliff's jaw, the boy very well might have gaped at him for taking his choice of toys away. A sudden self-check and a scowl brewed behind his grey eyes that was either more of that *brattyness* or he was bereaving himself for not taking the chance while he'd had it. Both were healthy for now.

VISIT #5

"I don't know if I can handle just being a sub." Cliff shook his head as he hovered at the edge of the room, the hallway directly behind him; a popular location at the start of their scenes together lately. The position told Pyotr, standing there at the edge of space, Cliff was ready to bolt at the first sign of his own big bang creation.

"That's only because you've never had anyone to be there for you. But I want you to understand the difference between being submissive and surrendering. These are not always synonymous. Your body needs to learn surrender. An experience you've been deprived of. Right now, you have a safe place to turn yourself over to it. And when we finish here, your strength will be restored as well as your control handed back over to you. When you leave, you will continue to be the Master of your home."

Cliff's eyes flickered out at him from under passive brows. Pyotr could see it in him, the fear that once turned over, he'd never have the strength to restore himself. Being in control for Kimmi and his self-depravation were the only threads holding the rest of him together.

Pyotr pulled a cushion from the sofa and dropped it to the floor at his feet, "Come sit here."

Cliff moved slowly but obediently, dropped down until he sat cross-legged between Pyotr's legs.

Pyotr reached out and softly combed through the tuft of hair around his forehead that was always blown up like some new youth idea for the latest distressed-look hairstyle. "You're ready for this. From now on, when you're with me, I will be in control. There is nothing in the world that is your responsibility in this very moment. When you are with me, I am in charge." When he said that, the young man seemed to nearly collapse. All the tension and strength washed away as Cliff slumped against his leg, his head resting comfortably on Pyotr's thigh, and he let out a hard sigh of relief as if he had been waiting all his life for someone to say *that* exact thing to him.

Pyotr continued to run his fingers through the thick tufts of dirty-blond hair. He loved how it felt in his hands, thick and soft, not silky or covered in a stiff hair product. It was also rather amusing to play with since it was always in a disheveled mess, which no matter which way it pointed, looked incredibly cute on him.

"Do you remember what we did last scene?"

Cliff nodded.

"Did you think about it more when you left?" Bluish-grey eyes blinked up at him and Pyotr could see, like himself, he probably had thought of little else over the last three days. "What is it you want today?"

Those same eyes diverted away and disappeared.

"Again, think in steps, rather than the whole package. A smaller portion of what you want makes it easier to ask for," Pyotr guided him to feel out the new territory of asking for the pleasures he wanted. Just simply allowing himself to want them.

Pyotr could feel some small amount of tension in the young man, but he also felt Cliff pressing his face into his thigh, and for a moment, he thought he could feel the young man's lips as they mouthed a kiss against his pant leg.

"I expect an answer, Cliff," Pyotr demanded, hoping to get a response while he was caught in the moment.

"I want to feel you pressed against me." Cliff dared himself to finally say it out loud, but it still came out in a whisper.

Pyotr shifted in the chair. He wanted to do far more than just press up against the young man, but like Cliff, he found himself continually having to remind himself, small steps. He just had to make sure his own body cooperated with that. He sat quietly, still stroking through the lad's hair, letting Cliff just sit and accept what he had asked for something before they actually got up and did anything about it. Cliff had verbalized his needs, now Pyotr was in charge and would take things in a stride as he saw fit for his new surrendered boy.

"Would you care for some coffee," Pyotr asked after they'd sat for a bit.

Cliff nodded compliance but then there was a noticeable hesitation.

"Out with it. I won't have you withholding anything from me."

"I prefer tea—" Cliff stalled in his honesty. "It's kinda like a comfort food for me." He didn't dare say why, but he hadn't lied that he did prefer tea. He didn't used to. But, he and his sister had discovered early on that tea helped Kimmi's stomach before and after a meal, so she was less likely to get sick. And since he couldn't really afford to indulge in both, he'd just grown accustomed to drinking the teas over having coffee. Besides, coffee gave him the jitters and that was one thing he didn't need more of on any given day.

Pyotr smiled. "Tea it is then." And he eased up and led Cliff upstairs to make some for the two of them.

Cliff hovered at the edge of the kitchen while Pyotr got the water started, but then called him into the kitchen. He leaned back against the counter and commanded Cliff to stand in front of him. Turning him away from him, then pulled him to lean against his chest, where Pyotr began to touch him.

Just slow caresses of his broad hands over Cliff's chest and belly. He stroked down his thighs and back up to do it all over again. "Tonight is just about us getting close." He spoke smooth editable suggestions of bait. Like window dressings of cakes and candies. "But we're not going to do anything but touch. Do you understand?" In other words, the shop was closed.

Cliff twisted, looking over his shoulder. He could not explain it, but he didn't need all this preliminary stuff, he already knew he wanted to be Pyotr's lover. At the first touch, though soft and slow, his body *zinged* for more. It had him stirring and surrendering at the same time. "What if I'm ready? What if I would like for us to do more?"

(◔ᴥ◔)

Pyotr pulled Cliff's face around, more so he could take a good look at the young man he intended to make his lover. Something in his eyes— yes Cliff did seem ready, but that didn't mean it couldn't back fire later. He smiled warmly, "That's good. However, remember that I am the one in charge, right now, and as I said, we won't be doing anything tonight."

The disappointment in Cliff's eyes was all too evident and he just couldn't leave that unamended. He repositioned his arm up Cliff's back until it caught him around his neck and pulled him into a kiss.

Like everything else Pyotr did, he kissed Cliff in a slow stride, his tongue pushing deep until it found his and held him just like his arms held the young man's body. His slow tantric approach rewarded him with the subtle sensation of feeling Cliff melt into his possession.

Pyotr moved his free hand over Cliff, taking in the sensation of every soft bulge of muscle and ripple of his body. Burning the man's shape to his memory, ensuring that even in the dark, Pyotr could kiss every part of Cliff in just the right way.

Pyotr pulled on his hips, crushing Cliff's buttocks against his erection, and nuzzled into the back of Cliff's head. He took a deep inhale of the young man's scent, just boy and some cheap sport scent shower gel. There was something about being with him, having Cliff next to him that was incredibly comfortable. He hadn't even taken Cliff to his bed yet and already he knew he was hooked. But, there was still one matter between them that needed to be covered. And he certainly couldn't expect an honest answer from the lad while he was palming up his shaft.

Pyotr pressed his face into the young man's head, nuzzling deeper into him, but the hand he used to stroke over Cliff's body stilled. "Do you know how old I am, Cliff?" Already he felt a twinge of regret, fearing the young man, who'd taken first seat in his mind, might quickly reject him because of their considerable age difference.

"Don't you dare." Cliff shot a heated glare over his shoulder at him. "If you're about to bring up some issue about me being too young for you, I don't want to hear it, 'cause I don't care. I want you no matter how much older you might be, and I want you now." Cliff pushed out in his arms and turned to face off with him squarely. "Hard enough, you're just like any other doctor, making me wait on you, but don't you dare try to tell me I'm too young to want to be in your bed. You keep at me about saying what I want. Well— you're fucking me and that's it!" Cliff finished his proclamation off with a stout position, crossing his arms over his chest, accentuating his bratty persona.

Pyotr let out a hearty chuckle at the sudden bravado, reveling in the warmth within his soon-to-be-lover's erupting pushiness. Guess that did away with all the smaller requests. "*Shejtan.*"

(ᵕ◡ᵕ)

Cliff dropped his arms and hooked his thumbs into his jean pockets, not sure about the chuckle that was still coming from Pyotr. "Come to think of it, if that's what's holding us up, then I think you should just push on, and let us get past it," he dared a second rhetoric in hopes he might actually goad the man into breaking the pace. He did say he was in charge, so he needed to go on take charge so he didn't have to worm up the guts to say what he wanted any more.

His heart skipped several beats when Pyotr snared his hips and yanked him into his body.

"The only thing I will be giving you tonight is a frot," Pyotr growled, kissing and grinding into him. "But it will be a damn good one."

Before Cliff could even think of a protest or what a frot was, his mouth was quickly consumed by Pyotr's demanding lips, crushing against his own, sucking at him to open. Cliff couldn't refuse and opened up to let him in and take the overpowering man's tongue in his. The soft heat of it scooping him up and drawing on him, it was like liquid sex in his mouth. He was melting into the man and he loved how it felt, like being bathed by a strangely dreamy kiss with deep undertones of luscious carnage.

Pyotr's fists tightened into Cliff's jeans and pulled their bodies so tight against each other even breathing added friction between their cocks, but he didn't leave it to just that. Pyotr's thigh forced its way between Cliff's legs his hands tugging on Cliff's hips which had him instantly dry humping against the powerful muscles of Pyotr's thigh.

Pyotr's cock was crushing against his own hip as his arms shifted positions, one pressing down to grope at his ass, the other smoothing up his back; a neurological tease of soft and hard at the same time. Pyotr's hips never ceased to rock against him. At every point the man knew where his body was and what each part was doing.

Cliff let out a guttural moan that was consumed by Pyotr's kiss. It felt so incredible, his whole body melting and drifting off into a pool of sensation. Pyotr's lips moved to his neck, a combination of kissing and licking. "Ouch." And biting.

"Don't fuss." Pyotr growled against his neck before resuming their kissing. Pyotr brought a hand around to Cliff's front and did away with the button on his jeans, next the zipper, and then pulled Cliff's eager cock out so he could stroke over the silky-smooth flesh.

Cliff's head fell back, and he gasped under the strong caress of Pyotr's hand wrapped around his already turgid shaft.

(ᵔωᵔ)

Pyotr looked down at the long rod of pink flesh. He nearly purred with the velvety softness of Cliff's skin against his palm. He grazed his thumb over the weeping slit, smearing the droplet of pre-cum over the tender glans, reveling in the twitchy response in Cliff's knees.

Though, having some fun with his new toy, Pyotr was feeling suddenly annoyed that the lad's jeans were in the way of him grasping all of his cock. He let go only long enough to grab the jeans at Cliff's hips and shove them down past his ass, then quickly picked up where he left off, fondling over the engorged erection.

Cliff was so damn hard already; his cock was standing straight up his belly. Pyotr had to pull it away from his body just to stroke him and even went as far as to amuse himself with Cliff's condition by letting it go, watching as it slapped against his belly. A slight purr escaped his lips and he repeated the playfulness several times causing Cliff's face to flush with an embarrassing color of red.

"So beautiful," Pyotr let out a husky whisper, Can't wait until one day I'm going to eat it up.". That alone made Pyotr's toying a little more bearable. "But, I still want you to know how old I am."

Cliff's blush took a turn toward alarm, his head struggling to break free of the fog just so he could stand his ground on this one. "I told you I don't care."

"I'm forty-six. That's old enough to be accused of robbing the cradle with you."

"No, it's not and like I said— *ahhh*—" His own gasp interrupting what he was going to say mid-sentence. God, he couldn't seem to think clearly, because Pyotr's hand never stopped stroking him. "*Ahh*— I- I don't care about that. I only care about being with you." Cliff popped his head up suddenly. Eyes meeting. Horror from Cliff's heart; he hadn't meant to be quite so open. It made him sound foolishly young at that point, which wasn't going to help his argument.

Pyotr's hand stopped and so did everything else, his gaze locked onto him. "You're sure about this?"

Cliff drummed up every ounce of energy he could just to dam up the whimper that threatened to escape his lips when he tried to say something else. Such a sound would also not help his cause. *Of course, he wouldn't care as long as he got off.* But, Cliff didn't want Pyotr to think that. He wanted this man to know he was here because he had never wanted to be with anyone else as strongly as he wanted right now with him.

"Positive." And just to prove it he reached for the bulge in Pyotr's jeans and palmed against it then tore into them to free the thick shaft from the denim. Pyotr's hand resumed movement and together they simultaneously stroked each other. Pyotr eventually pulled Cliff's hand from him and resumed their grinding.

As one hand brought Cliff higher and higher, Pyotr's other hand moved under his jaw and lifted him to his lips, kissing him in a slow languid caress of his tongue; taking the time to relish every combined texture and flavor of their tongues. And he never lost the physical contact of Pyotr's cock grinding against his groin. He kept pace with everything else the man did. Damn, Pyotr was like a symphony conductor for sexual contact and Cliff couldn't wait to get to the encore part.

"I love your lips," Pyotr hummed to him, "I imagine doing so many things with them one day."

Cliff was moaning. He couldn't stop the sounds anymore; he was so close.

Pyotr shifted. Once again, he directed their bodies to allow the full gyrating connection of their cocks against each other. Feeling the heat and the crushing sensation of the hard ridge against Cliff's own was mind-boggling. Their kiss deepened, became hungrier with the building anticipation, and when he felt Pyotr's hand once more, it was so he could stroke them both— together— in sync with the rocking of his hips.

Pyotr wrenched away from their kiss to looked down their bodies, watching as if fascinated by the both of them together. "Watch it, Cliff. Look how beautiful your cock is against mine." His hand tightened, flexed and tightened again, stroking up to capture more of the pre-cum that spilled from both erections, and then transferred a healthy amount of it back down. He shifted his fingers, spreading them out to tickle at the soft skin above Cliff's scrotum before repeating the process delivering multifaceted sensations of touch as he did so making it feel as though more than one hand grouped him.

Cliff tried to watch, but his head was reeling, his body already beginning to convulse with the inevitable. He was only being jacked off and yet it was more— way more. Far more intense and he gave no argument to fight the impending release and all the implications attached.

Pyotr seemed to know exactly how close Cliff was and responded by pulling them faster, his hand pistoning harder, both shafts together. "Keep watching," his gruff voice commanded.

Cliff tried, but what few brain cells not focusing on the sensational storm wrapped around his cock were concentrating on preventing his knees from giving out. They were growing weaker with every stroke. He had no idea how he was managing to stay on his feet as it were.

The room seemed to pitch and roll with each moan that came from his mouth. But, another sound was joining in his, a building raspy breath. God, it was sexy. Cliff followed the sound to Pyotr's lips, the man's eyes half lidded, and the sound was him sucking in his breath in rapid staccatos. It was unbearably erotic.

"Come with me, *dragi*," Pyotr managed to pant out in a husky growl.

Cliff had no idea he was already there, he had been so mesmerized by the sound of the other man, yet, when Pyotr told him to cum, his body obeyed.

Cliff's head kicked back on his shoulders and the groan that came out filled the room, and his ears. It was followed by a similar sound from Pyotr and it sounded like tantric music. His whole body tensed and he felt his knees finally give out. A powerful arm tightened around his waist, catching him from falling. Pyotr's arm displaying his strength as he held Cliff up against his body, keeping their connection together, while the earth seemed to shake beneath them both.

Cliff felt the hot cream gush with each pulse of their combined release, the pulse of his lover's cock against his own as more cum covered Pyotr's hand and splattered up their chests. Though, Pyotr's stroking never let up, making them ride out every nuance of their orgasm.

Time seemed to stand still in Cliff's mind just feeling Pyotr's body quiver against his. He couldn't describe it, but he loved how it felt; loved the chorus of heaving breaths that he fought to calm down.

Pyotr's hand came up, covered in the shared spunk. He licked a tasty amount in his mouth, then smeared some onto Cliff's lips then dove in to kiss the banquet from them.

Cliff had never thought to revel in the evidence of bliss. He knew some didn't like it at all. But, as Pyotr kissed him, his tongue dancing with his own, sharing the taste of their combined release, he decided right then and there he liked it, especially if this man got this much pleasure from it as well.

Pyotr and Cliff had since moved to the couch, spooning together in the darkness of the room, letting their hearts return to a slow pace and basking in each other's arms. Pyotr traced circles in the sticky froth that still dotted Cliff's chest with an idle hand, while delivering frequent kisses to his temple and the back of his head.

It was the last thing Cliff had expected out of a man. To have a fondness for cuddling. Another first in his life. "I've decided I don't want to wait three days. Can I come back tomorrow?"

Pyotr lifted his head to glance at him. "No. I have sculling practice tomorrow."

"Sculling? What's that?"

"Rowing. I'm captain on a sculling team."

Cliff ran his hands up and down Pyotr's arms, his fingers mapping out the multiple ripples of corded muscle. *Rowing.* So that's what carved his body so. "Like an Olympic team?"

"Hardly," Pyotr chuckled, "but we are in the competition master's circuit. We go under the name of the *Greenwich Queens, NY Rowers Club.* There is also a *Greenwich, Ct Rowing Club* that competes in this region, not surprising, of course, our encounter with them in our first year was amusing. Our name alone was goading enough to get them to accept a challenge when we first started out."

Cliff sat up, turning so he could face him. Pyotr rolled onto his back and urged him to lay over his chest. Cliff settled between his legs, resting on his elbows to either side over Pyotr's midsection. "I take it you're suggesting everyone on your team is gay?"

"That's kinda the whole point, *Dragi* ." Pyotr raked his hand through Cliff's thick tufts of dirty blond hair just as he had done before, amusing himself with the perception that no matter what he did to it, it never got worse. Or better for that matter.

Cliff shifted his weight and lowered down over Pyotr, completely immune to the man's playing as he rested his chin into his sternum. "What's *drag—* whatever it was you just said."

"*Dragi* —" Pyotr chuckled, "pronounced *dray-gah.* It means *honey* in Serbian."

"Like sweetheart?"

"Yes."

Cliff rolled his head to the side, landing on a cheek, falling silent as his head rode up and down on the man's breath. "*Dragi—*" he whispered his new pet name. But he paused, some ill thought finding its way in his head. "You must think I'm a real idiot, not knowing so many things." He only half dared to glance up Pyotr's body but didn't meet his eyes. He didn't want to see the disappointment in them.

Pyotr let out a gentle chuckle, his hand nuzzling against Cliff's head, turning it to look at him. "Not at all. I have twenty-two years head-start on you. And for the record, I don't know the first thing about emergency medicine unless it has something to do with a strained muscle." His arms moved to hook under Cliff's shoulders and like he was doing bench curls, Pyotr pulled Cliff up his chest and into his arms, his mouth coming over Cliff's in a tender wanting. Gentling him into accepting their differences needn't be measured in who knew what.

A few hours later and with some silent reluctance on both parts, Pyotr drove Cliff home as promised in exchange for the extra time they'd had together. But, no matter how many deep breaths Pyotr took, he could not slow the racing in his heart or his head. He wanted to hurry everything along to build a deeper connection between them. He could even hear himself asking Cliff to move in with him. Three weeks and already he wanted to make the young man a solid fixture in his life. *So much for taking strides.* He was actually grateful when Cliff began asking more questions as he drove. Questions about his rowing team and where they practiced, and when the next challenge was coming up. His lover's curiosity also showed a devoted interest as well as distracting Pyotr from his rummaging thoughts. Once he dropped his future off though, the thoughts quickly flooded back.

CHAPTER TWO

"Oh look! Here they come now!" Kimmi called out, pointing to several long, slender boats barely floating above the water's surface as they came skimming down the river looking much like water bugs skimming across the surface with its many oars. "Which one is his?" She grabbed Cliff's arm and was jumping with excitement.

"I can't tell yet. Settle down— we'll have to wait until they get closer." But even as the sculls drew closer, Cliff was having a hard time telling. Three boats, two of them had eight guys drawing oars, plus someone sitting in the tail end of the boat, calling out something that seemed to keep them all rowing in sync with each other. The third boat had four rowers, but no caller. Every one of the bodies seemed so similarly built with their backs to him— Cliff could only narrow it down by hair color.

"Well?" Kimmi bounced against him as the boats were drawing up under them and just then Cliff found him. Second scull. First man on the bow. Kimmi made a dash for the other side to which Cliff found himself rushing to catch up. He sure didn't want to miss the chance to see the beautiful man at work.

Cliff bent over the concrete wall, straining to catch the very first glimpse.

Like some athletic dream of motion, muscles flexed and strained against the oars. The boats were just slipping out from under them and there he was.

"Cliff!?" Kimmi tugged on him.

"There." He pointed, "On the front end of the center boat." And just then Pyotr glanced up, and in what seemed like nothing more than a blink of an eye, Pyotr saw him and completely stalled out. The clash of oars was instantly met with some curses from his teammates.

The one guy, who sat squatted in the tail end of the slender shell, twisted to see just what had their team leader kiltered out of sync. "Way'nuff!" the rear man called out as he turned back to his team. The other men stalled in motion, holding their oars straight out while Pyotr got back in position.

With another call from the man sitting with the rudder, all eight pairs of oars swept backwards then dipped into the water. Arms bulged with the hard first pull straining against the water only to come back up and repeat the movement. Returning them into rhythm with each other and pulling down river.

"I think he's in love with you." Kimmi wrapped around her brother's arm.

Cliff tried to pull away, but she held on like she always did. "What are you going on like that for?"

"His heart skipped several beats when he saw you."

"Kimmi those are called oars, not his heart."

"But, he stopped rowing because the sight of you stilled his heart." She beamed up at him.

Cliff turned red. "You're reading too many funny stories. Where'd you get an idea like that anyways?"

Kimmi shrugged and blushed. Ever since they got internet at the house, a few weeks ago, she'd been staying up late practically every night searching and reading, finding all kinds of things. She was like a sponge, only she couldn't keep up with the sources anymore.

"Come on." Cliff nudged her gently. "It took us forever to get out here. We'll walk through Macomb Park and catch the Number-22 there to start the trek home." He wrapped an arm over her shoulders, pulling her to him as they walked. It was a long trip when they had to go by bus, then train, and then another bus, but it had been well worth seeing Pyotr for that brief moment. Even if Kimmi was making too much of it.

Pyotr stood in the shower under the streaming water, his head lowered as he leaned on a hand, pressed flat on the wall. He hadn't expected to see Cliff. That did something to him— seeing the young man had come out to watch him rowing. And he could make a good guess the one with him was none other but his kid sister. That was a very positive action running in his favor.

He squeezed out a healthy amount of his favorite *English Laundry* scented shower wash and lathered up, spreading it over his chest and headed south as he brought up the image of Cliff and him entangled in heavily arousing kissing. He envisioned Cliff standing with him now, his lips beckoning him. Cliff really did have some incredible lips. Full. Pouty. Edible. Not a typical feature on a man, but it was an exceptionable bonus that it presently had Pyotr biting at his own, savoring the anticipation.

"Does it to you, does he?" the man stepping up to the showerhead next to him spoke through Pyotr's thoughts.

Pyotr opened his eyes, finding his brother, Pavle, standing next to him adjusting the shower knobs to get the right temperature. Pyotr smiled his acknowledgement. He felt like a kid with his new-found crush for the young lad and wasn't a bit ashamed for it.

"Yeah, well next time, try not to break the oars in the process, will ya?" Pavle teased before ducking under the water to let it rinse away the sweat and salt.

Pyotr turned, closing his eyes to do the same, but instantly the showers filled with boisterous laughter and cajoling. He scanned the showers, finding his teammates all laughing at him, along with the direction of their hungry eyes. He glanced down at the hard-on he was sporting, being the object of their amusement as it strove to row for the ceiling with a lively empowered bounce.

"Ya think the little blond twink caused that in him?" one of the men across from him asked, in general to the others.

"He must have. Pyotr broke out the good smelling stuff," another answered taking in a strong inhale then shared an expression of pleasure.

"He's not a twink. You know I don't go for that build," Pyotr moved to correct the stereotyping with a stern tone. He closed his eyes and moved under the stream of hot water, enjoying the feel as it cascaded down his skin, just imagining it was Cliff's tongue instead.

He felt exhilarated, his body pumped from their workout on the river, feeling the intoxicating mix of adrenalin and testosterone coursing through his veins— all the way down to his erection. He wasn't going to let the boys hound away his moment of fantasy and he quickly envisioning himself licking over Cliff's cock as he began to palm over his own.

"Come here, daddy. I'll bend over for ya an' you can run that beautiful sword up my arse," another one of the guys called to Pyotr in lustful offering.

Pyotr peeked a singular eye open to ward off the large New Zealander man. "You'll mind your talking so you don't interrupt my wet-dream again, Hemi, is what you'll do." It was a gentle warning. But, one that was not to be disobeyed either.

"Such a waste of a gorgeous cock," one of the others drew closer with hopes to tempt him.

Again, Pyotr peeked an eye open, this time it was Tim and standing intrudingly close. "A show is all you're gonna get."

"Hey, dinner and a movie. I'm up for that," another joked from the far end, calling Tim back to the lower ranks. "Come on over here, Tim. I'll stroke you up good and plenty, while you watch. Maybe even Hemi will back his ass over your cock and then together will how him how to actually row."

The shower filled with the ruckus of laughter. Pyotr did what he could to tune them out and stay focused on his cock.

They had a general rule, no dating between mates, but that didn't stop them from fooling around a little in the shower from time to time. Of course, Pyotr knew full well none of them would think twice about having a go with him; rules-be-damned for a chance to lie next to his well-kept body.

"Pavle is still making up for lost time. I'm sure he'd be more than happy to stick ya with his sword. And then you can give him a ride home," Pyotr suggested then went back to his wet-dream. He actually needed to hurry it up and just get a little release so he could get out of there and catch Cliff before they made it to the bus stop.

"Not like you to put forth the effort for a short fling," Pavle commented from his short perception, while Pyotr stroked himself to the edge.

Pyotr let out a hiss as the effects of his pumping fist started to draw him toward his release. "That's because it's not."

"Don't take this the wrong way, brother, but the kid looked a little young on the meter, don't you think?"

"He doesn't think so—" Pyotr sucked in a long-ragged breath. His hand throttling over his shaft as he held on to the vision of his soon-lover, pinned underneath him. "and he has the body of a man. That's good enough for me." His teeth rattle and despite all the disruptions his goal was reached. He let out a tight bellow. His body curling up, all his muscles tensing, and he shook in his own grasp. His cock blasting a steady spurt of cum out over the tile floor.

"Fuck! What a waste," one of the men mourned under their own panting, as several of them had begun jacking themselves off while watching Pyotr.

Pyotr shook off the last shudder and quickly rinsed, then turned the water off. He glanced at his brother, who was watching him keenly. "Find out why Sasha and Darko didn't make it in for practice for me, will you? Oh, and make sure one of these blockheads takes you home."

"Oh, I'm sure I'll get something to ride." Pavle shot him a mischievous wink.

Cliff and Kimmi had just reached the far end of the park when the black Audi Quattro pulled up alongside them and stopped. Cliff knew the car and expected the window to slide down, but instead, Pyotr was hopping out, coming around as though he intended to join them.

He looked good, fresh and clean from a recent shower with his hands tucked in the pockets of his relaxed Dockers. He almost looked excited, like he was forcing himself to hold back on some small detail. His eyes gleaming with some deeper happy thoughts and Cliff found himself pondering what they might be as he easily felt its effects, feeling a little excitable zing himself. Then just as abruptly, felt a sudden blush come over him that Pyotr's thoughts might have something to do with him.

"I thought it was you I saw." Pyotr glanced down at Kimmi and smiled.

Cliff watched and for the first time in more than he could remember someone's focus didn't go directly to her scarfed head. Not even with the festive colored bandana or the shortest strands of blond hair that poked out from under it, drew Pyotr's attention. Instead, his gaze went straight to her eyes then to Cliff's own. A slight grin emerged and then Pyotr looked back at Kimmi and it deepened into the genuine sparkling smile of his. "You must be Kimmi." He withdrew a hand from his pockets and offered to shake hers.

The smile Kimmi offered to Pyotr's reception was instantly welcoming and contagious. Before the first exchange of words, Cliff could see an instant adoration of her in Pyotr's eyes. Pyotr's hand went back to its hiding place, but the grin never left. "I'm famished. I usually eat at one of the local restaurants after practice. You should come join me."

Cliff hesitated, not sure what to expect or what to do at that point. To be asked to go eat with the man was outside any definition of a scene and he had Kimmi with him. Surely Pyotr didn't really want to be around him while she was there. No one else ever did.

"Please. I already ditched the others," Pyotr countered his hesitation as if on cue. "I know of a great place, the food's very good—"

"Kimmi has—"

"Even for the most finicky of stomachs," Pyotr broke in with a quick safety-net that suggested he wasn't about to be refused.

Pyotr was good to his word, having picked out a local family Italian restaurant that not only had Kimmi's favorite food, but Pyotr saw to it their white pizza was light on the basil, and extra heavy on the garlic and cheese.

They sat out on the terrace, overlooking the river, watching several more teams of sculls pulled by well into the evening, right along with kayakers and a few pleasure boats. They talked about a variety of things— the area and more about boating, Kimmi's fondness for glass painting, and where Cliff went to school for his EMT registry.

For dessert, they had gelato. Surprisingly, when Kimmi, of course, couldn't make up her mind which flavor she wanted, Pyotr ordered the grand slam dish with a scoop of them all. And pretty soon the waiter brought it over. The bowl s big it took two hands to carry it over then set it in the center of the table for them to share. It was fun diving in to try them all, pretending they were food critics taking notes of which ones they preferred, as they talked some more. Then at the first signs from Kimmi that she was getting tired, Pyotr offered them a ride home.

Pyotr pulled up in front of the single-story home, tucked length-ways on its lot, with hardly enough space between it and the next house to get a lawn mower past.

"You wanna come in?" Kimmi invited Pyotr as he came around to open the door for her. "I'll probably go straight to bed, but you can still stay and spend time with Cliff." Her tired expression held a mild hint that she knew fairly well enough what was developing between her brother and this new man— even if they hadn't dared a single touch between them in front of her.

Cliff immediately blushed and diverted his eyes, aware her invitation had openly placed them both on the spot.

Pyotr only wore a confident grin when he answered, "I'd love to."

Cliff's blush deepened to a darker red; well, okay, so only *he* was on the spot.

CHAPTER THREE

Pyotr followed Cliff down the stairs into the basement that made up his room. They'd crossed half way when Cliff stopped and turned to say something but froze, coming face to face with the lusty expression on the older man's face. Whatever thought process might have been intended, it was gone. He swallowed nervously, and his mouth went dry. He didn't move, didn't know how to move or what to say, if anything. He could only hope that Pyotr was planning on taking over from here, and real soon, because he couldn't muster up a single brain cell toward initiating anything.

Pyotr stood tall and still before Cliff. An almost unreadable expression on his face. Almost, because Cliff could still see a deep wanting in Pyotr's face staring right through him. And then Pyotr took the last few steps between them. When he stopped, there was barely a breath of air between them. Still silent, Pyotr's hands moved and slipped under Cliff's shirt. Like a liquid caress and just as fluid, the man's hands moved up Cliff's sides toward his chest and shoulders. A slight gasp escaped Cliff's lips at the touch and his breathing deepened. Anxiety and anticipation stormed inside him and he felt his entire body take off, flying away without him.

Pyotr moved his hands further up in a smooth motion, Cliff's t-shirt gathering over his wrists as he continued. Pyotr's fingertips tickling as they made it to Cliff's arm pits. "Lift your arms," the command was whispered and breathy.

Cliff found his arms obeyed on their own before his brain could consciously give the go ahead when Pyotr pulled his shirt up over his head, and let it drop to the floor.

"Keep them up," Pyotr whispered as his hands glided up the length of Cliff's extended arms. Pyotr's lips followed, kissing him along the inner muscles of his bicep, while his hand ran in a gentle caress all the way up to clasp around Cliff's wrists, drawing them down to wrap around Pyotr's neck. Once Pyotr had Cliff posed as he wanted, he reversed the course of his hands, finding their way back down streaming toned muscles, while Pyotr's lips found Cliff's. Pyotr's tongue flicked out to tease him, then rocked back each time Cliff tried to return the kiss.

After several tries, Cliff's arms tightened around Pyotr's neck to block any further teasing, but to no gain. Pyotr had enough height and strength on him to still cause him suffering in his playfulness.

"Do I frustrate you?" Pyotr teased him even more now with words as he dropped his hands down around Cliff's hips.

"And then some." Cliff made no attempt to hold back his opinion of his soon-to-be lover's fun with him.

Just then, Pyotr grappled under the curve of Cliff's ass and yanked him to his body, crushing the growing erections they shared.

Cliff let out a gasp and Pyotr's tongue moved in, licking into his mouth with a warm claiming, and tangled with his own to deliver a taste of lingering flavors of garlic and red wine.

Cliff felt the warm shiver pulse down the start of his spine, going in every direction once it reached his epicenter. He was melting and firing off under Pyotr's attentive touch. The few Cliff had been sexually active with before had been anything *but* attentive; it was just sex. A means to release some pent-up frustration or to play around. Right now, with Pyotr, it was like exploring sex while bungee jumping at the same time. Soft hands explored his back, sides and front, while Pyotr's kiss explored his mouth or brushed his cheek with his warm breath. Desire even came with a barely audible growling sound, but damned if Cliff could come up with a name for it. "Smoldering umber," he whispered aloud as his head fell back and Pyotr moved down his neck to do nothing but lick but was interrupted with a chuckle.

"What was that?' Pyotr asked in a husky lager red tone.

Cliff straightened, looking at Pyotr who waited for his answer, becoming acutely aware his brain was rambling and he had muttered something completely idiotic out loud, causing him to blush. "Ah-uhm nothing."

Pyotr's mouth curled up in a wickedly, wanton smile knowing full well he'd turned Cliff into mush already. He moved in on Cliff's neck, rocking his head back with the force of his returned kissing and suckling against his skin. Pyotr's hands moved over Cliff's body, exploring the curvature of his ass with one hand while the other palmed at the bulge in Cliff's jeans.

The man's breath was deepening, sawing out signals that he coveted craving to be inside him. "What do you want?" Pyotr asked with a husky voice.

"I want more—" Cliff could barely wrap his head around the concept of talking that very moment, but he was certain if he didn't say anything Pyotr would stop and he just couldn't let that happen, couldn't let anything stop or stall between them. He wanted this. "No more just frotting. I want more."

Pyotr gently pushed and held Cliff away from him, keeping little more than a few inches between them. But it was enough for Cliff to lose the contact of his body. Pyotr's eyes bore down on him with a severe expression. "You understand if we move past this point, it is no longer a scene for you to find yourself. If you give yourself to me, I will not go back to it. I won't want to give you up. And need I remind you; I've said as much how feracious I am."

Cliff felt like he was ready to crawl out of his skin and take the man himself if Pyotr didn't get on with it. He didn't need any more *scenes* to decide who he was or what he was meant to do. He knew already he was meant to bottom for this man and he wanted nothing more than to actively establish that right now. To prove it, he leaned into the hands that held him at bay to say as much.

Pyotr's mouth came crashing over the Cliff's, thrusting his tongue past his lips. Cliff's head pressed back, allowing him in deeper, surrendering to it. Letting the dominant man take possession of his new submissive's mouth— and making sure he would be left with no doubt that tonight was just the start between them.

Cliff's body was already responding to him, his hips pushing to meet with Pyotr's all while Pyotr undid his jeans and pushed them, and the boxers Cliff wore down off his hips.

Cool air wafted around his balls and his freed cock, but they were soon cupped by the warm hand of the older man, instantly working him with smooth confident strokes. The grip flipping from front-handed to back-handed, using his thumb to press firmly along the primary nerve along the underside of Cliff's shaft. Cliff let out a moan, his fingers digging into Pyotr's back.

Pyotr broke the kiss, his hand never ceasing the backhanded strokes he delivered to Cliff's cock. "Condoms and lube."

"Top drawer— *ahhh*— bureau."

Pyotr glanced at the bed, noticing the panel drawer in the headboard, then across the room to the tallboy, being the farthest piece of furniture from the bed. "Not in the headboard?"

Cliff's brain fumbled. *This was no time for conversation.* "Never a need. I'm not much of a frequent flyer."

Pyotr stepped in, taking Cliff's hips in his grip, then used his body to walk Cliff backwards and began heading them toward the bureau. "That will change."

Pyotr's hands were never still for long, moving all over him. One to tangle into his hair then down to his back; the other stroked over Cliff's side and then down to squeeze at his ass. A long finger slid teasingly between

Cliff's cheeks and back out. Cliff struggled to keep up, but he was fumbling just to get one act of fondling down.

Pyotr chuckled between his licking, "Don't worry— you'll find your comfort zone soon enough."

"What are you, psychic?"

"Psychologist actually, but the two tend to resemble each other at times." Pyotr grinned mischievously.

It was the first time Cliff had seen such a deviantly, playful look on the man and it was an incredibly wicked and sexy look on him. Pitching him off balance.

After some fishing through the drawer, Pyotr found what he was looking for and no sooner, Cliff found himself being shuffled across his room again until they reached the bed and Pyotr tossed the bottle of oil and a handful of condoms on the bed. Cliff glanced at the four or five squares of foil then to Pyotr who still had the sinful grin on. "Should I be scared?"

"Most likely." Pyotr leaned in, licking over Cliff's lips playfully. "But it's too late for that now." Pyotr's hands resumed their wandering and pulled him in for a deeper kiss, grinding the cock still confined in Pyotr's Dockers against Cliff's exposed body.

Cliff found himself desperately wanting the man as naked as himself. It seemed rather unsettling that for the second night in a row, Pyotr still remained clothed, but then the man had just tossed more than a normal night's worth of condoms on the bed. He had to wonder about the purpose of having so many. Perhaps knowing he was Kimmi's donor, Pyotr intended to double up on the protection for his own peace of mind. Which seemed to still be over-kill; Pyotr was a doctor, too, which meant he too had to keep clean. Not that Cliff would risk going bareback first time without paper and commitment. *Commitment.* He was getting way ahead of himself.

"Repeat your safewords to me."

There was a pause as Cliff gathered his thoughts well enough to respond with the correct answer. "Red, Yellow, and Green."

"Good. Give me one."

"Brilliant Lime Green," the words barely out of his mouth.

Yet once his colors spoken, Cliff found himself flying backwards, the bed catching the back of his knees and down he went. His back bounced on the mattress a few times, then he quickly got up on elbows just a little disgruntled, "Hey, that's not fair. You're still dressed."

"Shhh, *shejtan.* They'll come off soon enough."

"*Now* would be preferable." Cliff scowled up at him. He sat up then, reaching for the man's fly, but Pyotr caught his wrist and pulled his hand away.

"Stay where I put you and just watch."

Cliff furrowed his brows in silent protest.

"Do as I say *dragi* , and lie back," Pyotr insisted as he stood at the foot of the bed and slowly began to unbutton his shirt, pulling it open to reveal his physique for Cliff to see. "I want you to see what is about to bed you."

"If you're about to give me another *old man* speech, save it."

Pyotr undid the remainder of his zipper and pushed aside the denim, exposing his enlarged cock already fighting its way up his belly. His earlier release at the showers had done little to squelch his arousal that was now restored to full demonic need enough so the red-flanged tip protruded out from his boxer-briefs.

"No. Just the *man* part. I want you to be completely sure this is what you want. So that there is no panic when I push inside you. You're about to be fucked by a man, *dragi* . I want you to be perfectly content with your decision." He positioned his fingers, using them to deliver a gliding touch to his cock, causing an involuntary spasm that made its girth thump against his hand.

"I want this. I want you. For god's sakes push," Cliff fussed. "I don't want time to have second thoughts or doubts or even worse, feel unworthy of being with you."

Pyotr placed a knee on the edge between Cliff legs and was instantly coming down over him onto straightened arms, locking himself to plank just over the young man. His eyes bore down on him intently. "Prove it."

"How?" Cliff felt the sudden intimidation.

"Touch me. All of me."

Cliff's excitement went off the charts then. He'd been wanting to do that from the beginning, so he wasn't reluctant to follow Pyotr's commands. Immediately, he reached for his pants and pushed them further down, taking the briefs with them until they were clear of Pyotr's hips. Cliff brought his fingers up along the formidable shaft that bounced up several times with a jerk, pointing its imposing purplish red cap in his direction. *Jazzberry Jam Red*. Its single eye already glistening with droplets of clear fluid. Cliff touched at the bead, smearing it about then brought it to his tongue to taste.

The was a slight huff from Pyotr, "That's a nice start," he shared his approval.

Cliff next wrapped his fingers around Pyotr's shaft and slowly began to stroke it, lightly at first, just enjoying the soft, velvety skin.

Pyotr's mouth fell open letting out a soft, raspy breath and he closed his eyes, enjoying the attention. Cliff moved down the length, his fingers stretching out to grasp the tightening scrotum, catching them up in his palm and massaged gently then back up the long length of Pyotr's cock.

"You have two hands, use them," the next command came as a pleasant sigh.

Cliff glanced up at him and saw the need in Pyotr's eyes. For a man who quoted *in strides*, there was only so much slow his body would take tonight. Cliff snaked his free hand around Pyotr's neck to pull him down to kiss him, but Pyotr kept his arms locked and held his head up and out of reach. "Kissing is a distraction."

Cliff scrunched his face in a scowl. "You're impossible."

"Look who's talking, *shejtan*." Pyotr smiled at him, but still made no move. He expected Cliff to explore his body fully until both his brain and body accepted the fact he was about to be fucked by a full grown man. "I will feel your lips again soon enough. Right now, use your hands."

Cliff let his hand slide down the man's body, feeling his chest and abdomen then went back to embrace Pyotr's cock with one, the other slipping around to find his ass. He slid his hands all over Pyotr's body just as Pyotr had instructed until it was too much to bear. His own cock standing on end, throbbing every time it caught the slightest touch from Pyotr's cock as it hovered over him. Cliff wrapped around the older man's hips and pulled him to come down over him. But, it was the whispered plea that won the kiss he'd attempted earlier. And was rewarded with a healthy grinding that had him whimpering into their kiss before Pyotr crawled off him and rolled to his back. Cliff followed, grabbing Pyotr's Dockers and pulled them the rest of the way down, exposing long tan legs, and then dropped them to the floor.

Freed from the confinements of fabric, Pyotr returned Cliff to his back and came over him, subdued his mouth with small chaste kisses, working his way down the youthful flesh with a mix of kissing and licking. Enjoying the taste of Cliff's body, Pyotr found one of the small nipples and licked it over before sucking the small bud into his mouth. He heard the hiss from the young man, a sweet sexy sound. Cliff's body was a ticking time bomb of sensation, wanting sexual bliss that never had a lover to take the time to deliver the goods. That is, until now.

Pyotr moved to the next manly nipple to deliver equal attention then slowly made his way down the axis of smooth abs until he felt the young man's throbbing cock bounce against his cheek. He rubbed his face against it, rollicking within his privately, perverted thoughts with the added bonus that his young lover had such an impressive tool to play with.

He kissed the engorged glans, taking pleasure in the involuntary jerk of the young man's organ and even more so in the clean, healthy taste.

Cliff's mind was flooded with the sensation of Pyotr's touch. It felt so damn good. But, when he felt the man's mouth come over his cock, he nearly jumped out of his skin. "*Ahhh.* What are you doing?" He pulled up on his elbows, looking down his body at Pyotr, who hovered around his cock, his eyes glancing back up at him with a small amount of amusement that what he was doing seemed fairly obvious. When Cliff said nothing else, mesmerized by the man's expression and what he was about to do, Pyotr went back to indulging in the treat.

"No wait—" Cliff sucked in a hard breath at the instant touch. "You're a Dom, I mean a Master— you're—"

Pyotr's amusement only seemed to deepen. "Are you saying I am not allowed to do as I wish to my lover's body?"

Cliff's forehead wrinkled unsure. He shook his head. "No. Yes. I mean, of course you're allowed to do as you please." Suddenly unsure of just what that defined.

"That's good or we'd have to start all over again with our sessions until you developed a clear understanding of our roles here."

"But—"

"No buts, your body looks good enough to eat. Which is exactly what I intend to do."

Pyotr's hands slid up the young man's body, forcing him to fall back down on the bed, then made their way back down to Cliff's legs, taking each one at a time and pulled them to wrap around his torso as he went back to the impressive young cock that made no protests of what it wanted. Pyotr bowed his head and took Cliff's shaft all the way in his mouth, then swallowing it even deeper down into his throat.

"Oh god." Cliff's head snapped back into the pillows, his hands grappled for purchase on Pyotr's shoulders and held onto him. The very man that was both the reason for his body zinging off into space, and his anchor.

(ᵕᴗᵕ)

Pyotr rolled his tongue over the lad's cock, in a laving, caressing rhythm, completely separate from what the rest of his mouth did to Cliff. Interchanging his lips from soft envelopment to power sucking.

Cliff was anything, but silent as a chorus of hissing and moaning escaped his throat and filled the room. His fists thrashed into the mattress at his sides, only to curl up in the same instant to tug at his own hair then clutch the pillows around his head. Cliff's body jerked and quaked with the building euphoric tension. "Oh god— I can't hang on." He writhed with the torture of pleasure.

Pyotr released the young man's cock from his mouth and smiled from the enjoyment he got just feeling his new lover squirm. He would thoroughly enjoy watching him cum, but not just yet. He lifted up crawling over Cliff and ground his own hard shaft against Cliff's with a tight roll of his hips, but that was the touch that did his young lover in. Cliff was instantly jack-knifing, slamming up against him, crying out only to hitch back into the mattress when his contorting body had no other place to go.

The rasping whimper that came from his lips was the sexiest sound Pyotr had ever heard from a man and soaked up every detail of Cliff's violent shudders as Cliff's orgasm exploded. Thick streams of white pearly seed spurted out over the young man's chest and Pyotr ground against his lover's cock again to draw out the wave. Cliff's hands shot out grasping Pyotr's waist tugging then pushing him to stay at the same time, all while his body rode out the ecstatic convulsions.

As the hard shivers eased what should have been quiet bliss for Cliff was not what Pyotr saw. Rather, the young man was instantly mortified at what he'd done.

"I'm sorry. I-I'm sorry." Cliff quickly turned truly panic stricken that he'd cum so soon.

Pyotr was not, and he lowered over Cliff's body and slid across him, smearing the spunk between them, ignoring the misplaced panic.

"I didn't mean to. I couldn't help it. I'm sor-"

"Say sorry one more time and I may have to find some form of punishment for you, and that won't please me, because it won't go well with my expectations for tonight," Pyotr warned tightly. He shifted his weight to one arm and ran his fingers over Cliff's chest gathering up a healthy dollop of semen and served it over Cliff's lips. Without further words, he lowered down and helped himself to the banquet prize from Cliff's lips and a deep hungry kiss. When he was satisfied that he'd silenced his lover, Pyotr broke from their kiss and rolled to his side.

Cliff was silent, almost too silent. Pyotr pulled at his chin bringing his eyes around to look at him and saw the worry there. Pyotr strummed over the lad's lips with his thumb, and then pulled the lad to him to kiss once again. Like any kiss they'd had after their first, the touch of his *dragi 's* tongue was soft and inviting as he licked his way into his young lover's mouth.

Cliff pulled away and glanced at him, "You're not mad?"

Pyotr's amusement melted into a question. "Why would I be mad?" Pyotr chuckled with all his usual amusement, his eyes lowered down the body still smeared with his handy work.

"I'm not supposed to cum unless you give me permission. That's the way it's supposed to be."

"I don't believe I gave such orders this night. My pleasure doesn't usually come from withholding your release, but rather making you cum for me multiple times." Pyotr ran his hand over Cliff's chest, further smearing the spunk over his body then wrapped around the man's neck and pulled Cliff to him for a more forceful kiss. He chewed at his distressed lover's lip for a solid decade of hunger before releasing him. "Besides, seeing how you responded so explosively only promises sweet torture in our future." Pyotr smiled then.

Cliff's head popped up, "Can I do it to you now?"

Pyotr made a near chuckling sound, "Do?"

"Suck you off."

Despite the vocabulary, Pyotr never lost his amusement of his new boy. It wasn't exactly the most eloquent way to put it, but then his lover was young and young people were always in such a rush. Eloquence and etiquette weren't in their vocabulary. Then again, they didn't exist in many of his perversions either.

Pyotr rolled to his back, his hand gently bringing Cliff with him to take his freedom with his body. He wouldn't let his young lover bring him to orgasm, but he would let Cliff savor him in any way he wished, to explore a man's body as he desired. There was a mental difference between men who were gay from the start and those that were late developers. Pyotr had never been with a woman, had never desired to even try it out, but Cliff had, for the most part, only been with women. Girls, rather. And no amount of *play* compared to the real thing of lying beside— touching, feeling, tasting the body of another man. And for some, it could be disturbing their first time, only because of all the negative mental rejections placed there by other people's opinions. So it was important to take it slow and enjoy each other's bodies more so than the sex itself. Though, Pyotr was certain that was going to be beyond satisfyingly incredible once they crossed the threshold.

Cliff wrapped his fingers around the thick, hard shaft, just enjoying the look of it as it filled his hand, moving up and down in soft and slow movements. He could stack his fists one on top of the other and the length of Pyotr's cock would win out. He liked how if felt, soft like silk, stretched over a hard rod of iron. Cliff could feel the pulse in the protruding veins that ran its length like wild vines. A drop of clear pre-cum seeped out from the tip and he drew his finger tip over it and brought it to his tongue just as before. A surprisingly briny-sweet flavor touched Cliff's taste buds, which described only half of the male delicacy. The other half he couldn't put into words to save his life, but he liked it. And he certainly wasn't afraid of it. Cliff bowed his head and licked over the mushroom cap a few times then sucked it into his mouth. He skirted the broad tip with his tongue several times then made his way down, taking more and more into his mouth, until it hit the back of his throat and he instantly started to gag. His head shot up in a slight panic, choking down large breaths of air as if his body thought he had swallowed water.

Pyotr's hand was instantly there, cradling his cheek with the warmth of his palm, "Easy. Not all at once."

Cliff looked up Pyotr's body, finding his deep blue eyes watching him with the same gentleness that was in his hand. Pyotr sat up only slightly, with one arm crooked under his head to make the angled view possible for him to watch. The expression telling Cliff the man's enjoyment was only from watching his new lover take his first cock, rather than the sensation of a *virgin* meeting *wise & experienced*.

Cliff licked at his lips a moment, pulling them in thoughtfully. He wanted Pyotr to have more than just a show. He wanted Pyotr to feel what he'd felt. He licked his lips once more, opened his mouth and covered the broad tip again, using his lips to form a tight seal. He sucked on it, drawing out more of the pre-cum discovering the heady flavor of musk and semen soaking his taste buds.

Swirling his tongue around the head, he lifted his gaze to watch Pyotr's expression. He did his best not to stumble about like an inexperienced boy. More than anything, he wanted to please Pyotr, wanted to make the man feel as much alive as he'd made him feel. He couldn't think of a time, outside of his sister, ever wanting to deliver and serve so whole heartedly. Always struggling to just once cheat out some kind of pleasure for himself. But something about Pyotr made him feel like he'd already gotten all that with plenty more to come and he wanted to make sure he could give it back so that Pyotr would never be disappointed in him.

He coated each side of Pyotr's cock with the flat of his tongue, exploring the taste and the smell. A fresh tingling shower gel that gave off an alluring combination of a lime citrus, followed with something closely resembling— he took another inhale— spicy nutmeg. Neither of those took away from the hint of a deeper and more natural scent of male musk. In fact, as their bodies warmed up in their slow building fervor of pleasure the fragrance warmed with them and enriched the natural flavor of Pyotr's body. The kind of smell you only find on a man. And Cliff groaned instantly to show his enjoyment. He took a lasting deep inhale as he let the hairs around the base of Pyotr's cock tickle his nose and then he worked his way back up along the shaft and then licked over the slit seeking out more and heard Pyotr hiss each time he did it. The temptation of finding his lover's sweet spot was too much to pass up and Cliff tightened the tip of his tongue and jabbed down into the hole.

Pyotr practically jackknifed in the bed himself, an entire sentence or two spilled out in Serbian. None of which did Cliff understand as Pyotr's hands took hold of Cliff and pulled him from his cock, bringing him up to Pyotr's lips. The surprised man kissed him with a hungry growl, but made no other comment, just some fun wicked expression warning him not to tempt the beast like that again. Cliff smiled anyways. Like a kid with a new present on Christmas day, Cliff reveled triumphantly— he'd made Pyotr jump.

Pyotr's grip slacked, returning to lie back down and guided Cliff's mouth back to his cock, tangling his fingers into his hair, some reminder to behave, he was certain.

Cliff licked over the head, just savoring the feel of the bulbous glans and how it filled his mouth. Resuming some more of the playful exploring and just how easily he could use his tongue to extract a quivering response from Pyotr. Whether it was a hissing sound, a verbal praise, or just a twitch in Pyotr's thighs, Cliff liked them all. Even when his attempts were clumsy at best, he felt some small amount of self-confidence that it still rewarded the man with some amount of pleasure, until he could master the skill for making it awesome.

He sucked the cock further into his mouth, bobbing his head up and down several times then licked all around the underside of the shaft. Down over the tightening balls and back up to do it all over again.

Pyotr lay back, eyes closed, basking in his new lover's mouth, which was doing far more to his temptation than he had anticipated. He chewed at his lip, between the occasional escaped gasp, not that he bothered with trying to hold them back. A little bit of training and Cliff may turn out to be the sweetest pair of lips he'd ever had wrapped around his cock in some time. Adding to the erotica of it all were the glimpse touches of Cliff's erect cock against his leg as the young man continued to suck him down. It was an added thrill that his new young lover was still hard, even after such an explosive orgasm and it suited Pyotr just fine. He was going to enjoy watching the young man's dick, all red and swollen, bouncing up and down as he took him. Just the image in his head was enough to take him to the edge and threaten an early release. A reprieve he didn't want just yet.

Pyotr fisted his fingers into Cliff's hair and gently pulled him from his cock. A popping sound blasted from Cliff's lips as he tried to keep a firm suction going.

"Why'd you stop me?" Cliff fussed.

"*Shejtan,* there are other ways to please me. Ways other than racing to get me to cum."

"Such as?" Cliff looked up at him, his lips swollen from sucking on him, and Pyotr wanted to feel those swollen lips on his own.

"Kissing. I want you to lick your way up my body."

It was another thing that Pyotr wanted him to do, that would burn into Cliff's mind that he was with a man. Cliff didn't need any more tutoring on the matter. He wasn't in bed with just a man, he was in bed with Pyotr and there was nothing more erotic and arousing or more satisfying than that. "And when I have found my way up will you stop the gay 101 stuff?"

Pyotr laughed. "Alright, but I did try to break you in easy. Don't say I didn't warn you."

Cliff dropped back down, only instead of taking Pyotr's cock back into his mouth, he sucked one side of his tight sacks in his mouth, swirling the tender gland over his tongue then did the same to the other side. He wasn't afraid to be with a man, or to be gay. These mattered none to him. Being with the first person who'd given him time for himself, that was what mattered. And he was determined to show Pyotr just how open and ready he was for this. His ears filled with the sound of Pyotr sucking in a tight breath, which was what he was trying to get in the first place.

Cliff took a deep inhale and rubbed his nose into the soft skin between the man's leg and groin. He licked it over several times and started a wet trail all the way up Pyotr's belly to his chest and then his neck and gave him a triumphant nip on the jaw.

Pyotr let out a deep groan-like sigh and pulled the young man on top of him, rubbing their cocks together and kissed him, swiping over Cliff's tongue with his own. Lick— after rolling lick, soaking his lips with a laving caress of his tongue.

Pyotr pushed off, using his foot and rolling them both over, placing Cliff on his back, and putting Pyotr back on top. He kissed the young man several times more before breaking away and working his way down Cliff's body. His tongue grazing over the lad's cock with one long, teasing lick then did the same to each of his balls, following up with nibbling on the inside of Cliff's thigh. Pyotr raised Cliff's right leg up at the knee, tucked his head under and chewed on the back of his thigh then rolled Cliff the rest of the way over to his stomach to continue chewing on Cliff's backside. Biting into his left ass cheek then his right then trailed his tongue up Cliff's spine and lingered at the back of his neck to kiss and nibble there.

Pyotr could hardly maintain a steady breath as his need to keep exploring and enjoying the young man underneath him sent him into a new world of alpha heat. He reached across the bed and grabbed the bottle of oil, smeared a generous amount on his fingers and began applying it into the crevice of Cliff's ass, just slathering it on both sides of his cheeks. His finger pressed between them finding the tight puckered hole and massaging over it. Teasing the entrance gently with his fingertips, then pushed his hand under Cliff to wrap around his cock, stroking it a few times then coming back to tempt the rear entrance more.

Cliff pushed back on Pyotr's fingers, hoping to get a good slip. His body was burning with need, a yearning that was long overdue to be felt and sated. So, it would suit him just fine if Pyotr wanted to just get on with it and start fucking him right then. Several moans broke from his lips, mostly out of desperation for more of the more he'd asked for from the start.

Pyotr moved up on his knees, straddled over Cliff's legs, and slid his cock between his cheeks, letting his hard shaft slip in the oil against the forbidden crevice. Letting Cliff get a feel for his length against his body. It felt so good, even better with Cliff rocking back against him. He loved an active bottom, though he wouldn't expect a lot out of Cliff, not in the beginning. It would take him some time to discover a comfortable rhythm, but it still felt incredible, sliding against his tight ass, watching him push back, silently begging for more.

"What do you need?" Pyotr whispered, grinding harder against Cliff.

Cliff pushed back so hard that had Pyotr been lined up at that very moment, Cliff would have managed his shaft slide in to the hilt in one fell swoop. "I want that inside me— fucking me," he groaned.

"Give me a safe word."

"Green."

"Is that all? Just green. I have to wonder maybe you don't want my cock deep inside your hole after all," he teased.

"Soylent winter-fucking green." But it wasn't the angry *let's do this* brat that shot a look over his shoulder but a pleading wanton for their erotic connection to be finalized. To finally be claimed.

Pyotr moved back, grabbed one of the pillows, folded it in half then lifted Cliff's hips and stuffed it under him, positioning Cliff's buttocks perfectly for him. He tore open one of the foils and rolled the condom down his shaft, stroking himself a few times, then gripping his cock at the base, he lined it up until it was just right against Cliff's tight little hole. Pyotr eased up against him, the swollen cap of his rod pressing its way through the tightly muscled ring. Cliff hissed underneath him and Pyotr paused letting his lover's body adjust a moment before lowering into him further. Cliff's whole body tensed up and Pyotr pulled back.

"No. Don't stop." Cliff growled a protest into the bed covers.

"It won't be any good for either of us if I hurt you." Pyotr laid down the law with him. But was soon stroking over Cliff's hole with a slicked finger teasing the pucker to relax against him and slowly pushed in.

Cliff let out a heavy moan wallowing in the inner contact of Pyotr's long finger, pushing back a small amount and Pyotr rewarded him with a deeper penetration until the knuckles of his hand pressed against Cliff's ass. Pyotr picked up a slow rhythm sliding in and out a few times then added a second finger, and scissored them as they moved back and forth, stretching Cliff's hole open to prepare him to take Pyotr's cock easier. He crooked his fingers to catch his prostate making Cliff let out far more than a gasp this time and his hips bucked under Pyotr.

(ᵔωᵔ)

Cliff's head was swimming. He felt drunk, he was so damn needy right then his libido was screaming it wanted to be fucked with voracity. Pyotr taking his time was about to drive him insane. His fingers— how they seemed to know right were to go, finding a sweet spot Cliff had no idea he had. It was so good he wanted more of it. He rocked back on the other man's fingers harder, gaining deeper penetration and hopefully convincing Pyotr he really was ready. "Damn it—" Cliff gasped when Pyotr's fingers, lodged up in his ass, stroked over his prostate again. "Please."

Pyotr rolled off his legs and Cliff thought for sure he was going to freak on him.

"Get up and stand between the bed and the dresser." Pyotr gave firm instructions as he sat down on the edge of the bed himself and stretched his long legs out. Cliff jumped up, not sure what Pyotr had planned, but wasn't going to waste any time over preliminaries. He stood at the side of the bed where Pyotr pointed then let Pyotr guide him until he was standing straddled over Pyotr's legs which put him facing the dresser mirror.

"Place your hands on the dresser."

Cliff did as Pyotr instructed, the backs of his legs rested against the bed, and bent over, placing his hands on the edge of the dresser to hold his weight and brace against an anticipated pounding. He stared at his own reflection, then to Pyotr's, who peered around his side, watching their reflection together. He was leaning back on the bed, propped up straight on his arms, his legs stretched out between Cliff's and then he felt the first kiss of Pyotr's cock against his puckered hole as the man lifted his hips up off the bed.

Aligning the head of his cock, Pyotr gently eased in, slowly stretching its way into Cliff's hole. The tight ring of muscle resisting, but as Cliff willed himself to relax, his body adjusted, allowing Pyotr to slide in further, feeding the length of his shaft into his lover's body.

Oh fuck. Cliff's jaw clenched to stifle a guttural moan and his fingers curled into the edge of the dresser until his knuckles went white. His entrance flamed with its first stretching after such a long time out of use, and his passage awoke with a flurry of spasms he could not control, which resulted in his teeth chattering.

Pyotr eased out a little. "Take deep breaths and relax," Pyotr guided him.

It wasn't until that moment, that Cliff realized he'd been holding his breath. He closed his eyes, took a slow, deep breath and let it out nice and slow. Then he felt Pyotr's cock push up inside him a little more, this time with less pain and less resistance from his muscles.

᠆ᨆᨆ᠆

"That's it. Relax for me. Just let me be inside you a minute." Pyotr listened as Cliff took another deep breath.

Cliff dropped his head forward and just like that, Pyotr felt him relax and take him inside. Deeper. Hotter. Silken walls caressing and hugging his cock, he began to fill Cliff's nether.

Pyotr rocked his hips from side to side, letting his cock press against the sides of the walls as it slid in. One arm behind him held up his body, while he reached over and rested the other hand tenderly on Cliff's hips, drawing him further down onto his cock.

᠆ᨆᨆ᠆

Another sudden spike of pain had Cliff's teeth nearly chattering again as he forced his body to adapt. Pyotr eased out then rocked up inside him going no deeper than Cliff had already taken, yet the gentle micro movement of rocking eased the pain so pleasure could step in. The sensation was like a drug and Cliff wanted it all.

Inch by inch, Cliff began to work himself onto the older man's shaft, taking him a little deeper with every movement he made, and gradually learning how to relax around the thick intrusion at the same time. The walls of his rectum rippled, anticipating the moment it would feel Pyotr ramming his ass in a rough shafting. Cliff wanted that so damn bad it consumed him.

He heard Pyotr murmured his approval behind him as Cliff took him further and more fully inside. Feeding him the entire length of his cock, he inched slowly upwards, until, with a final grinding roll, Pyotr bottomed out deep inside Cliff's ass.

They didn't move, pausing to just let the final sensation make its imprint in them both. Soft skin of Pyotr's groin pressed against the fleshy globes of Cliff's ass.

Each sound of Pyotr's enjoyment encouraged Cliff. *He* was making the other man sound like that. By the time his new lover's cock was buried inside him to the hilt, Cliff's own moans had joined his.

Slowly, Pyotr started to move. Even sitting on the edge of the bed, the man's hips found movement withdrawing his hips until only the tip of his cock remained inside Cliff. Pyotr pressed upward, sliding his shaft all the way back inside. Back and forth he undulated, gradually increasing his speed and pressure until they were both caught up in a deep storm of moans. With his muscular arms braced back on the bed and Cliff straddled backwards over Pyotr's lap, riding him out, Pyotr was eventually pounding his hard cock into his young lover's tight hole. Taking them right to the edge, only to abruptly back off before starting up again in a torturously super slow pace and work his way up to the orgasmic building rhythm all over again.

Cliff gritted his teeth and his hands moved from the edge of the dresser to Pyotr's thighs where he gripped at them to keep his body from toppling over and perhaps hoping they'd keep his mind anchored as well. More moaning escaped his lungs. The friction against his prostate had him rocking with euphoric waves of pleasure that made it impossible for him to even consider being quiet. He'd never felt such exhilarating ecstasy and right now he was overwhelmed and consumed with it.

Shuddering, his head fell back and he squeezed his eyes closed, drinking in the earth-shattering feeling of Pyotr's silky, hard shaft, filling and stroking his prostate with every surge. The slapping sound of Cliff's cock against his belly, joined the erotic chorus of Pyotr's slick thrusts, which added to his delirium.

Pyotr shifted his hips, thrusting up harder— like a steam engine, pistoning into Cliff, aiming his intents— and reaching deeper.

The pressure on Pyotr's cock spun Cliff toward release. Rushing heat surged through his body and his balls drew up tight against his body until they nearly hurt. He was melting and shivering as his cock lengthened and hardened in a way he never thought possible. It bounced violently with every pounding. Dribbling pre-cum with every slap against his belly, ready to shoot. Heat and lust radiated around them, perfuming the room with the scent of nothing but pure male sex. It was intoxicating in a way Cliff had never experienced or ever thought could exist.

He wasn't sure he could hang on much longer. His throat burned from the relentless panting and whimpering. The nerves in his whole body, firing off like a thousand circuit breakers. The culminating wave of pleasure building into such an intense ball of energy, he was certain there'd be nothing left of him when he did explode. His moans were so loud and out of control, it should have startled him, but Pyotr felt so damn good, thrusting up into the rear nethers he couldn't convince himself to feel otherwise. It was too good to hold back.

"Ah yes— look at how beautiful your cock is, dancing for me while I fuck you," Pyotr growled with each thrust.

"Oh god," Cliff cried out, he was so damn close.

Pyotr's shaft slid deep then reared back until only the head remained inside Cliff's tunnel. Then he slammed up inside him again— and again. Cliff's cock bobbed with the timing and force of Pyotr's thrusts.

"Look at it, *dragi* . How it dances up and down for me," Pyotr's praises stopping only long enough to groan into Cliff's back and lick over the muscles in his arm before stating more of the obvious on Cliff's twirling and slapping anatomy. "Look how hard you are. I love how you stay hard for me while I'm fucking you."

Cliff tried to blush, but he just couldn't seem to submit to his embarrassment while Pyotr still lifted his hips, driving his cock inside him. The friction inside his tight walls had everything else swept aside. And it was clearly a huge turn on for his lover.

(ºωº)

Pyotr licked over Cliff's back, back and forth, tasting the saltiness of Cliff's sweat. He bit into the tender flesh below a shoulder blade and growled into him when Pyotr felt the walls around his cock tighten. "Ahhh—" Pyotr groaned more and he knew he wasn't going to last much longer with a trick like that.

He brought his legs in and pushed them both to their feet, his hips rocking Cliff forward farther and he bent over the young man immediately licking over the lad's neck and shoulder, savoring more of Cliff's taste. Pyotr's eyes filled with the sight of his young lover's cock, swollen and a completely dark crimson red from tip to stem. Angry and up right, it was primed to explode any second. Pyotr reached around, taking the fiercely engorged shaft in his grip and squeezed it, just as he thrust his own cock deep inside Cliff's ass once again.

Cliff cried out, his legs kicked, giving out underneath him, but Pyotr caught him up in his arm, yet still kept the shock and awe going. Pyotr's right hand continuing to jack Cliff's dick while he shafted into the depths of his hole.

He manage to maneuver Cliff back to his feet and took the opportunity while he could, to curl up around Cliff's side, taking his jaw and turning his mouth for him to kiss. Two more strokes, thrusting deep inside Cliff's ass then stilled just as every one of the younger man's muscles locked with the climatic force and Cliff's cock exploded.

With a low, strangled cry, Cliff lost it completely, obeying the demands of his hand with helpless pleasure. Heart pounding against the palm of one hand, his chest heaving for breath, while Pyotr felt the pulsing sensation of Cliff's cock spasming in the fist of his other hand. Cum fountained out, coating Pyotr's grip and the dresser with a pool of white seed.

Pyotr's hand filled with the hot cum and he used it to make a wet suction over the head of Cliff's cock, forcing him into a painful, bucking ride of post ecstasy. Another cry escaped Cliff, while Pyotr milked his cock further.

Keeping his hand relentlessly, expertly moved to ensure that each subsequent blistering jet was larger and more forceful than the last.

Like a jackhammer, Pyotr pounded him, spurred on by the vocalized orgasm. Muscles tensed— tighter— tighter— until Pyotr snapped. Euphoric waves washed over him. He powered through his orgasm, relishing each hot spurt of cum milked from his cock. Sweat beaded on his brow. His chest heaved and his body burned. He stared into Cliff's eyes in the mirror, thrilled at the rapturous glimmer staring back.

(•ω•)

"*Ahhh!* Oh fuck!" Cliff cried out his body tugging and towing against his lover's arms, but they tightened around him like a vice. Pyotr's cock shafted deep inside him once more, throbbing violently against his buttocks and Pyotr's groaning release was added to his own.

Cliff watched it all in the mirror, unable to take his eyes off the man as his face contorted with painful bliss. Cliff's own eyes fluttered, threatening to take the show away as Pyotr's groin rolled into him several times more, forcing that last swelled reach of his cock deep inside him, squeezing out every last aftershock and exquisite ripple through their bodies.

Pyotr's weight pressed down over Cliff's back and chewed on his shoulder. He kissed and then licked Cliff from shoulder to neck to cheek, spilling his hot panting breath over his skin.

"So good, *dragi* ," he whispered several times in his ear, the praises sounded as good as they felt as Pyotr breathed them out on his neck. And still Cliff was mesmerized just watching him. He'd never seen a man as sexy and alluring as Pyotr, like he was pure, walking ecstasy. Pleasure flashed across the older man's face—pleasure from being with him. And Cliff felt himself fall a little further for Pyotr. However, He already knew there wasn't much further left for him to fall.

A harsh breath rasped from Pyotr's lungs as the last of the aftershocks rattled through him. He volunteered himself to fall back into the mattress, taking Cliff down with him, his cock still lodged deep inside Cliff's nether. They rolled to their sides, Pyotr's arm wrapping around him possessively, even adding a leg to the embrace that had Cliff pinned down while Pyotr kissed the back of his head lazily. "So good, *dragi*." He stroked over Cliff's cock slathering it with the remains of his glazed spunk.

Cliff felt the exhaustion coming over them both, but he tensed preparing himself for the coming exit of his lover, left to sleep and wake alone. Cliff listened as Pyotr's rasped breathing slowed into a deeper rhythm and nuzzled against him until their bodies were fused in a seamless damp tangle.

"Never before have I enjoyed a man so intensely on the first time as I have with you," Pyotr whispered against his ear.

Cliff turned his head, being the only part of him that could move under the weight of the older man, "Never?" He could hardly believe such a claim with the experience Pyotr had. He had half feared he would be a disappointment to the man.

Pyotr licked and kissed along Cliff's jaw. "Never," he confirmed, "And I plan to enjoy you for as long as you allow me."

Cliff fell back into his pillow, "You can stay you know," he offered with too much hope that he might actually consider it.

Pyotr rose up on an elbow and pulled Cliff around to look at him, "Had you planned for me to leave?"

"They always leave."

"I'm not that kind of lover, *dragi* . If I'm to have you, it will be all of you, all of the time. No drive by quickies." He lowered over Cliff, kissing him, nibbling over his lips for the briefest of moments. "But you must also understand, I won't have anyone else but you, which means you'll have more of me than perhaps you're prepared to have. Are you ready to submit to a demanding lover, *dragi* ?"

Pyotr wasn't just staying the night; he was offering to stay period. For however long they were meant to last. It was more than Cliff had ever been given or promised in all his life. Ready or not, there was no way he was going to say no. Cliff reached up, his fingers tangling in the handsome man's hair and pulled him back down to him. "Yes," he hissed, "I'm ready."

It was early morning, and despite a late night loving-making romp, the habit of waking with the dawn was an unbreakable one for him. Leaving his young lover to slumber, Pyotr made his way upstairs and into the kitchen, finding Kimmi already up, working on one of an array of craft projects spread out on the table in the kitchen nook.

"Good morning, Kimmi. You're an early riser, too?"

Kimmi glanced over at him with a surprised expression that quickly turned into a smile and nodded.

"Which do you prefer, breakfast or tea first?" Pyotr helped himself to explore the cabinets, opening several until he found what he was looking for, and carried the electric kettle to the sink to fill it.

"Oh, you don't have to make me breakfast."

"I plan on cooking anyways. It'd be a shame if you didn't join me."

Kimmi's face melted into a much deeper smile and Pyotr had a good idea where it stemmed from, but he said nothing as he waited for her response.

"Tea first then, please." Then some thought marked her face and she was quickly making up for clarification. "Not that I get sick anymore. It's just habit really. I promise not to throw up at the table."

Pyotr nodded with a slight chuckle, but decided it wasn't of value to comment on, not wanting her to feel she needed to make any excuses. It was, after all her home. He glanced over the selection of produce and other items in the fridge then summed up there was plenty for what he wanted to do. "Any good at chopping?" he called over his shoulder.

"Excuse me?" Kimmi's mouth dropped into a long 'O' as she gawped at him from the table.

Pyotr pulled some groceries from the fridge and set them on the counter. "We're having omelets. I need a chopper assistant." He threw her a wink.

Kimmi's face beamed instantly and she jumped from the table in trade for one of the bar stools at the other side of the counter island. "That's me then."

Pyotr returned the deep smile he'd gotten from the girl. His suspicions confirmed. Whoever Cliff brought home on occasion, not only didn't stay the night, they obviously didn't include Kimmi on the social list either.

As they prepared their ingredients, Kimmi's face began to blush heavily and her lips quirked with some unspoken humor.

"What has you so amused?" Pyotr perked for her thoughts.

A giggle gushed from her, "Cliff was really noisy last night." She kept her eyes directed downward as she scooped up the chopped mushrooms and dropped them into a bowl then gathered a few more to slice on her cutting board.

Pyotr exploded with laughter and nodded in agreement. Yes, his young new lover had been a symphony of vocal expressions and Pyotr had loved being the cause of it.

The whistle on the kettle went off and he filled their cups, while Kimmi added the tea bags and dunking hers several times to speed up the steeping.

"So does it really feel that good?" Kimmi asked, this time her eyes filled with innocent wonder still accentuated with blushing cheeks.

Pyotr smiled and nodded to her. "When two people care about how the other is pleasured and take the time to see it delivered, then yes. It really does feel that good."

"It's never been like that for Cliff before." A tender amount of remorse for her brother's limited life showed on her face. "It's my fault yanno."

Pyotr kept quiet, it wasn't for him to pry or ask such questions. Not from his sister at least and certainly not without Cliff being present in a conversation about him.

Kimmi fell silent, but clearly her mind did not, and her blushing cheeks continued to deepen until the rouge color spread down her neck and down the top of her chest visible from under the drooping collar of her crumpled t-shirt. Her lips twitched as she fought to keep her smile at bay. "You must care a whole lot."

This time Pyotr felt a hint of blushing and his smiled deepened, nodded softly in agreement.

The two gathered in the breakfast nook, Kimmi drawing up on the bench seat in the bay window with her tea, while Pyotr took to the dining room table. As the morning light spilled through the lace curtains, Kimmi's glass paintings came to life. Each frame of paned glass was painted, sending a kaleidoscope of colors into the room in a faux twilight haze as they drank their tea.

Pyotr had talked with Diesel on her condition previously, keeping such conversations away from his sessions with Cliff. She had been doing well for the last six months, after a long recovery from a recent stem cell transplant and was appearing to be in a successful remission. But, he noticed her hair wasn't growing back. "How long does it usually take for your hair to grow out after you've stopped chemo treatments?"

"Oh no, I long since stopped letting it grow out." She racked the short strands of blonde with her fingertips, "I just can't bare going through the falling out stages anymore. So last year when I had to go through all the treatments, Cliff got me a pair of clippers, and we shaved my head." She made a sound as if she'd tried to laugh it off, "I still cried. So he shaved his own head too, right there for me." She gave a tearful smile then reached over to the window sill where she kept a carved, wooden box. She reached in, pulling out a plastic zip lock bag filled with a mix of blond hair in it and offered it to Pyotr for inspection.

Pyotr looked at the hair then the few other items he could see in the box. He slid his chair closer and reached over, plucking out the photo of Cliff and Kimmi, arm in arm, both with fresh shaved heads. In the photo, Kimmi was smiling, despite the red rims around her eyes, and Cliff's smile was soft and protective as a brother's should be. With it, were a couple more photos: One of them on a boat and right alongside it a large whale. Its massive head, rising up out of the ocean alongside the small water craft, eyeing the people onboard with as much curiosity as those on the boat looked at him, with wide-eyed wonder.

"When was this taken?" Pyotr held up the photos.

"Oh, that was last summer right before I had to go back in for treatments. The center took us all out on a sponsored fieldtrip. Someone from one of the other boats took the photos and sent them to me." She held up another from the same outing, showing a large white fin reaching up from the water and there was Kimmi reaching out making contact with the world's largest creature. "It's a Humpback whale." She bit down on her lip, her mind drifting to the memory as she glanced down at the photo in Pyotr's hand.

He watched her eyes. The same color as Cliff's only where his often seemed to reflect a storm about to come, hers were like the cool grey just after the rain has passed, when blue skies threatened to show through.

Pyotr placed the photos and the bag of hair back, noting the few other treasures inside it. She had only a few keepsakes for her treasure box, not nearly enough things that one would expect to be in a young girl's collection. But, he did want to hear about the pressed corsage. He pointed at it with an invitation to tell her story.

Kimmi's head fell to the side, a soft expression of fondness colored her cheeks, "At the treatment hospital, they have this prom night for the patients; one of the guys Cliff works with has a boyfriend closer to my age. He was my date for the night. He was dressed up so fancy. I don't know where my dress came from, but it was really pretty." She sucked in a dep breath that her entire body rose up with it until it landed a soft smile on her face. "I felt like Cinderella that night," she beamed.

"And your date? Did he kiss you at the end of the night?"

"No." She shook her head with a soft blush. "No, kiss." Her cheeks flushed even redder then.

Pyotr could see she would have welcomed the kiss had her date offered, but he had a good idea *who* her date was. It didn't take much to put the pieces together and no, he couldn't imagine neither Isaac nor Isaiah kissing a girl. But, it was kind of Sasha to arrange it for her. Knowing Sasha's twin boyfriends, whichever it was of them to be her *date,* chance were they'd been far more nervous than she had been.

Pyotr took several more sips of his tea when he noticed Kimmi's new expression. Something she was just dying to get out.

"Spill it," he commanded with a smile.

"There *is* a boy at the center. His name is Bryley. He's from Australia. I like it when he flirts with me."

"And has he kissed you?"

The deep blush quickly returned, she shook her head timidly.

"But you would like for him to?"

A smile melted onto her face, and the pinkish blush spread to her chest just like before.

They heard the stairs to Cliff's room creak and she nearly blanched, "Oooo, you won't tell Cliff, will you?"

Pyotr smiled behind his tea mug. "Mum's the word." He then pushed up from the table and headed back into the kitchen area so he could get breakfast started.

Cliff popped in, rubbing at his eyes and looking as if he was still half asleep, just as Pyotr was setting everything within reach next to the stove.

"*Dobro jutro, dremalo.*" Pyotr grinned at him, looking over his shoulder.

Cliff peeked up at him with a questioning look.

Pyotr's warm face brightened at the sight of his boy. "I said, good morning sleepy head." Pyotr felt a sudden rush at the sight of his new lover standing there in his lounge pants, shirtless and looking well fucked. He wanted to kiss him right there on the spot. He hesitated a moment, Cliff wasn't officially out and he had refrained from touching him yesterday while they were out in public and with his sister watching. But Kimmi was old enough to know good and well what they had been up to during the night, so he saw no need to harbor any closeting inside their home. In one step, Pyotr swooped in, taking Cliff in his arms, and crushed their bodies together— and before his young sleepy lover could even consider a protest, Pyotr kissed him on the mouth with something in between chaste and full on hungry devouring.

Willing himself not to push too far, Pyotr withdrew from their kiss, letting Cliff go and enjoyed the show of warm colors on Cliff's face.

Cliff fingered his lips, savoring the touch, though he also felt the building red in the face. He glanced over at his sister, watching with a bright expression, and bordering on giggling at him as if it was the most natural thing for her to see her brother do.

"What color would you call that?" Pyotr playful quizzed who he determined was the color master in the household.

Kimmi laughed giving it some consideration, "A mix of crimson sky red and magnetic mauve-mauve."

"Magnetic mauve-mauve— I like the sound of that and how it looks on him."

Cliff shifted his gaze back to Pyotr, watching with his usual amusement, "Are you going to continue to do that in front of everybody?" Cliff asked nervously.

Pyotr grinned down at him, "Eventually." And kissed him lightly on the forehead to either support the confession or sooth Cliff to his convictions. Either way, Cliff seemed content with the new knowledge.

CHAPTER FOUR

Two weeks had passed since their first night together and they showed little sign of slowing down; proving Pyotr to be true to his word that he had a voracious sexual appetite. As was his gentle command to be in charge of their relationship.

Cliff was just finishing up his shift at work, restocking the ambulance before he could clock out, when he happened to glance up and saw Pyotr standing just outside the garage. He froze, uncertain of what to expect or what was expected of him. It had him thrown off his guard a bit. Pyotr had never come by his place of work before.

Pyotr only stood there, a tall and handsome silhouette in the backlighting of the outdoor sunshine. So refined his lover was, but Pyotr's stance gave no indication of *why* he was there.

"Hey, Cliff!" Ozzy, their driver called back from the front seat of the ambulance, calling Cliff's attention away from the man standing at the drive, "Don't forget to grab a trachea kit and we gotta turn in an inventory count today."

"Shit, alright. I'll get it started in a minute." He turned back to Pyotr, but the man was gone.

It was as if he'd never been there at all. It was odd for Pyotr to not mention he might come by to see him. It was certainly one of those things Pyotr would have discussed with him. Cliff, after all, was at work and had not officially come *out* yet. Pyotr never once seemed to be in a hurry to push him either. *Everything done in strides.* Sometimes those strides felt to move so slow, Cliff could imagine a snail could gain the lead on them. He shook his head at himself— at his own thoughts. Chances are Pyotr was in the neighborhood and just letting him know he was offering a lift, and he'd be parked waiting around the corner or something. No big deal.

Cliff jumped out of the back of the ambulance and headed for the stock room for the trachea kit to replace the one they'd used at the start of their shift, as well as a few more IV lines. He pushed open to the hall, but before turning into the supply room, he heard Pyotr's voice— and Sasha's.

Cliff shot past his destination, instead following the conversation, his steps quickened until he reached the break room, and came to a full stop. Eyes snared on his lover standing squarely in front of Sasha. He felt the crushing pang in his chest, the feeling growing more intense when Sasha turned, looking at him. Cliff didn't even know what the look intended to say, but he knew what his heart was saying; it was screaming that he'd just lost his lover to another before he'd had the chance to realize how much he actually felt.

"You need something, Cliff?" Sasha asked, he almost sounded as if Cliff's presence was interfering.

Bastard— Sasha already had two lovers, he was even married to them. Now he wanted Pyotr as well?

Anxiety hit. And Cliff quickly turned, mind focused on his feet. He needed to get out of there—fast, but without running and tripping in his haste to flee. He cleared the hall; he could feel the panic boiling in him now, pitched up from a storm of feelings caving in on him. He passed the ambulance truck and out the roll door of the garage. Bright sunlight hit his face and for a moment he didn't feel like the world was caving in on him.

He stopped, leaning back on the brick wall of the building, eyes squeezed as tight as he could force them. He tossed his head up into the sun and tried to get his breathing under control. His thoughts and his emotions were beyond his command. But he knew how to keep them silent, years of watching his baby sister grow sicker and weaker— when he was lying face down in the hospital bed while the doctors drilled into his hipbone cavity with a special aspiration needle, drawing out the vital blood and stem cells. He'd always been wide awake with no anesthesia to dull the excruciating pain— he kept the pain inside then. That same day he came home from the hospital to find their parents had packed up everything and were gone— he survived all that in silence— he could get through this.

"Cliff."

Cliff tried to freeze at the sound of his name, but he couldn't prevent the quiver that went to his lip. He refused to open his eyes. *This time it was different*, he'd gotten through all those other things because he had to be strong for Kimmi. Here, Pyotr was the strong one; Pyotr promised that when they were together, the world didn't have to be carried on his shoulders. When he was with Pyotr, he was free, and that freedom found love. *He wouldn't get through this as easily.*

"Cliff." Pyotr's voice came directly in front of him now. "Look at me, Cliff," the command was tender.

Cliff took a deep breath and let it out slow and steady, then opened his eyes to see Pyotr standing just a few steps in front of him. Not too close that he would be in his personal space but close enough Cliff could see the concern on the man's face. And the question.

"You came here to see Sasha?"

"Yes, I did."

Cliff closed his eyes again, but he didn't drop his head. The only thing saving him right now was the warmth of the sun.

Pyotr watched him intently, watching the small twitches of muscle in the young man's shoulders, and Cliff's arms held straight at his sides, his palms flattened on the wall behind him as if hanging on so the sea of emotions could not wash him away. Cliff's face, save the quiver in his lip, was perfectly still, frozen in the sunlight. The bright rays glistening off his hair making the gold color all the more brilliant. Even in his emotional turmoil, his young lover was beautiful and dear, far more then Cliff gave himself credit for.

"What is it you are feeling, right now?" And then Pyotr saw it. Cliff would not have needed to answer the question for him to know what he was feeling; the pain was all over his face.

But, Cliff answered anyways, "It hurts."

"When you saw me talking with Sasha, it made you hurt?" the question designed to get to the root of the problem.

A deep breath expanded in Cliff's chest, strengthening him, "Yes."

"Well, at least it's a healthy feeling." Pyotr rocked back on his heels and shoved his hands into his pockets.

Cliff's eyes shot open, "What is so damn healthy about pain?"

"Had it been jealousy, we would have had a problem with it, but if you're hurting because you saw me with another man, and didn't understand, then at least we both know now that you have deeper feelings for me—feelings I share with you."

"Who is Sasha to you?" Cliff was through exposing his feelings and wanted the real answer. But, before Pyotr could answer his question, Sasha had stepped out discovering the two of them together.

"Pyotr? What is this?"

Determined not to lose Pyotr without a fight, Cliff snatched his lover by the collar of his shirt and yanked the taller man into him. While his other arm hurriedly shot around Pyotr's head, pulled him to his mouth, and kissed him in front of Sasha, and the whole world to see.

Pyotr felt his young lover's tongue brush between his lips, demanding entrance. A fun note clicked in his head. Pyotr knew what this was and decided that if this was what his young lover needed, he would allow it, even if it was being wasted on his baby brother. Pyotr pulled his hands from his pockets, moving them around Cliff's waist then down over his hips, and pulled Cliff tight against his groin. Holding their bodies firmly pressed into each other, seamlessly from cock to lip.

Pyotr was all about stride, but by god when it was time, nothing was allowed to be subtle or half expressed, and he took over their kiss. he laved his tongue deep into Cliff's mouth, swirling against his lover's tongue and licked at him drawing him to probe deeper in his mouth. Their lips separated from each other only enough so both could suck in a breath then deepened again. Pyotr never let go of his young lover's hips and Cliff didn't let go of him until both were satisfied their claim on each other had been fully announced.

Pyotr pulled back and smiled when Cliff tried to follow his lips. "And how do you feel now?"

Cliff let his head fall back a bit, looking up at his lover's face. And how he smiled at him; warm and welcoming. "Comfortable."

"That's a healthy feeling too, *dragi* . Look around you now. How does it feel to take your first step out?"

Cliff glanced around at the cars that drove by and the woman walking with a stroller on the sidewalk, but whatever he was hoping to think or feel from the new stepping stone came to a standstill when he glanced at Sasha still standing there gaping at them. Cliff looked back to Pyotr for an explanation.

"Sasha is my baby brother." Pyotr grinned as if he'd just let the joke out.

Cliff dropped his head on the man's chest, rocking it from side to side, "Now I feel silly."

Pyotr reached up and stroked the thick golden strands of hair, petting him then pushed Cliff's head to lift for him. Pyotr touched his face then slipped a finger under Cliff's chin. "My dear *Dragi*, silly looks good on you too." And he completed the compliment with a soft kiss. "How much longer before you are finished here?"

"Just a few more things to put in the truck then paperwork."

"Good." He gave Cliff a peck on the forehead. "We will spend the evening at your place tonight. I will be there waiting for you when you get home." Another chaste kiss and Pyotr stepped off, right past his brother.

"You?" Sasha gaped at his work partner.

Cliff's smile quirked to one side. *Mine all mine and you can't have him.* Then he turned on his heels and went back in to finish his work.

(•ω•)

Sasha took off after his brother. "Wait!" He ran up, catching up with Pyotr at the end of the building. "Cliff is the guy you've been sleeping with? Cliff Patterson, as in —*I'm gonna be the next Dominus*— Cliff Patterson?"

Pyotr stopped, turning to look at Sasha as he approached.

"You can't be serious?" Sasha protested at him.

Pyotr looked over to the spot where his young lover had just kissed him for all the world to see. The youthful display that shouted, *he's mine*— and Pyotr smiled at the recent memory. A silly little display really, yet, he had thoroughly enjoyed it. In fact, his heart was swelling that his little lover needed to stake a public claim. Perhaps the small act to claim territory had done as much for him as it had needed to do for Cliff.

"What was that back there? And don't think I didn't overhear you call him *Honey*— you'd never use a Serbian pet name on a casual fuck."

Pyotr's hand shot out. Too fast for Sasha to react and shoved him hard against the brick wall. His fingers splayed out just hovering over his younger brother's chest, asserting his dominance, that Sasha stay right where he'd just put him. "Do not over step yourself. I may be a gentle handler, but those limits do not include you."

"You can't possibly be happy with Cliff?" Sasha kept still, but not his thoughts or his opinion of his brother's poor choice for a lover.

"On the contrary, I find myself very happy with him. For once, I do not need to fix someone's head just so it's possible to have a relationship with them. He is a grown man and very capable. And his body fits my desires perfectly— lean, but enough muscle that he still feels like a man underneath me."

"A lot of the people we pick up are bigger than the gurneys we carry them on," Sasha quipped as if he'd said it a thousand times. But he knew what his brother meant; Pyotr would never sleep with someone who felt like a boy.

Pyotr forced a chuckled, "He said the very same thing."

"But Pyotr—" Sasha still pleaded for him to reconsider, "he's younger than I am."

Pyotr rocked back on his heels. There was that. Cliff was twenty-two years under his younger. A far stretch for lovers, yet neither seemed to feel it was worth getting in the way of them. "Yes. Yes, he is, and we have discussed it between ourselves, but we have decided that we are both very comfortable with it. *Perhaps* in ten years, we may feel differently, but then such is a thing in all relationships. Sometime down the road, one or both partners may feel differently about each other. We will deal with it when the time comes. But that is our decision to make, not yours."

"But you're investing in a relationship you know has an ending. Don't do this to yourself," Sasha half argued, half pleaded. Pyotr had a big heart; he'd kept their entire family together at the cost of not having one of his own. Now that everyone was grown up, Pyotr deserved a partner above them all, but one that he could take as his forever. Sasha just couldn't bear watching his older brother get caught up in the revolving door of lovers.

"If I have ten years of happiness or maybe only one, it will be worth having, because everything else is right. Do you not say the same about your Isaiah?"

Sasha sucked in a deep breath, almost daring to bow up at his brother, but quickly relented back against the wall again, allowing only his breath to escape in a hard huff. He was so protective of his boys it was hard not to react to Pyotr's comment. However, Sasha knew better. He knew Pyotr had not said what he did to be threatening or derogatory. Only pointing out that some relationships came with conditions, and as worrisome as those conditions may be, the most likely assumed futures weren't always predetermined either.

Sasha had been so young when the fled to come to America, but he remembered his parents. Pyotr was so much like their father in many ways but one— Pyotr was also just like their mother. He was the best of both, all rolled into one body. He was strong willed and strong in his body. Pyotr was the one who always brought an end to the fights between him and the rest of their brothers. And there had been plenty of those. Pyotr was even known to bring down a few street thugs in his time, dragging them down the middle of the street by their toes and sitting on them in the most humiliating ways until they agreed to stop wreaking havoc on the neighborhood. Most of that was set loose on the Irish in the neighborhood. But, Pyotr knew how to be gentle like their mother, and when you hurt, he knew how to make it better as if he had the box of band-aids for broken hearts. Their twin sisters gave him a lot of practice for that.

Eight brothers and two sisters aside, Pyotr had never had his own family, and Sasha could see how Cliff and Kimmi filled that need for him; perhaps too well, because that was an arrangement that was definitely predetermined.

"You know no matter what treatments Kimmi gets, she's not going to live much longer." Sasha made one last plea to convince Pyotr the relationship was no good. And the flicker in his brother's eyes told him everything. He was already locked into his little family— *just add Pyotr and stir*— and Pyotr was very aware it came with an expiration date.

Sasha felt an instant pain of guilt then. Pyotr deserved the world at his feet; it was disheartening that he should find something that fit his needs only to know it would be ripped away too soon. Sasha didn't want that to happen for his brother who deserved so much more. He swallowed hard, wishing he'd learn to keep his mouth shut.

Sasha dropped his head; his shoulders drooping along with it. He stared at the ground and kicked at a wayward piece of gravel on the sidewalk as if that might make him feel better. It didn't, when Pyotr walked away without another word.

"Fuck," he muttered, hanging back in silence for a bit. Sasha pushed off the wall, his hands buried deep in the pockets of his uniform slacks. Only one thing he could do now.

Sasha found Cliff back in the ambulance truck, putting the last few things in place. Sasha stopped at the step just watching him. Cliff kept his back to him, but the tension in his shoulders indicated Cliff was aware he was there.

"I'm really not ready for a conversation on how this changes everything between us," Cliff muttered, not looking at him, his hand counting out the inventory, and marking it down on the clipboard on the gurney already dressed in crisp clean sheets with a wool blanket folded over on the top, and ready for the next person in need.

Sasha kept his hands buried, took in a deep breath, and let it out, trying to rid himself of some of the tension he'd created on himself. "How much do you know about my brother?"

Cliff stopped in mid-count, but still his eyes stayed down, not meeting Sasha's. "If you're about to tell me some head-case story that's supposed to make me want to stay away from him, don't bother."

"No. That's not what I am about to tell you. I love Pyotr. He's not just my brother, but my father, too."

Cliff shifted, looking him dead in the eyes now.

"What I mean is, he's more father then our papa was. So when I tell you this, it is only because Pyotr deserves the best kind of love." Sasha took one last deep breath and began, "Pyotr is the oldest of eleven children with nine boys and two girls. We were living in Belgrade, he was in the university there, and top of the class. Pyotr would have been a doctor or a professor had we stayed, and he would have worked for the government. In Serbia, if you work for the government, you're rich. Work for anyone else and you're poor like everyone else."

Cliff sat back on the medic bench and listened. He and Pyotr had talked about many things, but his past had not been one of them. In fact, Pyotr had said little about himself. But strange how now, as Cliff listened to Sasha, who never had a strong accent before changed— it deepened and the more Sasha talked, the more he started to sound like Pyotr.

"Pyotr had the whole world laid out before him. But, shit was getting bad everywhere around us. Yugoslavia was being dismantled through uprising started by the

League of Communists of Serbia. In 1989, Milošević declared a decrease in power for several other republic sanctions. In 1990, the government declared complete media blackout. Freedom of speech was restricted. The Serbian Penal Code issued criminal sentences on anyone who *ridiculed* the government and its leaders, resulting in many people being arrested who opposed Milošević and his government. That was just part of it. There was also the KLA—"

"The KLA?" Cliff screwed up his face, not fully understanding.

Sasha nodded, of course Cliff wouldn't know what that was. "KLA, Kosovo Liberation Army. There were two power forces fighting for control— there was no peace between the two. It was a war in our country, between its army and its police, between Yugoslavia and Kosovo. Two conflicts running parallel and simultaneously, long before NATO got involved, and declared it an actual war. People died every day. Sometimes for no reason. Gangs were popping up and they were as much trouble as anything else." Sasha went quiet a moment. He'd been so young then, but Pyotr had always made sure they knew what had happened. And not just the side the outside world talked about. Not the history the deniers taught them. Pyotr made sure they all knew what had truly happened.

He took a deep breath, shifted then leaned against the door of the truck. He was only five then, but he did recall the time when soldiers barged into their home and dragged his papa away in the middle of the night. When papa returned the next day, everything would change for them.

"One night the police came and took my father away. The next day, he was back, and he and our mother gathered us all up and took us out of school. Next, we rode into the city to the university and got Pyotr. Our parents gave Pyotr all the money they could get from their bank accounts, along with a knapsack of food and a few suitcases of clothes. They drove us back out of the city where we met up with a crowd and we were loaded up in the back of a truck. My last memory of them was hanging out the back of the truck calling to them as they waved goodbye. Pyotr holding me so I couldn't jump out.

"For a day and half a night, we rode until we got to some shipping port on the shores of Greece. There we loaded up on a freighter heading here to the U.S." Sasha slid down the edge of the ambulance and sat on the step-ledge and stared out of the garage as the sun was dropping down in the sky and shining in on them with burnished orange tones. "I don't know how they did it, but we were allowed in. And Pyotr, from that point on, was our father *and* our mother. He took care of us all. But, at a sacrifice. Pyotr was gay, but he could not have a lover. Aside from Immigration, Children and Family Services were always watching him. Can you imagine what they would have thought— a grown gay man with eight little brothers? Suddenly, bathing us would have been deemed a mortal sin. It wasn't until we were all grown up and left the nest when he could safely allow a relationship in his life. But, by that time, he was pretty much set in his ways. Accustomed to raising kids and it seemed Pyotr often found himself playing doctor, rather than being lover, to men with too much baggage."

"So, what you're saying is I'm just another head-case for him to mother over?" Cliff forced himself to look away.

"No. There's nothing about you he needs to fix. He just sees you on the same level as him, someone who had to sacrifice himself for his family." Sasha twisted, looking squarely at him now. "You see, Pyotr's life was— put on hold because he was left with ten *Kimmi's* to take care of. Pyotr relates with you. The bonus that he'll get to mother-hen Kimmi at the same time probably makes him feel whle inside. No—" Sasha shook his head a moment, that was wrong, "—he feels much more. I think maybe he sees a family in you. One he can call his own."

Sasha stopped, using his fingers to wipe at his eyes. But, Cliff wasn't sure if it was just the sun or if there had been a threat of tears. Sasha got up, reached in and opened one of the organizer drawers in the ambulance, and pulled out a bandage. "Will you do me a favor when you see him tonight?"

"Sure." Cliff blinked at him.

"I hurt him when he was just here." Sasha took a deep breath then shoved the band-aid out toward Cliff. "Will you give this to him? Tell him, I'm sorry." He turned and stepped away.

"What happened to your parents?" Cliff quickly asked before Sasha could disappear and slowly stepped out of the truck, carefully as if any sudden movement might cause Sasha to take off.

Sasha stopped, his head hung low, eyes staring into nothingness on the concrete floor, "March 24, 1999

NATO moved in with their air strikes and bombed our country over the next four months. We never heard from our family again." Sasha glanced over his shoulder at him. "Go on. Go home to Pyotr. I'll take care of the paperwork." And then he disappeared down the hall.

Cliff couldn't get home fast enough, his whole body tingled. If Kimmi were sitting next to him right now she'd say he had ants in his pants. He grinned. The man sitting across from him on the bus shot him a disgruntled look. Maybe he was grinning too much for New York, but he didn't care. Six more stops and a dash down 79th street and he'd be in Pyotr's arms.

Cliff glanced at his watch. Unbelievable, a fifteen minute drive took an hour on the bus. Maybe it was time to start looking into a car or at least a small motorcycle. Before, it never seemed to matter. The ride home was time for him to shift from work to taking care of Kimmi, from one ailing injured person to his ailing sister. The long bus ride was the only time he had for himself, outside of hanging out at Club Pain.

But now, his lover was waiting for him. *Lover.* His grin deepened further. He'd never had a lover. The occasional short relationships, but any time he met a girl it was always the same. People just couldn't handle not being the center of his world, so they never lasted. Pyotr was different. Family was meant to be the central core of a person's life. Anyone else you *added* to it, instead of diverting your attention from it. And Pyotr was a man. His smile slowly turning to something far saucier. And he could feel the heat rise in his face.

Yes— Pyotr was a man— all man— tall, stout, and very debonair. His man. Cliff felt his breath deepen and his cock throbbed in his pants. He couldn't wait to get home and get his hands on the man who was waiting for him there.

The bus slowed, breaks hissed with a *squawlering* screech of worn down mechanical parts until it came to a complete stop. *Yes! 79th street.*

Cliff jumped from his seat, hopped off the bus, and instantly took off in a run. One block and two houses was all he had to get behind him.

Pyotr was in the kitchen den, sitting on the day bed with Kimmi when Cliff came rushing in. They were sipping tea which meant she had just finished eating and Pyotr'd prepared the tea to help settle her stomach so she wouldn't lose her meal.

Kimmi had on a delightful smile. She liked Pyotr's company. Anyone who came by and spent time with her was a hero in her eyes. But, when Pyotr looked up at him, the warmth that stirred behind that man's eyes and the way they brightened with the sight of him, Cliff could feel the beaming surge of emotions inside himself. He rushed over dropping to his knees in front of his lover, instantly wrapping his arms around Pyotr's neck and kissed him. He licked his tongue over the older man's lips until they parted for him and let him in.

Cliff eagerly dove into his lover's mouth until he found Pyotr's tongue and moaned at the treasure he so eagerly sought. It wasn't enough, he pushed on his knees, leaning back, and pulled Pyotr down from the daybed with him. They crashed down on the floor, Pyotr barely catching the weight of his body before crushing Cliff under him.

Pyotr broke from their kiss, letting out a slight chuckle. "What is all this, *dragi*?"

Cliff only grinned, hooking a leg into Pyotr's. He could hear Kimmi laughing at them and he didn't mind that at all as he pushed for Pyotr's lips again. Cliff let out a sigh of relief when his lover gave into his need, and then took over their kiss, deepening it. Pyotr's one arm wrapping around Cliff, while the other stroked down his side, pulling his leg up higher until it wrapped around his hip.

Pyotr grasped his ass, pulling Cliff into him, and crushed the bound up cocks together. The hard contact fired off so many sensations, Cliff had to break from their kiss just to let the excited gasp escape.

Pyotr growled out a light huff, "Is that what you were seeking, *dragi*?"

"Yes-*sss*— *Glavar*." Cliff hissed.

Pyotr rolled his groin into his young lover with a deep penetrating contact. Oh, he did like it when the young lad called him that. *Liked it very much.* "How did you learn to say Master in my language?"

"Google translate. Is it right?"

"It is, *dragi*."

Cliff managed to peek around the broad shoulders that nearly eclipsed him, "How was your day, Kimmi?"

Kimmi's face offered a melting smile when she caught a glimpse of her brother's smiling face peering out from under his new lover. "Maybe not as good as your night is expected to be, but I'm not complaining."

"Good." He turned his eyes back to the man laying over him, "I might be busy for a while." He heard her start giggling again and knew that she was perfectly fine with the evening's arrangement. It was one thing to have someone he felt happy with for once in his life. It was something far more stupendous that his little sister approved.

◖ᴗ◗

Downstairs in his room, Pyotr took over the mood Cliff had started. But he paused for a moment and pulled out a yellow slip of paper from his shirt pocket and offered it to Cliff.

Cliff's eyes shot up. He didn't need to ask what it was, he knew.

"I know it is very important you remain disease free. I wanted to offer this to you regardless of whether we decide to go skin to skin." Pyotr tossed the fold of paper to the headboard and came back down over Cliff to resume their kissing.

Cliff soon found himself on his back underneath the fierce hungers of his lover. Pyotr's hand stroked over his body and forced its way into his uniform pants to wrap around his cock and stroked him near to the edge. Even Pyotr's kissing seemed stronger, more forceful than ever, Cliff felt devoured by it, and tried to find space in his head to wonder where it stemmed from.

"You're thinking," Pyotr growled into his lips as he chewed on them.

"It's different now, isn't it? I mean—" his head fought to form words of his haphazard thoughts even as Pyotr's attention boggled his mind even further.

Pyotr's lips paused against his and waited. When Cliff didn't say anything, Pyotr demanded it, "Out with it."

"I mean, this isn't a scene anymore, is it? I mean, is this more?"

"This is far more, Cliff." Pyotr leaned in, slamming him with a quick kiss. "I warned you in the beginning, I had a voracious appetite. However, I've also waited for you to come out." Pushing up on his knees, Pyotr unzipped Cliff's pants, and yanked them free from his hips, then forced Cliff to roll over then finished freeing the pants from his legs.

Cliff felt Pyotr's tongue next, trailing up the back of his thigh, nibbling as he moved further up then bit into one side of his ass, causing him to jump in surprise.

"Do you wish to retract?" Pyotr paused to ask.

"What's the difference?" Cliff glanced back over his shoulder to the man he'd give anything to stay with. He watched as Pyotr lowered down over him, felt the man's hands part the cheeks of his ass, and suddenly felt the warm wet caress of his tongue lave right over the small puckered entrance.

"No restrictions," the warm whisper came from behind him then Cliff felt his lover's tongue again. Cliff slammed his face into the pillow to trap the moan there. Jeez, as wicked as it was, it felt so damn good.

❦

"No more restraints. Except maybe the ones I choose to put you in." Pyotr's hand slipped under Cliff's belly and wrapped around his erection, stroking while he continued to lick over his ass. "I spent most of my life hiding my sexuality. I refuse to do so anymore. To such a point, you could say I'm rather perverse in my openness. I refrained from displays of my affection for you for the sake of your own acclimation."

Cliff's stepping out, even as small of a step as it was, was also very bold, and it had made Pyotr feel extraordinary. He'd been waiting for this since they started seeing each other.

He moved up Cliff's back lowering his weight down on him, now taking the time to grind his own fully aroused erection into the crevice of Cliff's ass, teasing him with long hard strokes, while his hand still worked over Cliff's cock. "I won't anymore."

Cliff pressed back against him, lifting his ass in invitation.

Pyotr usually worked him over into a frenzy with foreplay, but not this time. It seemed tonight called for some direct approaches. Apparently, stepping out called for some unbridled pounding, and right away. And Pyotr knew Cliff wasn't going to complain over the new advancements. Foreplay or not, his young lover was always eager and ready to have him inside him. Cliff's engorged cock was close to exploding already, he was likely to cum the second Pyotr slid inside him.

He chewed on Cliff's shoulder then pushed up onto his knees, lifting Cliff to do the same. He slipped his broad hands down Cliff's arms, taking his hands, and guided them up to hold onto the head board. Pyotr crawled up against Cliff's bent over position, his cock throbbing against Cliff's ass. He pressed forward against Cliff and their bodies seemed to melt into each other, making Pyotr dizzy. He caressed his young lover, his chest and sides, growing more ravenous. He growled in Cliff's ear, "Grab a condom from behind the panel. I'm not going to be able to hold back much longer," Pyotr's hot breath instructed him.

Cliff pushed back keeping their embrace seamless. He dropped his head back and twisted just enough to offer up his mouth to be kissed, knowing Pyotr would grant it to him, "Nothing between us anymore."

"You're certain?" Pyotr stilled around him.

Cliff knew he was certain, because he knew he didn't have to ask if it was just them. Pyotr had made that commitment from the start. "Yes, *Glavar.*" The word solidified in his mind. His *Glavar.*

Cliff offered up the oil and nothing else. His Glavar pushing against him to lean forward, felt the dribbling tickle of oil down his crack, followed with the blunt fingertips that worked it in and around his hole, then the blunt tip of Pyotr's shaft, sliding up and down over his entrance, smearing the oil further.

Cliff bit into his lip and pressed back, Pyotr leaned back, dropping his weight up on one arm while the other guided his cock inside the tight sheath of Cliff's body that was purely his to enjoy.

Pyotr's hips rocked, soft pushes against the tight ring of muscle. His hand shifted to Cliff's lower back and stayed, steadying him to keep still as he watched the red head of his cock slipping in and out.

That was Pyotr; he loved watching and absorbing every detail of their pleasure. Some tantric energy he got from it, but Cliff's body was burning for more, and he pushed back on the length of Pyotr's erection to slide all the way in. Cliff's head kicked back with an escaped gasp and Pyotr was quickly pumping into him with long strokes to nurture those gasps along further.

Cliff's entire body tingled with waves of warm euphoria and he rocked back, countering into each of Pyotr's, until finally he felt every mind shattering inch of his lover's shaft filling him to the deepest regions.

Cliff's fingers curled into the headboard, hanging on because everything else made him feel like his body was being pitched over a rocky edge. Floating and falling all at once. Every moment he spent with Pyotr was like a new experience. A new shiver or a new warmth that spread across his body and his heart. There was no more falling for the man. He had hit rock bottom and fired off all his canons to be completely his. He'd never known such bliss and not just when they were in bed, but everywhere else. Pyotr was always attentive, and when Kimmi was with him, Pyotr's attention and respect were divvied out evenly. Yet, the best part was still during moments like now when Pyotr made love to him. Finding every electrifying nerve ending that needed to be touched, and ignited often, until Cliff couldn't stand it any longer.

Pyotr folded over him, arms carved from rowing encasing his chest, holding, and caressing as Pyotr's groin rolled up into Cliff. His lover's steady, pulsing movements over Cliff's body took on an almost hypnotic motion, sweeping them both into its sensual rhythm. Their bodies soon sheened with sweat only added to the seamless connection between them.

Pyotr's breath was deep and ragged. The very sound Cliff loved to hear. There wasn't anything sexier than that sound. Sounds that were paired with micro kisses and licking to the back of Cliff's neck and over his shoulders, as hard flesh penetrated into hyper sensitive interior walls. Cliff was on a steady incline to euphoria and he hoped to never return.

Pyotr caught Cliff's chin and pulled him around, his lips crushed against Cliff's. Their kiss was one of rapture and hunger, of longing and deep commitment. Pyotr sucked in a lung full of air and let out a deep, throaty growl as he pushed deeper, and Cliff pressed back, returning the rolling pleasure his lover offered him. Cliff matched the slow, steady rhythm Pyotr had begun; pushing out from the headboard, relishing the sensation of being completely filled each time Pyotr drove his thick rod into him.

Pyotr eased him forward with a firm hand on his back, shifting the angle of entry and instantly Cliff felt the tip of Pyotr's engorged glans slide past his prostate. Jolts of energy broadcasted out like some cosmic explosion rippling throughout his body. And he let out several moans.

Pyotr reached around him, wrapping his fingers around the base of Cliff's cock and pinched the underside flowing tube closed as he continued to ride inside him.

"I want to feel you cum around me, *dragi* ."

The wishful command was hot and breathy. Cliff could already feel the release coming. His cock aching to be stroked, just once and he'd be there, but Pyotr did no such thing. Instead, he kept him clamped off in his grip, while Pyotr's cock continued to pass over his prostate. Cliff's shaft throbbed in Pyotr's hand, pulsing out a mayday signal to have its release. His throat clamped shut around the moans that struggled to be expressed. He could hardly catch his breath. His knuckles went white against the headboard, his throat and lungs burned for oxygen as he gasped and moaned even more.

"Oh, God!" Cliff squeezed his eyes shut and he felt himself tumbling. Only the warmth of Pyotr's arms existed and the penetration that filled his rear nethers. Pyotr's cock sank in with a singular thrust then rocked in deeper, sending Cliff pitching over the edge into oblivion.

A shower of sparks burst behind his closed eyelids. And like a supernova it ripped through his body. His balls pulled up tight, and he cried out as he came. Pyotr's hand held tight, squeezing him off, sending his orgasm into double load. Cliff's entire body shuddering violently and he cried out again. Pyotr began thrusting into him, deep, hard penetrating strokes that slammed to his very depths.

He could hear Pyotr's own heavy breaths, growling out with each thrust. "That's it, *dragi* , cry out for me. Let me hear you moan for my cock." His growling became rough sawing grunts. Then Cliff felt the pulsing sensation in his ass. Felt it in addition to his own release, still fighting to break past the hand that kept it under its control. Then Cliff felt the warm fluid fill his back walls. A keen sensation he couldn't begin to describe if his life depended on it, but it was incredible. Soaking and saturating his body in his lover's seed. And just then, Pyotr's hand let go; instantly white cords of semen shot from Cliff's own cock, spilling across his pillow and against the headboard. Both men let out rasping expressions of exquisite rapture.

Cliff tightened his anal muscles around the still pulsing shaft, rewarding his ears with a heavy groan from Pyotr who bent in to lavish a long hungry lick across his back. Pyotr drew Cliff's mouth around for another deep savage kiss as they rode out the last shudders of the release, as if he hadn't begun to be sated yet. But Cliff could hear it on his lover's breath, Pyotr was pleased. The kiss was the last hungry morsel, which was followed with small nibbles on his bottom lip, nuzzling against his jaw, across his neck and shoulders. Like some wild animal marking him with his sweat and masculine scent by rubbing against him. *Postplay*. It was as equally erotic as foreplay with this man.

Pyotr kept wrapped around him for a long still moment while they both caught their breath. Then he slowly eased out and guided Cliff down to the bed on his back and lowered over him to lick over Cliff's softened cock.

Cliff jackknifed instantly unable to remain still with Pyotr's wicked tongue bathing his sensitized flesh. But Pyotr's hand caught him flat across the chest, pressing him back down and ate him, despite his moving about, then made a trail of kisses up his abdomen, along his chest until he slowed over his final destination. Deep blue eyes like the evening sky looked down at him, electrified with a look of pure satisfied bliss.

"Tell me you love me." Pyotr nudged Cliff's chin, then licked at it teasingly.

Cliff stilled, but quickly corrected his hesitation and sent his arms up, wrapping around Pyotr's neck. He did love him but had been fearful to tell him. Because he feared saying as much so might send him away. "Why?"

"Because I have something to ask of you, but I need to hear what I know you feel, before I do. One must come after the other."

"You won't leave me, will you?" Cliff was suddenly worried over what sort of response his answer was going to get, but he knew he wouldn't be able to lie about it.

Pyotr caught Cliff's jaw holding him firmly in a locked stare, "You would have a hard time convincing me to let go."

"I don't want you to let go." Cliff's arms tightened and he lifted up to kiss Pyotr.

Pyotr kept the kiss short then lifted away. "Then tell me."

"I do love you. I have for some time already," Cliff said it softly, because that part of him was so vulnerable to injury and he'd just exposed the hidden wound.

Pyotr dropped to his back, pulling Cliff with him, and letting his young lover's head rest over his chest, waiting for what was about to be asked.

"I want you to move in with me." Pyotr bent in to kiss the top of Cliff's head, just as it was instantly coming back up.

"What?" Cliff's head popped up, wide eyes and opened mouth like a carp. Pyotr couldn't help but let out a chuckle. He ran his fingers through Cliff's tussled hair, but Cliff brushed them away. "Stop. What did you just say?"

Pyotr just grinned. "I want you to move in with me."

Cliff's mouth shut, looking at him— face blank and Pyotr waited for the gears to start turning again, amused by the minor hiccup in his lover's head. "But, what about Kimmi? I'm not leaving her here alone."

"Of course not. She comes, too."

"I—" Cliff swallowed hard. God it seemed too good to be true. He loved Pyotr's home. Even better since he would be with him all the time and not have to worry about Kimmi because so would she. "I don't know. I mean, I don't even know how to spring this on her."

"I do. So, I have invited the two of you to spend the weekend with me. Then, Sunday night you can decide with her if you want to stay."

Cliff glanced around his room. It wasn't much, but it was theirs. "What about this place?"

"Keep it if you like." Pyotr wouldn't dare suggest they get rid of it. Though it would not please him more to see Cliff stay forever, he did have to be realistic about this. "You can rent it out to generate some extra income for you and Kimmi. That way it's always here if you change your mind. Though, I hope once you move in, you never leave, but there may come a time, Cliff, when you will only see an old man—"

"Stop. I told you— I don't care about that. If you were my age, I would not like you more. Maybe less. You are so much more because being older," Cliff scoffed at him.

"So, then it does matter," Pyotr redefined him.

"I-" Cliff stuttered, "yes but in the way I want you not reject you."

"Now you don't, but one day you might." Pyotr placed his fingers to Cliff's lips to silence more of the protests. "I'm only trying to say is whatever time I have with you, I want us to be all the way. I want you in my life and my home, because I am very much in love with you, *dragi*."

Oh god. How could he possible say no to this man? Cliff hadn't just heard the words; he could see them in Pyotr's eyes. Cliff kissed him, soft and tender, lazy embraces of their lips as they surrendered to the submersion of relaxation.

Cliff rolled over to his back, his neck notched into Pyotr's arm pit with his arm falling heavily across his chest and he stared up at the ceiling just day dreaming of living with Pyotr. And for the first time in a while, Cliff had too much energy zipping through him, despite their spent sex, to doze away before they started up again.

He thought about what happened earlier that day and about what Sasha had told him. About Pyotr being more father than their real one, as he grew up. Funny how he hadn't put the two together. But Sasha didn't look much like Pyotr at all. Not like their brother Pavle, who not only lived with Pyotr, but also worked at Queens General where most of Cliff's EMT calls were taken to and he saw him often in the ER. *Him,* he could see the genealogy. Pavle looked a lot like Pyotr, only lighter colored hair, sable or hazelnut. He grinned that Kimmi's way of seeing color would just pop into his head all the time.

Cliff rolled in place, feeling too fidgety to lie back any longer, and he looked up at the sleepy gaze of his lover, whose eyes smiled back at him. "Your accent is stronger than Sasha's."

"Because I actually grew up in the Republic of Serbia, Sasha was barely five when we came to the United States. I was twenty-five at the time."

"Tell me more, please."

Pyotr reached behind his head, jamming the pillow up a bit to raise his head and smiled warmly. "I was born in Čačak. Eventually, my father moved us all to Belgrade where there was more work and I attended the University of Belgrade up until the time we left—"

"Do you ever wonder how your life would have turned out if you didn't come to the states?"

"Oh, I suppose the time would come when I would have been arrested and publicly executed."

Cliff pushed up on his arms, his face filled with the alarm he felt, "Why do you say that?" Cliff couldn't for the life of him think of any reason why a man like Pyotr would be given a death sentence.

"Because I am gay *and* I had an Albanian lover. Our government considered them the *dergs* of our nation."

"What was his name?"

"Kostandin. He had a sister, Ljena, a few years younger that lived just outside of the city. We'd go there on weekends so we could be together and not be confined to our dorm room. We told everyone I was courting her. So, it seemed natural that we were together all the time. In our society, men hung with other men, not their wives."

"Did you love him?"

Pyotr closed his eyes a moment, remembering those far off times. "Yes, very much so."

"Do you think you'll ever fall in love like that again?"

Pyotr reached down scooping Cliff up under the arms and pulled him up to wrap around him. "I believe I already have."

Cliff surrendered to Pyotr's arms and they kissed like there was no tomorrow, slow and playful enjoying that small moment. Cliff dropped his head to Pyotr's shoulder, tucking his face under the man's jaw. He could feel sleep coming for them finally yet still his mind raced. "So, do you really have eleven brothers and sisters?"

Pyotr chuckled, "Well, there are eleven of us in total. I'm the oldest, then Jovan, then Pavle, Darko, Artyom, Trofim, Stanislav, Rury, and Sasha. Then our sisters, who are twins, Andjela and Varvara."

Cliff now understood why Pyotr's house was so big. He never understood before why the man needed eleven bedrooms. "Is that why you have such a big house?"

"Yes. When we first came to New York, I walked over neighborhood after neighborhood, deciding which ones were the best to live in. I fell in love with Astoria. I picked out several homes that suited our needs. And as the years went by we grew from one rental home to another as we could afford. During that time, I made friends with the homeowners of the houses I had on my list. So that should any one of them ever go up for sale, I had a shot of making an offer before it ever went on the market."

Cliff looked up at him, surprised to hear this methodically calculated plan. "Are you serious? You really did that?"

"I had a plan to have a home we all fit in and it had to be in the right neighborhood. Of course, by the time I got it, Jovan and Pavle were both married. And Artyom was engaged. But, it's here if they ever need to return."

"Like Pavle?"

"Yes," Pyotr agreed with a sleepy nod, "like Pavle."

"Do you mind if I ask?"

"Pavle's ex-wife, Maggie, is a wonderful woman and they have two great kids, but Pavle is also gay and as much as he loves Maggie, he couldn't stay in the marriage anymore."

"But, they're still close?"

"Absolutely. Then again, she knew from the beginning Pavle was gay, so there was never any *coming-out shockers* between them. Maggie use to go on dates and dinner functions with him for sake of appearances. They were best of friends, and there were a couple of times when they'd had too much to drink they became friends with benefits. Then she ended up pregnant. So, he did what he thought was right. They had a good life together, but at the same time Pavle was being unfair about his needs and it was starting to sink in. With the boys older now, they both decided it was time to set each other free."

"Wow." Cliff returned his cheek to Pyotr's chest. Just then Cliff remembered the favor to Sasha and was instantly jumping out of the bed. He found the pile of clothes in the middle of the floor and fished out the bandage Sasha had given him, then crawled back into Pyotr's arms, and handed it over.

Pyotr took the bandage and held it up thoughtfully. "Sasha?"

"Ah-hmm," Cliff hummed nodding into Pyotr's shoulder.

Pyotr let a smile come over him. His arms tightened around Cliff, curling around him completely, and kissed his head. They snuggled into each other and were soon drifting into sleep. Now everything seemed warm and perfect.

Pyotr and Cliff were both up, getting ready for work, which seemed to take longer than their normal routine did when they weren't together, as they often stopped just to kiss or tease playfully.

"So, will I ever get to meet them?" Cliff looked up, watching Pyotr with his final grooming touches including a splash of day fragrance cologne.

"Meet who?" Pyotr asked as he watched Cliff snatch the bottle of cologne and test it on himself. "My brothers and the girls?"

"Yeah." Cliff uttered the auto response while still investigating the cologne, having a near sudden minor panic attack when he splashed too much on. To which, he was quickly trying to rub the excess around his chest and then a note of bratty-ness flickered in his eyes, and he dove a hand down into his shorts.

Pyotr chuckled watching him. "I most definitely expect them to honor me by coming to meet you," Pyotr turned matter-of-fact as he made the comment.

But, it struck Cliff as an odd thing to say. "What do you mean by honor you?"

"I'm the papa by proxy; I laid my life aside to raise them all with the exception of Jovan and Pavle. But, I still carried them through college since both pretty much had to start all over again. So, when I call on them, I expect them to respect my wishes."

Cliff walked over, yet hesitated, keeping just out of arm's length, "This is a cultural thing, isn't it?"

Pyotr turned, his face drawn in a serious expression, "In part yes. But, I also raised them all to respect family and the bond. We don't leave each other. We don't turn our backs on each other. That includes our extended family as well." Pyotr closed the gap between them and wrapped around Cliff, "You and Kimmi are *my* family. They will come honor me." Pyotr delivered a slow lingering kiss before going back out into the bedroom to gather his overnight bag and tossed the holster strap over his shoulder. "Now, I will come get you and Kimmi after work. Be packed and ready then we'll go out for dinner before going home. I have training in the mornings both Saturday and Sunday, but the rest of the day it will just be the three of us. So, if there's anything special she wants to do then that's what we'll do."

Cliff right away let out an incredulous expression, "Oh god! Just don't say the word *anything* to her. Ever since Diesel got us internet, her head has swelled with all kinds of ideas."

Pyotr let out a laugh, grabbed Cliff's hand, and towed him upstairs.

Kimmi was already in the kitchen with a bowl of oatmeal and her morning tea. He looked at Cliff then back to Kimmi, "Anything, Kimmi," he proffered a wry grin like he was leaking out the secret answers to win the game, any game. "The sky and seas the limit."

"Wha-?" Kimmi's eyes shot from Pyotr's to her brother's and back again.

"What did I tell you?" Cliff tried to scold Pyotr, knowing damn well he could only get off with playful scoffing.

Pyotr only grinned, yanking on Cliff's arm, pulling him against him, and kissed him hard against the lips. "It's my treat. Therefore, anything she wants."

Cliff pushed off, shooting him a scowl. "You're gonna spoil her. I can see it already."

Pyotr laughed as he leaned out and planted a kiss on the top of Kimmi's head as he passed her and headed out for work.

Kimmi gave her brother a perplexed expression, despite the amused curl in her lips, and the light that showed in her eyes, a happy glow that had scarcely existed over the years. "What was that about?"

"Nothing," Cliff mumbled, pulling a dish down for his own breakfast, "What are you doing today?"

Kimmi shrugged. "Library for the teen group."

"They picking you up or are you taking the bus?"

"Picking up."

"Okay, but don't stay out all day. We're gonna stay the weekend at Pyotr's. So we have to pack."

Kimmi's eyes lit up, as if there was room for more sparkles in there somewhere.

He shook his head. He could tell already, they were gonna have to start looking for boxes. And frankly, he was okay with that.

CHAPTER FIVE

Just last weekend, they'd had the little *family* outing, which had consisted of a concert in Central Park and shopping. Lots of it. This weekend, Pyotr had plans for dinner with some work associates. So rather than stay at home pacing the house anxiously, Cliff decided to hit Club Pain for a night. He hadn't been there in a while and was missing the crowd.

He caught his friend, Gina, just as she was heading out, and she agreed to swing by to pick him up on the way. Though once accomplished, Cliff felt awkward.

Gina's fingers tapped on her bare skin thigh as she drove one handed. It was one of her *tells*. She knew the art of drawing a man's eyes where she wanted them with the simple movement of her fingers. Cliff wasn't any different. He caught the movement and looked, but quickly diverted away, feeling the heat rise in his face. But not with any sort of blushing, he was angry suddenly, that he should respond at all.

"You know, I'm really glad you called," Gina struck up the conversation, "I've been in the mood to be a naughty slave girl. After I've been *good* at Pain, we can go back to your place, and you'll let me be bad to you." She nearly hummed her excitement at him. Not at all questioning whether he was actually game to be her play thing.

Cliff swallowed hard and glanced out the window. He felt the pang of regret twist in his gut. It even annoyed him that she would just assume he'd be up for it. Then again, he'd never actually played hard to get on the few times they got together. He was always up for whatever crossed their minds. Only now, things were different because he had Pyotr.

Pyotr— the man's face popped in his head. Would Pyotr be pissed if he found out he'd gone out to the club without telling him? It wasn't like he'd done it purposely; Pyotr was already out for the evening when he'd gotten the idea. And it wasn't like he was trying to go behind Pyotr's back or anything, just a spontaneous outing. Okay, so he could have called or texted, but that would be rude, Pyotr was with friends of his own.

Cliff ran his fingers threw his hair, pulling tuffs of it straight up until it stung, before dropping his hands back to his lap. He could feel every nerve in his body start to jitter. He was fucking up somehow. He wasn't in the right place. And for the first time in as long as he could remember, he began to fret uneasily.

Gina didn't even notice as she pulled off the overpass onto Delancey Street, taking them toward Club Pain. That's how intuitive she was. That or she just didn't care. Pyotr would have already pulled the car over and they would've sat there until he was ready to talk about what emotions he was overcame with.

Pyotr. Cliff knew he wasn't where he was supposed to be. He was supposed to be with Pyotr and while he would like to go to the club, he wanted to do it *with* Pyotr. Panic was setting in now. If he stayed with Gina it would be cheating. He hadn't done anything, but she was already expecting something from him, and if he didn't get away now, the questionability of how the night would end would not look good.

His eyes flickered to the girl as she pulled the car into a parking space in the garage. Without a moment's hesitation, she was out of the car, and heading for the stairs.

Cliff knew he meant nothing to her. He was just a thing, not that any of it mattered, he'd only wanted a ride. However, the abrasion was enough to remind him in a harsh manner he was in the wrong place and it would cost him the one man that did matter.

Cliff got out. Yet, when his feet hit the sidewalk, he stopped, and watched as Gina disappeared through the doors of the club. He stood there, staring at them blankly. He liked it in there. Liked the people and what it offered, even if he had not gotten to truly experience its offerings, but now he wanted Pyotr more then he wanted what was behind those doors. A stinging wind swept down the street and brushed his cheeks, delivering a chill through his long coat that was meant more for show than warmth. It wasn't supposed to drop under the sixties tonight, but in the city, it always felt colder. He gripped its lapel and closed it around him. Thankful for its trench coat length at least. It was going to be a long, cold walk home, but a punishment he deserved. And with that, Cliff turned and started walking.

Pyotr was glad to finally be freed of his company. The dinner meal had been good. Though, afterwards Pyotr found himself hustled into joining them at the Pink Flesh Club, a local strip club. It was only in his favor that he happened to know the owner, Dane Masters, and was able to show off a little to boost the guys' faith in him to hang and let loose.

Nonetheless, the whole display was scorching to his personal appetite. Rather than watching the girls as they danced around, peeling away layers of already skimpy attire, and the dollars that made their way into leg garters, Pyotr watched the men watching them, seeing, for the first time, beyond perfunctory observation.

It was fascinating really. Take a group of men and place them in the company of a pretty naked girl, and all manners of civility vanished. The way they carried on was beyond just complete civil disabling. They were worse than a locker full of naked gay men when boundaries were set aside.

The girls, how they tolerated such uncouth behavior was a wall of mental defenses Pyotr built his career around breaking through. Now, he was watching it being built. He glanced about, eyeing the changed behavior when a man was alone, and his attitude toward his subject of arousal changed. Lust burned much hotter in them, rather than a game of boisterous rudeness, the man's mind was often consumed with acquisition on how to seduce the woman to come home

THE DOMINION OF BROTHERS SERIES
A PLACE FOR CLIFF

with him either by words, a glance of finger tips to her thighs, or just out-right offering more money.

Fascinating, yet, abhorrent.

After two and a half hours and four rounds of drinks, Pyotr was finally able to excuse himself from the fun on the pretense that he had practice at 8am sharp the following morning, and he said his farewells.

He'd just turned onto Houston Street to take him to 2nd avenue, when he spotted a familiar shape walking down the other side of the street. Only, he wasn't alone.

Pyotr wasted no time jerking the car to cut across the several lanes of Houston Street and up on the curb just feet away from the five men crowding in on Cliff, doing all he could to keep his back from being steered toward the brick wall of a nearby building. He barely managed to set the car in park before jumping out and approached the five. "What seems to be the problem here, boys?"

"Piss off old man. This is none of your business."

"Oh, but that would be where you are wrong. This is my business— run along before you get a lesson from me," Pyotr, for all his calm, responded fiercely, like a man not to be reckoned with, but the punks he was addressing weren't going to give in so easily."

"You're gonna give me a lesson, will ya? I'll show you." The bolder of the five started to push his coat sleeve up, but the flash of an arm was the ending to that.

Pyotr's fist came up and down like a sledge hammer into the man's face, and in the blink of an eye, the young man was on the ground, and out cold.

"What the fuck?" One of the others cursed, but kept cautiously back, despite his home-boy on the ground.

"Talk of fighting is a waste of time. Let us just commence. Any one of you ready?" Pyotr held out his arms. Pumped and primed to bash the next contender.

The boxy-hair-cut guy in the group, looking like a jock out of place, took Pyotr up on the challenge, and rushed him. Pyotr took an instant side step to the right, dropping his left arm just behind the jock, catching the man by the back of his coat, and snapped him back, twisting him to come about-face just in time to have it pounded by Pyotr's fist.

There was a crack and the guy's face erupted in a splatter of blood from his nose. He stumbled back into his friends and swiped the blood from his face with a sleeve and gave it an inspection. Obviously, it was more than he cared to lose, and he pushed back behind the defenses of his gang. He exchanged glances with the others, then gathered the pal off the sidewalk and took off.

Cliff just stared on with a gaping expression. He managed to get a few stories from Sasha of growing up, some of which were of how Pyotr would whip some of the boys in the neighborhood into shape. But those stories didn't come close to what he was just had ringside seat to.

Pyotr was the arcane hero, complete with buff body. The one you secretly whacked-off to as a boy. And suddenly, Pyotr turned and stared straight at him, carnal fire burning in his eyes. Pyotr walked toward him, slow and cautious like he was fighting his own control. Cliff could only gape and his eyes followed Pyotr's hand as it reached out to clap his shoulder then moved him firmly for the car.

Without a word, they were driving off down the street. A few blocks down, Pyotr pulled into the small parking lot of a nearby quickie store, "Wait here. I'll only be a minute." And he jumped out running into the corner mart.

Cliff didn't say a word. Hell, he wasn't sure what to say. He was afraid Pyotr was mad at him, to tell the god's truth. Or worse, to be disappointed that his young lover turned out to be nothing more than just some runt kid who needed to be rescued. Cliff's hand flashed to his hair, raking and tugging at it again. How could he have been so fucking stupid? First time he runs off on his own not thinking it through, may have very well cost him everything he ever wanted to keep in his life.

The door swung open and Pyotr dropped into his seat, his eyes locking onto Cliff with intense heat. But, the tension in the man's jaws had Cliff questioning his emotional state the most. Pyotr started the car, and once again they were heading down the street. Only, they were heading straight for the boathouse— not his home.

"Climb into the back seat and remove all your clothes. I want you completely naked when we reach the boat house."

Cliff eyes darted up at Pyotr in shock.

"Do it now."

Not wanting him madder then he already was, Cliff quickly unbuttoned his trench coat, and shrugged it off. He twisted up in the seat and climbed into the back, doing as he had been told. He glanced up at the man watching him in the rearview mirror while his heart was pounding like a herd of a thousand horses, and his body twitched in nervous waves. He couldn't help but feel aroused by the eyes, shadowed in the car, staring— watching him intently, barely breaking away to watch the road. Fuck, that was hot.

☙❦❧

Pyotr pulled around into the parking lot of the boathouse and stopped in one of the spaces just under the light pole. He would have preferred the dark corner. But he knew the cops in the area and they knew him. As long as his car wasn't parked out of habit, they would leave them alone.

He glanced back at the man, now completely naked as he'd instructed him to be, waiting. Pyotr sucked in a deep breath, feeling every bit of his emotions surging inside him. Opening the bag from the quik-mart, he pulled out the tube of lube then got out of the front of the car and into the back seat with barely enough time for his heart to beat once.

In nearly the same motion, he unsnapped his slacks and shoved them down around his thighs. "Come here," Pyotr growled. Cliff had no sooner moved to obey him than Pyotr's arms were already snaking around his waist and pulling his lover over his legs. Positioning Cliff's knees over his lap and then folded Cliff over to ravish his mouth with a deep probing of his tongue.

Seeing Cliff getting corralled by a throng of street bullies was more than Pyotr could bear. Had anything happened to his *dragi* , he would likely have beaten all five of the boys into a pulp. As it were, it had taken only one knockout and one slightly broken nose to get the message across. But now, Pyotr's body seethed to have its prize. The instinctively carnal behavior of ancient man demanded that once battled for his mate, he had to claim him, and that was exactly what Pyotr intended to do.

He fisted his fingers into Cliff's hair, tugging him down in a tight hold while their kiss continued— deepened— licking in and over Cliff's mouth. Pyotr's hips tensed up, sliding his cock under Cliff's sack. *This was his.*

He quickly released Cliff, allowing him a brief moment to catch his breath. But, the assault of attention didn't stop there. Pyotr pulled his prize's hips up and immediately swallowed his young man's still partially flaccid cock into his mouth. Pyotr mouthed and tongued over it, groaning as the flesh hardened against his tongue just as his lust demanded. When he released Cliff's cock, he watched it involuntarily bounce to get back where it had been. "Yes-s-s, that's it, make it dance for me," Pyotr growled then sucked it back into his mouth. Without even looking, Pyotr's hand let go of Cliff's hip and moved for the tube, flicked the cap loose, and squeezed a healthy dollop out onto his fingers. He tossed the bottle and quickly slicked the gel over Cliff's sphincter, and without hesitation, slipped two fingers inside his tight hole.

Cliff's head fell back, pitched in an awkward tilt against the roof of the car, but damned if he was going to complain about that right now.

"Ah, fuck—" he gasped as Pyotr's fingers slid into his hole and twisted inside him. "Fuck." His nether muscles bit down on his lover's fingers and Cliff began to pump in the hot wet mouth swallowing his cock at the same time, like the fingers inside his ass, pumping in and out, faster and harder.

Damn, he could already feel the rising pressure. He was gonna cum soon if Pyotr kept this up and just like that, as if his lover had heard his thoughts it all came to a stop.

"No! Fuck, please don't stop," Cliff snapped up, not afraid to beg at this point for what he wanted.

"Shhh— I know what you need. And right now, you need me to fuck you."

Pyotr was quickly repositioning Cliff's legs pulling him up off his knees, so he was squatted over him, his feet flat on the seat. He next pulled Cliff's arms around his neck to hang onto the headrest behind Pyotr's head, then guided Cliff's ass down until the thick shaft, already seeping with pre-cum, pressed his hole, nudged at it a few times then eased its way in. The mind rocking sensation of being stretched and filled was like no feeling Cliff had ever had with anyone else. He loved it. He loved being impaled by this man and he couldn't imagine there being another in the world that could make him feel this way. He had no desires of searching either.

Pyotr's hands cradled each ass cheek, lowering him down over the hard shaft of flesh, spreading his crack wider so Cliff's body would take in every exquisite inch.

"That's it, *dragi* . Take all of it in— just like that," Pyotr hissed at him, watching as his dick disappeared inside his young lover's body.

Cliff's ass settled on Pyotr's lap. Every inch of Pyotr's cock sunk deep inside his bowels and it was euphoric. Pyotr's arms wrapped around Cliff, holding him, while his hips curled up, finding that last, sweet, extra nudge. And then the claiming began. Pyotr's arms tightening just under Cliff's arm pits, lifting him then slamming him back down several times. Pyotr traded his arms out for hands and the ride widened and quickened.

Cliff added in the rhythm, bouncing up, and down on Pyotr's cock. God damn, he couldn't believe how deep Pyotr's shaft sank inside his body. Stroking the inside walls, sending out waves of frenzied pleasure that tormented his sanity.

Pyotr rode him harder and faster; no longer just a man, but beast— brutal and driven. He growled with every pounding into his gut, his breaths panting heavily. God, it was sexy.

"That's it, *dragi,* show me how your hole belongs to me." Pyotr's eyes locked on Cliff's cock, hard and red, flapping up and down between them.

Cliff was so hard it hurt and he pitched his weight to one arm, freeing a hand to grab his cock, pumping his fist over it, only to have Pyotr quickly slap it away.

Pyotr rode him for what seemed like hours, interchanging from hard and pounding— to slow and agonizingly easy. They changed positions and were at it again until they switched to another position; changing out several times and not *all* conducive to being attempted inside the backseat of a car.

Cliff had already cum twice; the first still coated their bellies with the sticky mess. The second, Pyotr had swallowed up, and those were just the ones that made Cliff ejaculate. As if his mind wasn't already in a whirlwind and the car rich with the scent of their carnage, Pyotr already had Cliff well on his way toward a third cliff of release.

The windows were completely fogged over and the leather seats slick with the sweat from their bodies. They were both panting and grunting, but Pyotr's relentless hunger showed no signs of letting up.

Cliff felt completely melted into and over his lover. Completely content with surrendering to his passion, not wanting to ever be set free from him. Utterly drunk and addicted to this man. His *Glavar*.

Pyotr's cock dug into him in one last desperate thrust, reaching to the farthest reaches of Cliff's nethers. His body locking up in a tense sculpture of muscle, and then Cliff felt the hot fluids fill his channel. The drenching warmth was all his body needed to fire off again, and soon his own orgasm and cries echoed off his lover's anguished grunts. Cliff bucked against Pyotr, controlled only by the strong arms wrapped around him. Then they both dropped to the seat with Pyotr's face smashing against the back of Cliff's head, kissing him with an exhausted effort.

Too soon, his dominant lover pulled out and rolled the mess that Cliff was, over to be cuddled and kissed inside Pyotr's arms, though he himself didn't have the strength to kiss back. Cliff wasn't even sure if he had tried. He heard the tired chuckle from Pyotr that said he hadn't and Cliff realized he was even too tired to care enough to blush. It was too much effort to even breathe normal.

Pyotr's hand swiped up his chest, playing in the bath of sweat and spunk. "I apologize if I have been too aggressive with my *dragi* . Seeing those boys wanting to hurt you—" Pyotr's confession drifted a moment, "I warned you I was an insatiably possessive lover. I couldn't stop my feral drive to reinstate my claim on you."

Cliff struggled to keep his eyes open as he listened. His heart swelling with every wondrous emotion and some he'd never thought could exist for him. Claimed. Possessive. Pyotr's. He loved them all and he loved this man. If only he had the strength to tell him. The last thing he heard was a promise from the man to take him to the club whenever he needed.

Cliff woke up in the small bunk room of the boathouse and rolled over finding the crumpled space of sheets empty. Not that it was any surprise— well except the part about getting from the car to here. He kinda didn't remember that part, but he at least knew where Pyotr would be. Cliff spotted his pants folded over a chair and decided to get dressed and go down to the dock to see if the crew were within view, snatching his trench as he headed out.

The chill morning air swept up against his skin greeting him like the New York early winter always did and he

pulled his coat tighter as he walked out— just in time
to see the team coming back from around the bend.

The morning sun cast the water with a blanket of gold
sparkles so bright that it hurt his eyes. Cliff squinted,
watching as the three boat teams rowed in sync with
each other, two eight-man scullers and one four-man
shell. Moving like water bugs gliding across the surface.
Odd, because that meant two people were missing.
Usually there were two single runners and they had a
Region's Master's Race coming up at the end of the
month—

The Masters were being held up in Boston this year and
Cliff really wanted to go, but he had long since agreed
to cover Sasha's shifts at work, just so *he* could have
the weekend off to be in the race.

☉ω☉

Pyotr climbed out on the deck, right away
positioning himself so he could hold the shell steady
while the rest of the men offloaded. He glanced over his
shoulder, spotting his lover up on the bridge, watching,
and waved him down. Cliff always held back as if
waiting for permission to approach and it was the last
thing, he wanted Cliff to think he needed permission for.

Perhaps that would all disappear once they moved in.
Watching his frumpy lover bound down the stairs for
him, Pyotr couldn't wait for this week to be done with
and he could have his little man with him all the time.
An endless supply for contact and raw sex. Along with
moment of just sitting with him in between.

"Good morning, *dragi* ." Pyotr stood and smiled, pulling
Cliff into his arms to wrap around him tightly. He

lowered his lips to Cliff's ear and whispered, "How does that sweet ass feel this morning?" Pyotr laughed, feeling the heat rush to his lover's cheeks that quickly.

❀

Cliff pitched in, helping the guys wash and rack the gear, but as the men began to strip down and make their way into the showers, he lagged behind. Pyotr held at the door looking at him as if expecting him to keep pace— but the open raciness and touching that had already been put on display between all the men had Cliff glued to the spot of floor where he stood. And then he watched with a pang of regret as Pyotr turned and went into the showers without his lustful smile.

❀

"What's the matter, Pyotr? Your boy too shy to come play in the water with you?" One of Pyotr's teammates razzed openly.

Pyotr tried to make the deep hit of rejection roll off. Even going as far as to silently persecute himself for his selfish wanton to be with his lover. Cliff had every right to maintain some privacy rather than being a show for the others.

He closed his eyes and ducked under the spray of water, letting the sound of the shower drown out some of the roast he was getting from his teammates over the withdrawal of his lover's shyness. It was more than banter this time, they were scolding him for having one so young, and one still closeted by their terms that he couldn't keep up, and keep the great Pyotr Laszkovi satisfied. Cliff satisfied him quiet well, he was just being selfish to want to take even more and wanting to do so with total abandoned inhibitions into voyeurism in front of everyone. In truth, Pyotr acknowledged some part of him wanted selfishly to show off his lover, and how Cliff moaned and whimpered under his touch.

The touch startled him. Pyotr snapped a hand out to snare the one who dared touch him without his consent, only to find Cliff standing before him. The young man's eyes flaring with a defiant rage he'd seen there on more than one occasion or two.

"*Dragi* ?"

"Make them stop talking about you like that." Cliff's face scowled, but his hands took Pyotr's and drew them to his naked body were they belonged. One on front and one behind, offering himself up like a sacrificial lamb to be Pyotr's shower toy.

Pyotr took a deeper look into his young lover's eyes, had there been even the most remote sign of nervousness doubt there, he would have turned Cliff's approach down, and spared him the open display. However, Pyotr found none. Just his bratty lover angry that the teammates would dare accost them for being mismatched and Cliff was determined to display otherwise.

Pyotr had loved fucking this man from the beginning. It seemed he could never get enough of Cliff. Each time they were together, only spurred Pyotr to want more. So, at this very moment at Cliff's offering, Pyotr's lust was damn near brandishing, and he could not refute that he wanted to plunder inside him yet again.

With one hand, Pyotr took hold of his lover's cock, finding it already swelling for him, but his other arm abandoned the firm ass offering to come up and wrap up behind Cliff's head and crushed the young lad's mouth to his own.

"Put your arms around my neck and keep them there." Pyotr instructed Cliff as he moved along the young man's jaw chewing at the bony edge then along his neck. One hand was still stroking over Cliff's cock, while the other moved down to take up the rest of his body that had been given over to him.

Cliff felt the first digit circling around his still sensitive ring, then the length of Pyotr's finger dragging over it; caress the crevice between his ass cheeks. Pyotr's touch was like a violin bow, drawing his long fingers over strands of nerve endings that instantly sent out notes of explicit heat, and electricity bolting out through Cliff's body. His knees quivered under him and his hips battled in jerks from one hand's touch to the other. Cliff tightened his hold around the man who controlled his body at that moment, grateful someone thought about his ability to stand. It didn't occur to him, it never did, though it should— Pyotr's touch swept him off his feet and yanked thoughts from his mind, every time his lover touched him.

"When you are mine there is no one else," Pyotr told him at just the moment before Cliff felt Pyotr's finger push past the ring of muscle and instantly sought out the tender prostate gland. Cliff's entire body lit up from the contact and he shivered when it withdrew. "And nothing else exists but what I want you to feel," he whispered against the shell of his ear. The deep groan in Pyotr's voice was like a dulcet command played against a background of white noise, caused by the running water.

Cliff stared up into those deep, blues that burned with smoldering lust for him. They held him and just the resonate voice told Cliff there was no one else, just the two of them. He let out a deep breath and his whole body relaxed, surrendering to the awe of pleasure that swept over him in that moment and he let the moan out. No one but them and the euphoria he felt being consumed by Pyotr's touch. And before the second rasping moan escaped his lips, Pyotr's mouth came down over him attacking his with a ferocious kiss.

"That's it; it's just you and me," Pyotr hardly tore from their kiss to growl out the commands just as he positioned his finger to press at Cliff's pucker, then circled and pressed again. When Pyotr sensed Cliff's body relax, he eased two long fingers through the tender entrance, and sank in all the way to his knuckles.

Cliff's head fell back, the groan that started clutching at the back of his throat when Pyotr's fingers caught his sensitive glory spot. He was still explicitly sensitive from last night, so it took near to nothing for Pyotr to have his ass cumming from just the caress of his fingertips deep inside him. Cliff leaned into him, hanging onto his neck, panting as he watched while Pyotr had him shooting out to splash the tiles with his spunk.

Cliff's body shuddered and his head lopped over onto his lover's shoulders. "I'm mush now," he nearly pouted the confession for only him to hear.

Pyotr chuckled, "Good. Mush is the best compliment your body could give me."

And just then, Cliff let go of Pyotr's neck and dropped to his knees in front of him. His hands gliding down Pyotr's wet sides then tightened around his hips, fingers pushing into the flesh of his ass in order to crush his body against his face.

Cliff rolled his nose around into Pyotr's genitals, inhaling the clean musky sent of his man. He made broad strokes of his tongue over the scrotum, dragging a wet caress all the way into the soft crease of Pyotr's groin and chewed into the flesh, then returned to do it again and again. Pyotr's legs willingly accommodated him, parting enough to let Cliff chew into tender, soft skin, then hitched his hips forward, burying Cliff's face in his balls on each return.

Pyotr raked his fingers through the wet strands of hair, following as Cliff moved to suck him into his mouth. His fingers fisted, clenching tight as Pyotr's hips pushed his cock down into his lover's throat. Gasps broke from his lungs in short notes, surrendering to the swallowing indulgence of Cliff's throat muscles, and the tongue that licked over his shaft like a greedy boy eating candy. All while everyone else watched with envy.

It was intoxicating for Pyotr. All his life he had to hide who he was. Only when reaching the point, he didn't have to hide anymore, he'd developed an unquenchable perversion for exhibitionism and voyeurism. *Let the world know he loved fucking men over the edge of delirium.* It had been a heavy demand on his past lovers. But, here, before him, sucking him to a delivered euphoria was the handsome young man who sated that need. Cliff surrendered to Pyotr's perversions one after another only to come back to mirror him in his own explorations. Making it all the more perfect, was Pyotr felt like *just* a man with Cliff, not the doctor, and *that* Pyotr welcomed into his life with open arms.

Pyotr let his head fall back against the tiles, the shower washing over their bodies. His lover swallowing his lust so perfectly, he could feel his release closing in.

"Yes-s-s, *dragi* —" Pyotr arched his back away from the wall and in doing so pushed his shaft deeper into Cliff's mouth. "Mmmm— that's it," he growled open appraisal, "Love it when you swallow me up, *dragi* —" Pyotr closed his eyes letting his lover's tongue do him in. He didn't need to watch the others, he could hear them. Their heavy breathing— their moans as they jacked themselves or each other off while they watched. He may not be mush— borrowing the words from his lover, but he was a happy fucking pig basking in his mud right now. And that was the best compliment his mind and body could ever give Cliff.

CHAPTER SIX

The week moved like a blur for Cliff as it took every spare moment, they had to get everything packed and ready. Nevertheless, by the end of the following week, he and Kimmi were moving in with Pyotr. Cliff had been so nervous the whole time that there were a few times his stomach was doing so many flips he thought for sure he'd be the one getting sick. Kimmi, however, was forever elated and her health seemed to beam like springtime. She was just that happy.

Cliff walked the block to his new home after getting off the bus. He'd actually gotten off early to cut back on his hours, but the slightly longer commute home still had him arriving at dusk. Their move into Pyotr's home had gone smoother than his nerves anticipated. Plus, one of the nurses from the cancer center was going through a divorce and needed a place for her and her two daughters. So it was quickly settled on a rent and the new tenants would be moving in this weekend.

Kimmi took to her new environment faster than he did. Cliff was still trying to get used to other people in the home, even if it was just Pyotr and Pavle. And he also needed to learn to stop asking for even the simplest of needs like a glass of water. Pyotr, of course, was as patient as a saint and not once made Cliff feel guilty for being so foolish at times.

As he reached the house, Cliff spotted someone in the courtyard messing around with an old beat up motorcycle. The dude, to his surprise, looked vaguely familiar.

"Hah," the dude chuckled as Cliff stepped through the gate, "I would never have believed it if I hadn't seen it with my own two eyes."

"Darko?" Cliff's eyes widened as he looked at him. He knew Darko from Club Pain, but now it was just starting to sink in he knew him by another means as well. Darko was Sasha's older brother— which made him Pyotr's younger. And the resemblance was almost a spot on match right down to the same blue eyes.

Darko shook his head with an expression of humored disbelief. "The mighty Cliff Patterson sleeping in my brother's bed," Darko chuckled. "You may not have triumphed as being the next Dominus, but you definitely triumphed where none ever could with Pyotr."

Cliff's face dropped into a deep scowl. The longer commute, now nearly twice the time, had him tired and moody, he wasn't prepared to be hounded by another one of Pyotr's family members. He got enough of that from Sasha.

Darko ignored the scowl and tossed something at him. Cliff's hand automatically flashed up, catching it just as the tossed item hit his chest. "Here you go, Dominus." Darko smirked at him.

THE DOMINION OF BROTHERS SERIES

Cliff's eyes dropped to the item, finding a single key attached to a ring with a worn out key tag that read *Norton*. His gaze shot up to Darko then over to the old bike that coincidentally also said *Norton* on the side.

"What is this?"

Darko let out a laugh and shrugged, "Most people call it a motorcycle."

"He's here!" Kimmi's excited voice shouted from the frontsteps rail overhead.

Cliff looked just as Pyotr came out the door, taking his sister by both shoulders, and steered her down the stairs. By the time they hit the courtyard, Pyotr had Kimmi pulled back against his chest in a tight hug, as if she were the only thing grounding him from flying off with all the excitement that danced in those blue eyes of his. Together, the two playfully came up to greet him.

"Well, what do you think, *dragi*?" Pyotr's eyes motioned to the bike.

Cliff blinked up with a blank expression. "It's mine?" His hand fisted over the keys.

"For a bit," Darko butted in. "This here is the banger. You'll ride her for a while until you've learned how to handle a bike and get through New York traffic without getting killed. She has double crash bars, both in front and on the back, so if you dump her, no harm done."

Cliff's attention snapped back to his lover who was beaming proudly.

"When you're ready, we'll get you a nice bike that will be all yours," Pyotr added.

Cliff was floored, but far from being speechless, "But why? I mean, why're you giving me a motorcycle?"

The amused flame that always seemed to be there, sparked to deep wickedness. "Your commute home has another hour added on it— time better spent in my bed."

Cliff could only grin at that, but it had Kimmi blushing under Pyotr's arms. Darko was only shaking his head in more disbelief. Just then, a car pulled up front and honked, breaking the varied levels of embarrassment being passed around.

"Hemi?" Pyotr gave his brother a questioning glance as he recognized the car to belong to one of their teammates.

"Yeah, told him to swing by and get me, so you didn't have to take me home."

"You sleeping with him now?"

Darko's face squinted up and again he shook his head, "Nah— not after spending the last month and a half playing service boy to Diesel for his fallen angel." Darko's lips nearly puckered as if savoring a fine wine, "After that man, I'm ruined— at the least spoiled for a while." Darko's eyes flickered to Cliff and gave him an amused smirk. "See you around, *Dominus*." And he headed off for his ride.

Cliff snapped around to face Pyotr, anticipating a response to Darko's comment, and the shocked look on Pyotr's face said it was definitely coming. Pyotr's arms immediately let go of Cliff's sister and edged her away, stepping for him. "Why did he call you that?" The tone revealing Pyotr was not in the least bit entertained by Darko's teasing banter.

Cliff cringed and kept silent.

"You will answer me, *dragi* . Why did my brother just now call you the Dominus?"

"I— I— he was just being sarcastic. I swear it."

Pyotr took Cliff's arm and for all the force Cliff knew to live in that arm, it was surprisingly gentle.

"You cannot use that title. Not even in game, *dragi* . A lot of work went into establishing the meaning behind it and someone going around in false parade could destroy everything we've worked for. Do you understand?"

Cliff started to nod, but then he didn't understand. Why was it so important? It was just a club and some crazy convention with an auction for sex play. Cliff's answer reflected his confusion when his head jerked back and forth.

Pyotr sucked in a deep breath and let it out like a heavy sigh. "BDSM is very serious— it's a Lifestyle for many, and it is sexy play, but it can be very dangerous, as well. Establishing Trenton Leos as the Dominus over the community in the area has provided a safe harbor for those who live it; keeping it healthy and safe for all those who want to be involved. However, Trenton's position must *never* be undermined in order to maintain it. There is a black market lurking in New York. Women and young boys disappear and die from it every day. He protects us from that. Now do you understand?"

Cliff just blinked up at him a moment.

"*Dragi* ?" Pyotr's voice softened, then coaxing a painful understanding from him.

He nodded. "I wanted to be him. I wanted to be the one in charge that everyone looked up to." Cliff's face dropped to the ground and he shrugged, "I'm sorry. I was kinda a brat about it, too."

Pyotr caught his chin and pulled him up to look at him. Every bit of understanding looked back at Cliff and then kissed him. "I'm sure you were." Pyotr smiled and kissed him again.

That evening, Pyotr prepared a special dinner as his celebration, now having his new family with him. Serbian dishes he considered family favorites, to which his brother, Pavle agreed fully.

Cliff and Kimmi both had extra helpings. Though, Kimmi's stomach didn't take to the hoarding and Cliff soon found himself watching over her in the bathroom as she wretched her stomach out. Pyotr, to Cliff's surprise, was right beside him the entire time preparing a warm tea with honey to help settle her stomach when she was able to cheat a few sips in here and there. He even insisted Pavle check her vitals regularly; one of the benefits of having an ER doctor in the house.

Regardless, even with the shared concern, Cliff felt the deep fear lurch closer as he carried his burden. He'd heard the question more than once. *Won't it be a relief when you don't have to worry about her all the time?* He couldn't picture his life without Kimmi, so the question was more than just offensive, it frightened him. Because losing her was still a shadow that walked only a few paces behind him, never taking over, never disappearing.

ʕ•ᴥ•ʔ

Pyotr's feelings were beyond ecstatic to finally have Cliff and Kimmi living with him. All his life he had wanted a family of his own, one that was not just his siblings. Watching his brothers grow up and have children— it was both a joy and a sorrow. Cliff, for all his frumpy youth, filled him in ways Pyotr had always hoped to find for himself, and Kimmi, while not his own, he adored her as if she were. Now, watching over her as her mortality showed its horns in her life, he also felt the pending grief that came with it. The one Sasha had tried to warn him of.

The worry that marred his young lover's face was equally painful to watch. There was so much more going on inside Cliff and Pyotr realized that his lover had yet to *spill* as he had predicted when they first met. Pyotr had gotten so swept away with their growing relationship, he'd become distracted from the one thing Cliff needed most— and that was to come apart, so he could be mended back together properly. A task, now daunted with the realization they'd grown so close, Pyotr wasn't sure he could do the job alone or objectively.

ʕ•ᴥ•ʔ

Kimmi was just finally drifting to sleep in her bed; Cliff curled up against her, equally tired and drifting. Pyotr touched them both, brushing his fingers across their foreheads as if he could erase the worry lines they both wore. He glanced at his watch. It was late, but his thoughts could not wait. He slipped from the bedroom and went to his office downstairs. If there was one person he could go to and count on, it was the Dominus Trenton Leos, and Trenton would take his call even at this hour.

CHAPTER SEVEN

Pyotr held Cliff in his arms as if he had no intention of letting go anytime soon, while he stole several kisses to hold him over while he was gone. Most of the rowing team was already loaded up in one of the Ford Excursions, supplied by one of their sponsors, Marcus Scriven who owned *Scriven's Armored Transportation.* But that didn't stop the guys from watching like wide-eyed children behind the windows, as well as offer a few snickering comments their way.

Cliff scowled up at Pyotr, who as usual, was wearing his amused expression, "Can't you make them stop?

Pyotr's brows shot up and he nearly laughed aloud, "Who? Them?" His head nodded back and forth. "Never." His arms tightened, crushing Cliff against his chest, and kissed his young lover one last time. Devouring his lips for a long moment before finally releasing him and loading up in one of the vehicles, each one towing the trailers loaded with their team color glossy racing shells. It was amusing in a way, while the team didn't need armored protection, they weren't about to turn down the luxury the sponsored vehicles gave, as well as capacity. Free of charge was good, too. Not to mention all three trucks came with drivers, allowing the team members to rest and relax during the long drive to Boston.

Quentin, who was sitting in the passenger seat up front, turned to goad Pyotr. "So, don't you think maybe you're going a wee bit fast? Fucking the good lookin' lad is all good, but you got him all moved in now. We've never seen you move so fast with anyone before."

"That is because I have never been as sure as I am now." Pyotr's face dropped a bit, but only to feel the beaming emotions and confidence he felt in his relationship with Cliff.

"But, how can you be sure?" Quentin asked.

Pyotr looked back up at the stout New York Irish man and then the others all rubber necking at him, waiting for some magic word. He shrugged, "You just feel this certainty and you have to trust it if you want to enjoy it."

Darko looked at his older brother. He'd been worried over this from the start and now seemed the best chance he'd had to ask him, "But what if you're just letting your desires to have a family cloud your judgment, making you see what you want to see, and not what's really there?"

Pyotr slapped a hand on his brother's shoulder and nodded confidently. "Where would we be today if we let fear be the deciding factor for us when we first talked about competing?" And his friends and teammates finally understood and nodded.

Tom, who was sitting behind him, leaned up over the back of Pyotr's seat, unable to pass up a chance to razz his buddy to lighten the mood. "So, you're not at all worried about leaving your boy-toy unattended?"

"Who said I've left him unattended? He knows he belongs to me," Pyotr chided confidently, still allowing his mates to have their fun with him. At least here, his lover would not feel such urgency to defend them, so all was in good fun.

"Don't let him fool you." Quentin chimed in, "Pyotr probably put saltpeter in the boy's food while he's gone." The comment got the guys laughing.

"Say it isn't so." Tom stammered.

"And risk ruining that beautiful pecker on him?" Pyotr tucked his chin, managing to keep a straight face, but his eyes were already laughing, giving him away. "Absolutely not. I put a cock cage on him instead." Pyotr's response got the men roaring and Tom slapped him on the shoulder then sat back as the trucks pulled off.

The morning after their arrival in Boston, Pyotr watched his men carefully as they unloaded the trailers and walked the long shells down to the water, then began reassembling the rigging.

The Greenwich Queens Rowing Team had long since earned their keep in the district and for the most part, the slander among their peers had stopped. But *this* was a new level; the Regional Masters Head Regatta was hosted by both the British Rowing Club and the Essex Rowing Club, and it was bringing in teams the GQ's had never raced against, until now. Meaning the smirks and whispers— the strange looks— and the silent hate were back. *And his team could feel it.*

It wasn't good for them. They had two days before the race and Pyotr had decided a long hard day of rowing on the Merrimack River to acclimate themselves would do them some good.

He spotted York Sterling, one of the district organizers from New York, over at the boat house and decided to go check in with him and say hello.

"Ah, Pyotr." York took Pyotr's hand as he stepped up. "You and your boys have made it. And already setting up for a trial run on the river, I see."

"Yes, first time to the regional is putting some jitter in them, its best we row it out." Pyotr gave him a cordial chuckle.

York's face tightened and he leaned closer, in confidence, "There have been some unpleasant murmurings among some of the unfamiliar teams already spreading. I won't have this Pyotr. Anyone give you problems, you come to me right away. We won't tolerate bad sportsmanship. We're gentlemen here."

Pyotr could only offer a smile for his friend. York was a true gentleman, who once confessed privately with him, he was uncertain if homosexuality was a sin or not. But, such things mattered not in the sport of rowing and York Sterling had always seen to it that others followed by his rules. York had always seen and treated them as an inspiring team to the sport, just like any other. For that, Pyotr had always been grateful. "If we hear of any, we'll just wink and blow kisses at them as we pass their asses on the river."

York let out a hearty laugh, "To the duels then." They shook hands again. "Check back with me before you leave, I'll have your credentials ready when you boys come back in."

Race day. Pyotr and his crew sat lined up in their sculler. To their right, floated their team's second eight-man; making two out of only nine contenders that had converted away from the commonly used one oar per man *sweep*-rowing to traditional scull-style rowing in the eight-man class. The remaining eight-man teams in the competition had yet to change over and stuck with the sweep method, thus had a race class of their own.

Pyotr glanced over to Quentin on the second squad, who, like him sat in the first slider bow-seat. He gave him a nod. They both spoke to their teammates, to talk them through the tension, drawing their minds into focus. All of them— on the ready— waiting for the start of the race.

"Glistening water— smooth and waiting for us. Like bugs skidding across her surface— we will glide," Pyotr whispered to River, sitting in front of him, who then whispered it to Mitch. From Mitch to Cody, then to Hemi, Andreas, Trofim, and lastly Zane who had the stroke seat.

To their left, a Michigan team snickered homophobic verbiage at them, but Pyotr only minded his men to keep their focus. Only the race mattered in this moment.

On the bridge, just behind the starter point where the rowing teams floated, fans and spectators filled up and spilled down along the river banks. Several groups mixed with both men and women stood waving rainbow flags and homemade posters that declared their love and support for the New York Greenwich Queens. For them, it balanced it out. They had become one of the most popular sculling teams around. Bringing in long sought after attention to a near forgotten sport. Of course, having twenty-six men, most of which were pretty damn hunky, did help, and the girls didn't seem to mind one bit that none of them were straight.

A temporary docking station floated across the river with fingers that jutted out. Each one contained a young boy or girl tender, presently laid out on their bellies holding the sixty foot sculls in place. Watching over like a monarch, the official Aligner stood at the bank directing each tender to assure all boats were positioned equally for a fair start— down to the inch. The rowers sitting quietly, motionless— their oars up and positioned back for that vital first dip that made every bit of difference of positioning.

Calon was their coxswain, while his twin brother Calob had the cox'n seat in the second eight-man crew. Their job was to call the rhythm out and keep the time in time, as well as maintain the small rudder located in their tight space of a seat in the aft section of the scull.

All eyes swept their starboard side to a man dressed as if he planned to greet the British Royal stepped up on the elevated dock built out from the river bank and took position.

The men's arms tensed— oars easing back but keeping clear of the water— heads bowed— backs arched over— and the anticipated pause that stretched out for a millennia.

The gun fired off and nine long shells of men dipped and lunged forward with a myriad of chanting cries from the men who oared them. Only, none so predominant as the one the Greenwich Queens had. While chants were usually called out by the coxswain, Hemi was pure blood New Zealander Maori and he had been given a *Strong Haka* by his *Kodo* back home for his team; a type of chant used by the warriors to warn their enemy they were coming.

As they're oars dipped into the water in unison, Hemi called out the first verse from the second crew, and together they all slid forward on the tracks of the seats, bearing oars back and then the crew all responded as they dipped and pulled with all their strength for the most vital catch in their start— arms, legs, and souls.

"*WHAY CHAY HOWA!*" Hemi charged out the chant from his lungs with each pull of the oars.

"*HOYH!*" the team calling back in the motion of the reset.

"*KQUATAH QUATAH HAY HO!*"

"*HOYH!*"

"*KEE OCUHEE NAM ME TAH!*"

The shells sliced through the water's surface, surging forward with every pull of the oars, and in those first two or three pulls, Pyotr's team took the lead position.

In momentum, the coxswain now took over keeping the *Haka* chant to set their cadence, leading them in unison with the words that told their enemy what would be left of them once their crew was finished with them in this race.

Calon and Calob called in together, *"Ka mate! Ka mate!"*

And their teams all responded, *"Ka Ora! Ka Ora! Ka mate! Ka mate! Ka Ora! Ka Ora! Tenei te tangata Puburu huru! Nana I tiki mai Whakawhiti te ra! A. upa— ne! A, upa— ne!"*

While some might have thought it would be distracting it was anything but. It was the roar of their strength, commanding body and mind to surge with every ounce of focus and strength as one great body of war. And they wear killing it on the water.

Pyotr strained with all his muscles, his mind working in balance with his body, watching his men. Each set of oars a nano second behind the first. They worked like a precision time piece and he couldn't help but feel a boost of pride just then. Legs pushed and straightened, while backs and arms pulled for that extra effort. The Haka they sang out— part war cry part aggressive grunting— to kept them in focus and in time like a drum beat. Slide and pull— sweep and catch.

"A upane, ka upane Whiti t era— Hi!" They all called out the final verse of the Haka and took off down the river in the lead.

While the rowing strokes looked fluid from an outside perspective, they were made up of four sequential elements: the catch, the drive, the finish, and the recovery. And as the crew moved down the river, the movements became a hypnotic cadence, counting in their heads with only the cox'n keeping them monitored and controlling the rudder.

As the race reached the last bend in the river, muscles burned like hot coals from a fire. Sweat soaked their bodies and stung in their eyes. The prime eight-man team was in the lead, but just barely. The next two shells, another New York team, and the Michigan team still keeping a close pace to them, and it was time to leave them behind. Zane had the stroke seat and it was up to him to implement the up-take on their strokes. But, not until Calon gave him the call, and as he monitored their position to the other boats, in accordance to the remaining distance in the race, he would not call for the double-pace until just the right time.

The New York Rowing Regiment was drawing up beside them and that was a position they couldn't afford, and the call was made.

"Up-step!" Calon called out, Zane heaved with a will of super strength on his next catch and the men lined up behind him followed, forcing their bodies to pull harder and faster into double-time for a count of twenty strokes. Growling, burning, and pulling, Pyotr's teammates stayed focused on keeping their lead position. They didn't pause even a breath when the other team suffered a collision of oars and suddenly fell back and out of the shot for second or third place.

The twenty up-step had given them the lead they needed, pulling ahead of the others, but the race wasn't over, and though they dropped back to their primary cadence, they all knew the pressure was on.

The world fell away; the brain surged with every slide and growled with every catch of water in their oars. Burning adrenalin tainted the air around them, along with testosterone. And just as they reached the end of their twenty, Calon called for a power-10. Ten strokes of their hardest, most grueling strength, and to see to it they felt it, he called out the Haka once more. Giving them what they needed to keep their mental strength.

"*Ka mate! Ka mate!*"

And their teams all responded, "*Ka Ora! Ka Ora! Ka mate! Ka mate! Ka Ora! Ka Ora! Tenei te tangata Puburu huru! Nana I tiki mai Whakawhiti te ra! A. upa— ne! A, upa— ne!*"

One final grueling pull and Pyotr saw the ribbon slip past them and snap as they sliced past it. A quick glance to the digital board onshore gave him a proud read out of 14.9 miles per hour. Cheers and rainbow flags met them from all sides of the river. Relief made Pyotr's body melt in that instant and he slumped over, too happy, and too tired to do anything else. *They had won*! The championship was theirs!

Shortly after, the four-man crews came in sight— Pavle, Stefan, Theo, and Noah were holding fourth place. Even more exciting was when the singles started coming up the river and Pyotr's brother, Darko, was pulling ahead to take his win by a landslide in an intense race against nearly thirty other single scullers. When Darko crossed the finish line ribbon, the guys hardly gave any hesitation to the matter, and they all bounded into the water to celebrate with him.

Pyotr scooped his brother up right away and planted a deep kiss on his lips, then hoisted him off his feet.

They all gathered around, rejoicing in their accomplishment with loads of cheers. Their hard training and perseverance had paid off today.

The final high was standing on the temporary platform, all lined up in their matching uni-suits: black with slightly slanted broad strips in each color of royal-blue and heather-grey sashed across the chest. They were ceremoniously handed over their trophies and they collectively felt like kings on top of Mount Everest in that moment. They stood proudly while sport journalists took photos and the presidents from both host rowing clubs shook their hands to congratulate them.

The awards ceremony wasn't a long one, but before it ended, someone unexpected stepped through the crowd that brought a sudden concerning memory to the fore. Pyotr quickly glanced at his younger brother, Trofim, who had also spotted the ex-partner, Shay Wilks, charging up fast.

Pyotr quickly brushed past Zane, who'd been standing between them, but Trofim was already backing away so fast he nearly went crashing of the back edge of the platform. Trofim spun and darted down the steps and took off in the other direction.

Pyotr followed his brother down only to head Shay off at the pass and caught the young man by the arm, bringing him to a stop.

Shay, tall and handsome, had certainly matured over the past five years. But one thing apparently didn't change in him; he still loved Trofim madly. It was written all over Shay's face. An excited expression colored the other man's features in awe and torment, but they quickly melted away when he turned, glancing at Pyotr, and recognized the roadblock for what it was.

Pain and weariness filled Shay's eyes just then. "I want to see him. Please!" It was almost a demand if it weren't for the hurt and pleading deeply rooted inside his tone.

Pyotr wished nothing more than to let these two be together again, but the price for his brother's life was too steep to not intervene. Pyotr was suddenly aware that Shay was also in uniform and he looked out past Shay— to the crowd of spectators. Benjamin Wilks had to be out there somewhere; this was too good of an opportunity to boast about his son and to look positive in the political world. "Your father is probably looking to congratulate you."

Shay's face went stark blank as if all will to live or fight left him. Now, only an empty young man stood before Pyotr. Without another word, Shay slowly turned and walked away.

CHAPTER EIGHT

The night had finally come for Pyotr to bring his lover to Club Pain. After a brief chat of *catch-up* at the door between him and Vida, Pyotr and Cliff walked inside the club and were surprised to find the Dominus Trenton Leos at the bar already waiting for them.

Pyotr felt the immediate tension on his young lover as they slowly approached what, essentially, was Cliff's final *coming out*, though it was not the purpose of their scheduled evening. Still, it was something that could not be dismissed and Pyotr closed his arm around Cliff to comfort him and assure him they were doing this together. Cliff was not alone in any of this.

Since they had begun their relationship, they had done a number of activities publicly. However, it was often more that they were doing *anything* that revealed Cliff's lack for an active life outside of work; his club nights, being his only personal escape. So showing up at Club Pain now, as a *surrendered-lover* and not the Dom he tried so hard to convince other he was, was understandably unnerving.

(·ω·)

Cliff felt every bit of nerve-racking adrenalin racing through him, his stomach twisted and flipped. And nothing, not even the familiarity of Trenton's demeanor, put him at ease. He watched as the Dominus shook hands and greeted Pyotr, a slight glance shifted his way and that was all the recognition he was afforded. Not that he had expected a friendly greeting in the first place, but Cliff perhaps thought he would have received more than just a glimmer from Dominus since he was here with Pyotr.

After the two spoke into each other's ears to hear over the music that already thrummed and pounded in the club, Pyotr's arms snaked around Cliff's waist and brought him about-face, pulling them together. "Keep your eyes on me," Pyotr whispered to him and began to kiss him lightly. Instead, Cliff closed his eyes, trying to escape into that kiss, but it was over too soon, and his insides still felt as much the pretzel as he did a second ago.

(·ω·)

"Patronus isn't here yet," Trenton leaned in toward Pyotr as he spoke to be heard, "Would you care to join me in my room for a drink and some privacy to start or would you prefer to go ahead and move upstairs?"

Pyotr listened but kept his gaze on his lover. He took Cliff's chin, lifting his face to look up at him for a moment and could feel his young lover shaking as if he were standing naked in the cold rain. "Perhaps some privacy at first would be best for both of us." And Pyotr gave an agreeable nod to Trenton.

"What do you drink?" Trenton asked.

"Vodka."

"And some wine?" Trenton raised the question to Pyotr as a matter of courtesy. Both he and Pyotr knew who the wine would be for should he decide, as it was the only libation a sub or slave was permitted, to help take the edge off before a hard scene.

Pyotr rolled his lips in thought for a moment before answering. "Yes, some wine would do well, something fruity—" He kissed Cliff's mouth fully with growing expectations. "To go with his sweet lips," he added with a playful whisper.

Trenton turned to the bartender, "Derek, tequila for me, a flask of Gromoff Premium Vodka, and a small decanter of either a Icelandic Ice Wine or a Chianti. Whichever we have available, please. And then have someone bring them to my booth when they're ready. Oh, and let Patronus know where we are when he arrives."

The bartender nodded and was already grabbing a flask and glasses to fill the order. "Yes, Dominus. Anything for the mouse this evening?"

The Dominus declined the offer for his own slave and turned, sweeping his head out to lead Pyotr and Cliff in the direction of the VIP booth on the far side of the club.

Pyotr moved Cliff to walk in front of him as they followed their host, dropping a firm hand at the small of Cliff's back to show his possessiveness. It was a severe difference to being a submissive. An aspect his toy likely wasn't educated on.

✿

Once inside, Cliff glanced around the VIP room, encased with one way viewable glass, taking his first glimpse of the additional luxuries Dominus had kept away from public view. Off to the side, he instantly spotted Katianna Dumas.

The small woman who was both a well-known author of erotica and the Dominus's collared Life-slave, sitting in a funny shaped upholstered lounger along with the laptop he'd rarely ever seen her without. Her fingers typing away. And just like before, her eyes never left her work to look at him. He almost smiled, except he was still feeling those butterflies flipping in his stomach. They were still the same, though. He was the one changing.

"Cliff?"

"I think I'm gonna be sick," he confessed knowing there was no sense holding anything back. It was all gonna come up anyways.

"Cliff," Pyotr tender tenor called to him.

He turned to see Pyotr looking at him carefully, waiting for him to find his comfort zone and join him where he'd already taken a seat on the sofa. Cliff tried to smile, but he wasn't sure it made it to his face. He then followed over to where he was called, and as he often did, slid to the floor at Pyotr's feet and rested against his leg, watching with silent admiration as Dominus went to his little woman, and spoke quietly with her. Katianna willingly gave up her attention to him, giving Trenton the kiss he apparently requested, and then went back to her typing when he came to join the two of them on the moon shaped sofa.

(◕ω◕)

"How is she?" Pyotr asked gently, not wanting to push the subject too much in her presence or for the night. Yet, he had always been concerned for the two of them since her kidnapping. Pyotr had offered to council them both together and/or separately. But, Trenton had declined his offer, choosing instead to handle her care privately, himself. And that alone had kept Pyotr's concerns awash. Trenton, too, had endured the trauma, and Pyotr had seen the dark pain the incident had caused the man. Yet, he didn't push the matter and only had gone to visit him once since then. Yet, even now, he saw how Trenton's eyes always went back to her, some shadow still there, fearful that any moment someone else might try to slip in and snatch her right from under his arms.

"She's recovering well. She doesn't dare go anywhere without myself or Diesel anymore." Trenton pursed his lips and hi gaze finally shifted from her to Pyotr. "That's probably best for my sake right now."

"Trenton if you need more time—"

"Yes, she and I will need plenty more time," Trenton interrupted, "But, did you think I would disregard your needs?"

Pyotr offered a sympathetic smile. No, he couldn't even imagine Trenton denying him or allowing anyone else other than Diesel to handle his private needs. "We won't be disturbing her?" Pyotr offered a mild shift in the conversation.

Trenton shook his head. "She listens to music when she writes. That pretty much keeps everybody out."

Pyotr took that opportune moment to change the subject to completely divert away from tender issues. "What does she listen to?"

"Everything. Whatever fits the mood she needs. But, it's usually instrumental. Stuff I'd never heard of before her," Trenton chuckled.

As they both continued to talk, Pyotr stroked the side of Cliff's face with the backs of his fingers, thinking long and hard. Not so much of what was said, but more of what was ahead of them for the evening. His lover glanced up at him. Cliff was feeling it, too. For tonight was not a night for partying or dancing, it wasn't a night on the town, it was a purging. And it was not going to be an easy one for either of them. And Pyotr was putting his faith in Trenton to see them through it safely.

A light rap on the glass and one of the club's employed subs poked her auburn-haired head inside. "Dominus, I bring you your drinks."

"Enter. Set them on the table."

The sub, dressed in patent leather club-wear, stepped in carrying a serving tray, and knelt beside the center table. She set out the decanters along with three empty glasses and a glass of ice water. After pouring the first round of drinks, she sat back on her heels waiting patiently to be dismissed, though her eyes shifted to Cliff and locked with his.

Cliff's guts locked and the breath in his lungs hitched into a knot.

"Thank you. You may go," Trenton dismissed her and leaned over, taking up the shot of white tequila on the rocks.

Pyotr ignored his drink at first, picking up the wine instead, and brought it to Cliff's lips. But Cliff didn't accept.

He was too mortified. The auburn haired waitress that came in and served them had been none other than Gina. The girl he had messed around with and the very one he had nearly placed his relationship with Pyotr at risk when he rode with her to the club a few weeks ago. To now sit here, despite how he felt for Pyotr, it was not easy coming out in front of everyone, especially in light of how he had acted here.

☙❦❧

"You're too nervous. Perhaps some practice right here before we go upstairs," Pyotr suggested to Cliff who gave a voluntary nod. Agreeing to any form of distraction.

Pyotr unzipped his pants and pulled his cock out; already hard as he anticipated the evening. Though not entirely meant for pleasure, the thought of watching Trenton work a scene with his own *dragi* was too much of a visual to control his pleasure.

Cliff's eyes glanced around to the people just outside the glass partition, still visible from the inside, which for Cliff meant so was he.

"Look at me," Pyotr called Cliff's attention back to him. "There is no one else that exists for you but me."

Cliff's eyes wavered under his stare and shifted, glancing over his shoulder to see if Trenton was still watching. "But, the Dominus, he's—"

"Hush. He does not exist for you." Pyotr brushed Cliff's lips with the backs of his fingers, then caught his chin, lifting it so his young lover looked only at him, "Our scene together has begun. You are mine and no other's. You are not to look at Dominus, nor speak to him, or anyone else for that matter. You're to never respond unless I tell you otherwise."

Cliff looked trapped suddenly, his eyes widened, "But— but Dominus— everyone must follow his commands. How—"

It was clear Cliff had earned more than a few warnings from the Dominus in the past and now that he was trying to set his tracks straight— the last thing he wanted was to be directed to disobey any command the Dominus might give, landing Cliff right back on Trenton's wrong side.

"Hush," Pyotr whispered again, not once losing his patience, not once raising his voice. "Yes, he is the Dominus and that does seem to strike a conflict of interest. But, then he knows not to speak to you. He knows you belong to me and would never put you in a position to disobey my command or attempt to undermine me. That is part of what makes him Dominus. Only in extenuating circumstances might he break that protocol or when I say otherwise, such as later tonight. When we go upstairs for our session with the Patronus, he may give commands to which you will follow. But again, nothing he will say will override my own commands. He knows not to create that kind of conflict. Do you understand?"

It was hesitant at first. Perhaps it had never occurred to him that some much protocol went into being a Dom of all Doms. But eventually Cliff nodded.

"Shall we practice then?"

Again, Cliff nodded and Pyotr took his lover's head and guided Cliff's lips down over his cock. He let out an instant hard sigh as the pleasure of his young lover's mouth eagerly swept over his flesh. "Mmm, that's so good, *dragi* ."

The strong muscular build of Diesel Gentry was suddenly at the door and Pyotr crooked his fingers several times to signal his entry would not be an interruption. "We're practicing," Pyotr explained as Diesel stepped in to join them.

(ꞷ)

However, the sounds spilling in from the nightclub just beyond the door had Cliff tensing up nervously all over again, and the additional audience of Diesel, of all people, added to Cliff's panic. He began bobbing his head frantically, sucking harder and faster over Pyotr's shaft until it was more a race to run away than to deliver any form of pleasure.

(ꞷ)

Pyotr grabbed Cliff by the back of the head, his fingers gripping in his hair and peeled him off, pulling Cliff to a stop. "Slow. Take a deep breath and relax a bit and remember your *Glavar* likes it slow." Keeping a firm grip on Cliff's head to keep him steady, Pyotr guided his young lover under his control, setting the pace for how he wanted Cliff to suck him. "That's it— lick it. I'll do the rest." Keeping his fingers fisted in Cliff's hair, Pyotr moved his head up and down over his hard shaft, slow and steady, taking his pleasure with his lover's mouth in stride. Like everything else he did.

He glanced over at Diesel as the well-built man watched the scene, and Pyotr gave him a smiling glance. "Young people are always in such a hurry. Especially in play. I am always having to slow this one down." Pyotr dropped his eyes to Cliff and caressed the side of one cheek as it swelled with the length of Pyotr's shaft sinking all the way into his lover's warm, wet mouth.

Once he was satisfied that Cliff would not start rushing again, Pyotr released his head, and settled back in the sofa, letting the climbing sensation come over him. "Our age difference has presented some challenges. I normally wouldn't take on a lover as young as he—" he licked his lips, closing his eyes, letting the pure pleasure wash over him a moment before he continued with what he was saying. "But, I could not resist Cliff. And despite that I am twice his age, we seem perfect for each other." Pyotr took in a long deep breath, rolling his lips, and let a soft grumbling sound rumbled out from his chest, "Hmm, that's it—" he let out a deep husky breath. "I'm going to cum soon."

Cliff swirled his tongue around the head and lifted his gaze to watch Pyotr's expression then mischievously stabbed at the hole.

Pyotr's hips jerked; he quickly snatched up Cliff's head and pulled him from his cock. The tight suction his lover had on him made a popping sound when released, and Pyotr's shaft twitched to get back to the pleasure. Which only served to please his young lover a great deal. "Are you trying to make me cum so quickly?"

Cliff slipped his tongue out, catching a dewy droplet of saliva from the corner of his mouth. His eyes half lidded with the bratty possessiveness Pyotr'd grown so attached to. Once Cliff got started on something, especially his cock, Pyotr's young lover was quite greedy. Not wanting to give up a single drop of his *Glavar's* essence no matter how miniscule. Cliff wanted it all.

How could Pyotr not grant him the vulgar pleasure and he released Cliff's head, who triumphantly went right back to what he had started, and sucked Pyotr's hard, throbbing flesh all the way to the back of his throat in one, long swallow.

Pyotr pushed back in the sofa, taking Cliff's head in his hands once again but only to caress the sides of his cheeks as they swelled with his cock, riding as Pyotr pitched his hips up, pumping slowly into his lover's tight wet mouth. He hissed with the pleasure and then let the pent up energy go, felt the orgasm coil up in his balls then shoot out into Cliff's waiting mouth.

"Mmmm— so good, *dragi* ," he groaned, stroking over Cliff's head as he licked Pyotr clean then like a dutiful submissive would be commanded to do.

Cliff tucked his *Glavar's* cock back into his slacks and rested his head against Pyotr's thigh. Calmer now.

"Good boy," Pyotr sighed.

A silent twitch from Diesel in his direction beckoned Pyotr to step out of the VIP booth. The stoic concern readable on the man's face had Pyotr concerned as well. Tonight's session would not be easy on either of them, so any concerns had to be addressed properly and before they began. "Excuse me, *dragi* ." Pyotr sat up, folding over to nibble on Cliff's upturned lips a moment then pushed up to his feet and followed Diesel out of the booth to talk in private.

Diesel stopped at the rail that looked out over the dance floor, but his focus was only on Pyotr. He waited until the door to their booth floated closed before saying anything, "When I sent Cliff to you, I thought you'd do a few sessions with him, and yes perhaps a few scenes— private ones. I did not expect you to make him your lover."

Pyotr relaxed then. Still a genuine concern, but none that would hinder tonight's needs. "I understand your concerns here. In mine and Cliff's coming together, I too learned he is perfect for me. I knew this right away. But, believe me when I tell you, I did not take advantage of his emotional state. We are both very aware of what we are doing."

Diesel took a deep, long breath and leaned back on the rail. He wasn't fully accepting of this situation yet wasn't sure what to ask to better decide how he should react. Nevertheless, he was putting his guns away. Of course, Pyotr would not take advantage of the young man. That wasn't like him at all to do. Only that their relationship seemed to be developing on a rather fast track which was also unlike Pyotr. "Tell me he's not being forced to be here."

"He is not," Pyotr assured, "Though, it was my choice for our session with you; it was his choice to come to the club."

Another long breath and Diesel held himself in deep thought.

"I appreciate your concern for him, Diesel," Pyotr offered, dropping his hands in his slacks as he spoke, "It only shows that you, too, will one day make a great Dominus like your brother, especially in light of Cliff." Pyotr paused a moment then chuckled lightly, "Cliff told me that while coming here he was—" He grinned. "a bit of a brat."

Diesel let out a slight chuckle. That much was true. Cliff had put a great deal of energy into pushing everyone to accept him not only as a Dom, but the kid wanted everyone to think he was the next Dominus. If Cliff had been honest about that with Pyotr then perhaps they had gone into this openly, even if it did seem to be rushed. Perhaps finding each other was far better than Diesel thought it would be. He took another breath and rubbed at his mouth. "My apologies, Pyotr. I should not have questioned you."

"Don't be. But, now that we have cleared this issue with mine, what of yours? What happened to the beautiful man I saw you with a few months ago? Did you ever give yourself permission to be with him and enjoy his affections?"

"I had. I only regret not giving in sooner." Diesel's eyes dropped to the floor in thought.

"Had you, it would have been too soon. There was quite an emotional tug of war between the two of you, beautiful and powerfully potent. Such things can also explode. And now?"

Diesel looked into the blue eyes that watched him, knowing more than Diesel cared for anyone, other than his brother, to know about him. Though he knew Pyotr's trust was worth ten men's weight in gold. "Paris works down at the resort. He did not take separation well."

Pyotr nodded a moment, taking it all in. "And neither have you obviously. Take it from me— as a friend, Diesel—" and he waited for Diesel to look him in the eye. "The best loves are the ones you have to grow into. Go to him and let him know that."

Inside the booth, Cliff had been watching Katianna. He felt guilty, and that he was here with the Dominus only made it worse. "I want to apologize to you, Dominus." Cliff looked over at the domineering man and saw he, too, was watching Katianna, like she was a moving painting or something. Perhaps a touch of wickedness in his eyes, but Trenton heard him and responded mildly.

"For what?"

"For the way I acted."

"Accepted," Trenton answered, his eyes never leaving the small woman who had ceremoniously been claimed as a slave companion for life not too long ago.

Cliff was quiet for a moment. In a medical office, he knew what he was waiting for, knew what was expected of him. But, right now, he knew neither of those, and without Pyotr's calm demeanor to be his anchor, Cliff found himself starting to fidget for the first time in his life. "Do you want to apologize to me?" The nonsense blurted out before he could even consider how spoiled rotten it made him sound. Wasn't the first time though. Not with this man.

"No."

"Why?" Cliff was surprised, but not offended. Maybe it did hurt a little, that somehow Dominus's refusal to apologize meant Cliff was still not accepted, not even as a person.

Trenton turned and looked at him just as he would with anyone else, eye to eye and direct. "Because anything I may have done was never an act of cruelty toward you. Despite your affluence in my club, I never once bullied you. Steered you away from your intentions on my property, yes, but I never brought harm on you. Neither was I cruel. I reacted as any other might, in the way you presented yourself."

Cliff let out a long sigh. Damned if Trenton sounded a lot like Pyotr in a way. And strangely what he said made sense. Why would anyone apologize for acting the way they did when all along he instigated their actions with his own? Somehow, he was okay with not getting that apology after all.

Trenton smiled suddenly, as if he was holding back a chuckle, "Pyotr tells me you're still a brat."

Cliff glanced up and saw the slight smile on the Dominus's face and he felt the heat of his blushing pride warm his own face as he grinned at the notion. "Yeah, I guess I still am."

Upstairs in the private members club, Trenton and Diesel led their guests to a private room in the back, away from the watching eyes of others, where Pyotr watched as Trenton and Diesel began the night scene.

Tonight was not about sex or kink; it was about therapy for his young lover. Cliff's mental barriers had forced him to latch on and seal himself up tight, in order to endure for the sake of Kimmi and her failing health issues. So well cocooned, Cliff was on the verge of a nuclear meltdown on the inside. A self-destructive existence that needed to be healed and tonight would be the means to pull the tattered threads of his cocoon that had managed to hold Cliff together all this time.

Pyotr stood in front of Cliff, touching him as reassurance as his lover stared back at him stoically, withdrawing inside his tough-boy shell. Trenton and Diesel began the process, using the same colorful ropes they had used on Diesel's absent Unicorn, coiling them over Cliff's arms and legs into the skilled knots the men were known for.

Trenton held a bamboo wood stock behind Cliff's shoulders, bringing his arms up and out, while Diesel latched arm and bamboo into one. Careful placement was given to each and every coil of rope to prevent slippage that could cut into his Cliff's circulation. The coils of eight wrapped around Cliff's forearms and six more around his biceps would hold the young man's weight in balanced proportion.

"Look at me, *dragi* ," Pyotr called his attention to him, drawing his lover out of his shell. It was extraordinary watching the Dominus and the Patronus at work, and Pyotr felt no shame in having them handle his lover. There was a gift these two possessed like artists of precision skill.

He, however, was more the voyeur type of artist. But he knew this was what Cliff needed in order to break past the walls he'd imprisoned his emotions behind.

Cliff's deep rooted pain was because he'd put every moment of his life into Kimmi's care and guarding against some darker knowledge that it would all be for nothing when he would be alone when she was gone. Burdened further that there would be no one to catch him and hold him through his mourning.

Pyotr would be here to catch Cliff when he came apart tonight. And if and when Kimmi lost the battle to her illness, he would be there for him then, too. This was the only way to let Cliff know. But, Pyotr didn't want Cliff injured in the process, so it was sensible planning on his part that he asked these two men to help them.

Cliff's eyes followed him. A small glint of worry marring them despite a well anchored trust. They had talked this over— discussed every detail before agreeing to proceed. But, even now, Pyotr felt Cliff's strength waver, which was the point, Pyotr gave him nothing less than his usual expression of pleasure which wasn't all that difficult. Watching intently as the next set of black ropes draped down the center of Cliff's chest in a sloop knot that then separated in opposite directions just under his pectorals to wind around Cliff's torso several times then repeated above his pecs.

After the block lines were set in place, next, Cliff's body was dressed with ropes of red silk, woven into a maze of netting that caged his body, then looped one leg— and up he went, with both legs snared and positioned with feet behind his ass. His ankles were looped and leashed into the system of ropes that held him slung up by the bamboo rod. Every piece, every slip and knot, precisely placed to be quickly unraveled with the pull of one single cord.

Cliff's face bit tight, a pulse at his temple throbbed as he willfully resisted all sensations.

"There's his wall," Pyotr confirmed.

Right away, Dominus took a horsehair flogger, and started the task of whipping the skin of Cliff legs, catching the sides of his ass, and much of his back as he worked up his subject's body, then back down.

Diesel took a long thick strand of string, holding it as it hung down Cliff's front, and proceeded to pin it to his skin with standard style clothesline pins. Making a line of them down Cliff's chest, then down one leg before swapping places with Trenton to do the same on Cliff's other side.

Cliff's body broke out into its first cold sweat and he shivered as the repeated session of clips and flogging began. But, he uttered not a word.

Pyotr kept close, monitoring Cliff's bodily reactions as well as reading the storm that battered behind a dam of gray blue eyes. He reached down, finding Cliff's cock, hard, and dripping with pre-cum. He gave it a firm slap, watching as it bounced back up to slap against Cliff's belly, stimulating a groan from them both with the delight.

Still Cliff kept quiet.

Pyotr kissed the side of his lover's face. While he offered reassurance, he still knew the importance of Cliff surrendering to his fears and so began to coax him to reveal them. "You need to feel, my pet." Pyotr whispered in Cliff's ear.

Cliff swallowed back a gulp when the stinging swipes from Trenton's flogger came across his developing reddened skin again. "I do." He sucked in a deep breath with the automated determination to keep composed.

"No, you need to feel all of it."

Cliff shot a glare at him, eyes flaring with every question. Pyotr glanced passed Cliff's shoulder to Trenton and gave him a nod, and the flogger was soon replaced with a bamboo beater.

Cliff moaned as Dominus placed rapid snaps of the cluster of bamboo reeds across his thighs, one after the other. Even the rattled *WHACK* sound, the beater made, reverberated in the room, adding to the sensation that was finally starting to consume Cliff. "Please," he moaned.

Pyotr was instantly before him. "What do you need, my dragi ?"

Cliff shook his head, like a rattle, twitching back and forth— it was clear he didn't know. His eyes searched, not the room, but his mind— his emotions— he didn't even know what he was looking for.

"Feel, *dragi* . Let it happen and let go of your walls." But then the bewilderment turned to refusal, and Cliff continued to shake his head.

"I can't," Cliff nearly pleaded as the next set of six canning reps came down on the fleshy part of his right hip then another six whacks on his left side.

Pyotr gave Dominus another nod and once more, the instrument was exchanged for another. Diesel moved to the wall, taking the hoist line and yanked Cliff up high where his genitals were set on display at chest height, and the leather striped flogger was brought down like a whirly gig on the inside of Cliff's thighs, just to the side of his scrotum.

Trenton kept his swings tightly measured to follow Pyotr's request that Cliff's cock would not be marred. But the strikes were close enough that an occasional suede strip left a single red welt across Cliff's balls.

"Feel, my pet. Open up and tell me the one thing you fear the most. Why have you been avoiding a life for you?" Pyotr deliberately refrained from using his name, under Trenton's advice. Using Cliff's name was a source of strength, one they needed Cliff to let go of because it was part of his resistance. "Stop being walled in and let go. Stop fighting it and surrender."

"No, I can't. If I do—" Cliff's quavering words broke off.

"What, *dragi* ? What will happen?" Pyotr nodded and three more strikes to the left landed on soft flesh.

Cliff's head thrashed, his teeth clamped hard, and his cock jumped.

"What's going to happen?"

Cliff shuddered. "It'll all come out. I don't think I will be able to stop it."

"What are you afraid of, *dragi* ?" Pyotr's voice deepened to a tone of base support.

Cliff gritted his teeth fighting back what screamed to get out and dropped his head to hide the coming tears that welled in his eyes.

Pyotr circled around Cliff, setting his hand on Trenton's shoulder, and the Dominus stopped, taking a step back. Pyotr drew closer. Bring a hand up to feel the heat of his lover's stinging flesh. The young man hissed under his touch— there was but one more thread holding Cliff together— and yet he clung to it with all he had. "What are you afraid to feel, *dragi* ?"

Cliff didn't want to feel. *Not that.* Anything, but that. Tears began to stream down Cliff's cheeks then stopped as if a dam had been instantaneously constructed to wall them up. A combination of fear of what he did not want to feel and the brazen sensation that suffered his skin relentlessly. His cock bobbed, hard, aching to be touched. But Pyotr never did, touching only where the radiating sting from the leather that had whipped his body into an overload of sensation.

Cliff fought inside himself, the pressure in his mind ticking away just inside his forehead, like an ice pick just tapping to get out. His cock swelled until it ached. The tears in his eyes threatened to break past his final defense and spill out along with everything he'd fought to keep bottled up inside. He had to be strong for Kimmi because if he let it out who would be strong for him.

His flesh stung, hot like crimson coals— sweet and brandishing at the same time, sending tumultuous waves over numbing static across his nerve endings. Every time Pyotr told him to feel, Cliff's grasp slipped a little more. Until finally when his lover ripped the string that ran the length of Cliff's body, taking with it the twenty-five or so clamps that pinched at his flesh and that soft loving voice once more told him to feel— he did.

Feeling emotions— thoughts— words— they detached from Cliff's mind— his control failed. It all came rushing out of his mouth at once like a tsunami, followed by it were the sobbing tears, and the vocalization that he was afraid for himself if Kimmi died. He was afraid of being alone without her. He was afraid someone would judge him for being selfish in the wake of her death. That once she was gone—

Cliff couldn't hold it back anymore; he tossed his head back and screamed what he had tried to hide from even himself. "I WON'T BE NEEDED ANY MORE—!" he belted out, "BY ANYONE! I WON'T HAVE A PLACE!!"

The trapped emotion was too much to bear and Cliff felt fractures— the last thread unraveling and withered away, undoing the walls of his fortress. Fear seized his heart and sorrow freed it. The tide was rushing through now, breaking its way through the fissure and gaining momentum beyond his control.

Cliff felt none of his defenses, along with his consciousness, he crumbled.

Pyotr snapped his fingers and with a pull of a rope, the weave of bindings that held Cliff's body in suspension came undone, dropping Cliff right into Pyotr's arms.

"Shhh— see there? I got you." Pyotr kissed him instantly— his cheek— his temple— the side of Cliff's head, all the tender, emotional spots that needed reassuring that told the boy he was not alone. "I'm here for you and I'm going to catch you whenever you need me. Your place is going to be with me. In my arms forever, *dragi* ." Pyotr held him, hugged him, and rubbed out the soreness where the bindings had been as Diesel and Trenton silently unraveled them, while Cliff continued to come undone in Pyotr's arms. "Because I need you," Pyotr whispered for him and felt Cliff surrendering his mental state to his *glavar* completely.

When Cliff was free, Pyotr shifted his young lover's body then scooped him up in his arms. He carried him over to the bed, laid him down, and crawled in next to him.

Diesel set a bottle of salve for Cliff's back and thighs on the bedside table, along with some lubricant in case the two decided to make love later, in addition to a condom package, not knowing where they were in their relationship. Then he and Trenton left them to their privacy.

CHAPTER NINE

Kimmi radiated from one ear to the next as she shared cake and ice cream, and rainbows of party favors with the staff and other patients that joined to celebrate her 19th birthday at the Cancer Treatment Center. For some, it would seem the worst place to have her party. But for Kimmi, nearly all of her friends came from here and many would not have been able to attend if she didn't bring it to them. Friends, she wasn't willing to do without and as such, the recreation room of the oncology ward was transformed into a Kimmi-kaleidoscope of color and birthday festivities.

Of course, it didn't go unnoticed by her brother when a young man, she'd met there, came in and gave her more than just a friendly hug. When the young dirty-blond male picked her up off her feet and kissed her, Cliff nearly jumped out of his seat— or rather he did and Pyotr quickly snatched him by the leg of his pants and pulled him to sit back down.

Cliff snapped a glaring shot at his lover, "You knew about this?"

Pyotr only smiled. He'd raised all his siblings, these things just didn't go unnoticed, "I suspected there was a boy she was sweet on." Was all he confessed to having known.

Cliff's scowled only deepened. "And you didn't think to tell me?"

Pyotr chuckled at him then and pulled Cliff in roughly by the back of his neck for a kiss. "My dear, *dragi ,* there was nothing to tell."

Cliff's face only barely softened, the expression protesting that that had been something Pyotr could have told him.

Kimmi eventually traded the new boy hugs for the gifts piled up at the table. Lots of oooo's and ahhhhs around the table and plenty of volunteering hands to share in having a turn of inspecting each present, ensured even those still in medical care got to participate in the fun.

Pyotr had held back, saving his gift for last, but finally it was his turn, and he slid a stack of papers with a decorative bow tacked to the upper corner in front of her. Kimmi's eyes danced from the beaming smile on Pyotr's face to the offering placed before her.

(ᵔᵕᵔ)

Six nurses, all scrunched in around the table, barely containing their excitement as they sat anxiously, each with a pen in hand. Another eight hospital staff stood behind them, all sharing the same expression. Making Kimmi's face turn a bright pink.

She finally tore her eyes from them so that she could inspect the mystery stack of papers and that's when she saw the print across the top that read:

—Petition for Agreement for Parental Rights and Adoption. —

Everything stopped. Just then, the world hummed in Kimmi's ears, as she read the words again, and then one more time— *just to be certain.*

At the bottom of the page, a small red tag, cut in the shape of an arrow, pointed to a blank signature line, along with several more tags sticking out from various places within the stack of forms. She flipped through them, each red arrow pointing to a line that required another signature. Kimmi's eyes shot up to the man beaming just as brightly as ever. Her brother, sitting further back in the room, chewed on his nails, and nearly every nurse she knew from the center was elbowing against one another as they squished themselves into the few chairs around the table. Outside of Cliff, they all were starry eyed with hopeful expressions that made Kimmi laugh. "What is this?" she asked.

"Well, what does it say up top?" Pyotr mused.

She read the title page again— this time reading aloud, *"Petition for Agreement for Parental Rights and Adoption."* She shook her head at Pyotr, "But, I don't understand. Who's adopting who?"

Pyotr leaned in, his hand sliding across the table, and he pointed to the two names on the document. Kimmi's eyes followed his fingertip until she read Pyotr's name and just below it was hers. —*Doctor Pyotr Laszkovi* —

"It would mean so much to me if you would agree to let me adopt you." Pyotr smiled deeply.

Kimmi started to burst into laughter. Pyotr was great, though, she'd never known him to be a prankster, so the papers were such a surprise. But, her laugh stopped dead as she met his eyes and she saw he was quite serious. "But, I'm nineteen now— how can you adopt me?"

Pyotr glanced at his watch, then reached down to the open satchel next to his chair. He pulled out a slip of paper and laid it down on the table, turning it so she could read it. "According to this—" He tapped the time and date on her birth records. "You are still eighteen years old for another twenty-two minutes."

Just then, a woman came in walking briskly, as if she were certain she was late. Kimmi noticed she was wearing the kind of robe a judge wore. Only, she hadn't taken the time to button it up yet and Kimmi could see she still had on her Saturday clothes. The woman joined them, stopped just behind Pyotr and smiled at her. "Hello, Kimmi Patterson. I'm Judge Annette Georgian. You may not remember me, Kimmi, but I'm the one who cleared your brother's custody of you some years back. It'd be my honor to approve one more for you, if it is your wish."

Kimmi's face lit up like fireworks on a birthday cake. She shot a glance at Pyotr, to Judge Georgian, and finally to her brother, Cliff, who was still looking nervous, but was showing some of the same hopefulness she was currently feeling.

"And Cliff?"

Judge Georgian smiled warmly. "Nothing changes there. But you may find it awkwardly funny to explain one day," the Judge finished with a chuckle.

"What do I do?" Kimmi stammered, grabbing the papers and flipping back to the first page with the red tag.

All the nurses piled in, pointing, and giving directions all at once as Kimmi quickly signed, followed by the signatures of her two witnesses plus a dozen more that wanted to be a part of the prompt ceremony.

On the last page, Pyotr's name was already handsomely written in acceptance.

And then, Judge Georgian bent over and added her own. With the final signature set in ink, she set her pen down then stood hands clasp before her and her shoulder straight and square as she warmly basked over her. "Kimmi Patterson, it is with great honor upon compliance with the State of New York, I now declare you the daughter of Pyotr Laszkovi."

Kimmi let out a high-pitched squeal that lent a number of fingers to an ear, while she jumped out of her seat, instantly climbing over the table, and spilled into her new adoptive-father's arms.

It wasn't even a day later when Cliff was bee-lining it for Pyotr's office without even a word, passing Pyotr who was at the front desk looking over the center's daily schedule.

Pyotr saw the blur of dark blond hair and brooding scowl go by and he didn't need to ask why. It was part of their relationship, part of their understanding. When Cliff needed to talk, he taken a preference to doing it in the office. A definition of the arrangement a healthy one for both Pyotr and Cliff, because when they left the room, it was the switch for Pyotr to stop fussing over his lover as a doctor and just be Cliff's lover. The unspoken habit worked well for both of them.

Pyotr followed his rushed unannounced client into his office, closed the door, and moved over to his desk. He leaned back in his chair, resting his hands stitched together behind his head, stretching his long legs out, and waited as another habit of their sessions played itself out. Cliff always had a tendency to tour the room for a few minutes, asking questions, sometimes relevant, most often not— a warm up to what Cliff really wanted to say.

Pyotr watched as Cliff began reading some of the titles of the books on one shelf, his head tilting sideways. Cliff pulled one out, but just stared at it in his hands, not ever opening it. Pyotr knew which one he had pulled: *The Demedicalization of Self-Injury: From Psychopathology to Sociological Deviance by Adler and Adler.* The subject of non-suicidal self-injury was a phantom medical condition. But, Pyotr knew first hand from treating his baby brother's lovers, Isaac and Isaiah, just how realistic and dangerous the condition was, and yet so few publications on the matter.

Cliff slid the hardbound book back into place and glanced over his shoulder to Pyotr, who waited patiently, always content to just watch him, "So have you always been Isaiah's psychiatrist?"

Pyotr nodded. "Ever since we discovered his condition. While his emotional problems started at home when he was younger, the emotional trap for him developed while they were in college."

"There's no hope for him, is there? I mean, of him getting better."

Pyotr dropped his hands to his lap, folding them together as he spoke, "He has his hope right now. Someone who loves him and understands the implications of his illness enough to know how to not only control it, but feed his medical needs when the addiction must be dealt with in a scene in order to keep the illness contained and manageable. I'd say that is the best care he could hope for."

"But, that's not a cure."

"Perhaps— but I feel that often we put too much emphasis on finding a cure and that we overlook the benefit of just finding a means to manage our illnesses and enable ourselves to have a fulfilling life."

Cliff shuffled over to the window and peeked out the curtain, looking out without seeing, listening as Pyotr spoke. He closed his eyes a moment, his mind finally coming to the topic he'd come to talk about. "You mean like me letting Kimmi have a boyfriend."

"I wasn't implying anything. But, since you bring it up— her illness is under control right now. She is doing well. Why not let her have an experience for herself. She's a young woman, let her explore some part of the world as such. It's time."

"And that's what you think I should do?"

"Cliff, I do not deny my feelings for you or those I have being a part of your family, but the choices you have to make for your sister are yours and yours alone. I will listen if you need to talk, give advice if you ask of it, and I will support you no matter what decision you make, but the decision is yours, not mine."

Cliff let the curtain drop closed and he rolled against the wall, never bringing his weight from it as he turned so he could look at Pyotr. "Did you help Katianna after the kidnapping thing?"

(•ω•)

Pyotr rocked back further in his chair. "I did not. I do tend to two others that were rescued from that same incident. But no, not her. Trenton hasn't allow anyone anywhere near her since that night. Save that evening we met with them at Club Pain." Pyotr pivoted once or twice in his desk chair, then rocked back again. "Now, let me ask you something."

Cliff's eyes shifted to Pyotr, but he kept to holding up the wall.

"What answers are you looking for, Cliff?" All these questions his partner was asking— they were irrelevant, yet they hovered around something, attempting to fish out answers for a question Cliff had yet asked. A bush-beating tactic, Cliff was too good at doing. Often to such a point, Cliff often evaded himself, if allowed to go on for too long. So it was up to Pyotr to prod him to zero in and be out with it.

"I just—" Cliff's eyes wandered into a distant stare, which told Pyotr his mind was wandering. But he waited; he knew Cliff would return to him— to the moment. "I just thought that if perhaps someone like Dominus could let someone else make a choice, then maybe I could, too."

Pyotr tucked his chin a moment, considering where this was leading. "This is not the first time you have tried to put yourself in Trenton Leos' shoes. Do you relate yourself to Dominus Leos?"

Cliff was instantly looking at him with a near snap of his expression. "No." Cliff took a deep breath, letting it out through his nostrils this time. "I've just always been in charge of Kimmi," he huffed, "I'm not a parent I don't know any better yet I don't even let the doctors have the final say."

Pyotr smiled. "Come here."

Cliff kicked off from the wall and circled around the desk to his lover who sat up in his chair spreading his legs for Cliff to kneel between them, and he did so willingly. It was as welcoming as a hug. And he dropped his head down over Pyotr's thigh.

Pyotr stroked the mop of blond hair. Such a strange fondness that he should be developing— enjoying petting his pet.

"What if I asked you to make the choice for me?" Cliff asked without looking up. "What if I gave that up?"

Again, Pyotr smiled, but he shook his head, refusing the surrender of power from his lover. Cliff may have verbally offered, but because Cliff refused to look at him when he said it, meant Cliff could never actually let go.

Just wished he could. "No matter what choice I made for Kimmi, you would inevitably find something upsetting about it, and it would come between us. And I would come between you and Kimmi. Cliff, you may surrender all things about you over to me, and I will lovingly care for you and your needs, but Kimmi must remain forever under your command. To do otherwise would offend you."

"She's too young to have sex." Cliff muttered suddenly, his brow furrowing.

Pyotr choked back his chuckle, recalling how he'd struggled himself when the twins had grown up, and began exploring boys and their sexuality. Even from Pyotr's own perspective, he viewed the girls with different rules than the boys. And he had been far more sheltering with them. "Perhaps you are looking at this too hurriedly." Pyotr offered an important evaluation to the discussion.

Cliff finally looked up, "What do you mean?"

"I mean, let's only consider her going on a date. Just a dinner date— it could even be a chaperoned date. No one said she had to have sex."

Cliff's face returned to the scowl he'd had on a few minutes ago. "But, it will lead to it, eventually."

This time Pyotr couldn't keep the light chuckle back. His *dragi* was too damn cute to not allow it. "Yes, eventually it might. But, why worry over it now?"

CHAPTER TEN

Well under way of their third hour, Cliff had long since grown bored with the game app on his phone, having stuffed it away in his pocket.

Waiting in the lobby of the cancer treatment center, sitting quietly as his mind wandered to something not here and certainly not now. He was used to this—*waiting.* He couldn't count the number of times he'd sat a half a day away just *waiting.* He felt his eye lids growing heavy and the faint weighted bob of his head, as stagnant sitting was putting him to sleep, but the crash of a door against the wall had him snapping back awake.

Kimmi came out from the back in a rush; Cliff was already on his feet to follow her out. But, then he made out the fright in her eyes, not to mention the rush in her step. She practically brushed past him, catching his arm in her hands, and was instantly tugging him to follow her. "Come on, Cliff. It's time to go."

Cliff knew right away something was wrong. Something that had her wanting to run and she tugged even harder on his arms when he didn't budge.

"Come on, let's go. I want to go, please," Kimmi stammered.

Cliff's attention went back toward the hallway where she'd come from and saw Dr. Lee coming toward them. The doctor was wearing the same *not so good news* look on his face as Kimmi was attempting to hide on hers. Cliff wrangled his arm out of her hands, brushing off her attempts to grab him again, and stepped for the doctor, who was already shaking his head as they met.

"It's not looking good this time, Cliff." Dr. Lee again shook his head.

"What do you mean, not looking good?" Cliff asked, the alarms going off in his head. He sucked in a hard breath, battering up the walls inside his head, like an emergency preparation for a hurricane.

"It's so spread out, we can't consider surgery."

The doctor's vague response only got stupid questions from him. He didn't want to hear *wide spread*— no *this* or *that*— he wanted specifics of what— What— WHAT! "What do you mean spread out. What is?"

Dr. Lee took a firm breath then decidedly answered with the full sprectrum, "To start, her physical exam. There was some notable swelling and tenderness in her left arm pit. Furthermore, concerns were raised when we found some swelling in the upper right quadrant of the abdominal cavity and some tenderness in the left upper quadrant. We decided to do an immediate biopsy on both her liver and her spleen and ran the samples while she went down for her x-rays and bone density tests. While the x-rays don't reveal anything conclusive yet, the biopsy found a combination of infectious fluids and some bleeding in her organs. Her CBC tests came back with an alarmingly low white blood cell count."

"But what about the gallium and the MIBG? What did those scans turn up?" Cliff disregarded the tests results until he had all of them to calculate it in his head. *This wasn't their first time. They'd gone through a few close calls, a few scares only to have everything to turn out to be a minor infection because of pain meds or a tolerance build-up of antibiotics.*

Dr. Lee drew in a deep, heavy breath, dropping his arms, still holding the clipboard in his hand, down at his side, and he shook his head at Cliff in slow motion.

Cliff wasn't ready to accept defeat. Kimmi had just gotten better from the last battle. It was too soon to go through this again. "Well, if that's all you can tell me, what the hell has taken so long back there?"

"Every red flag was getting thrown up. We couldn't risk her walking out until we were sure. So we've squeezed her in for an MRI. Her red blood cells are breaking down inside the marrow and bleeding out in her organs and lymph nodes. Cliff, the cancer is wide spread."

Cliff's voice was instantly rising with his next response, "She was in here just four weeks ago! If it's that bad, why just now?!" He was almost yelling, "Why didn't you tell us then?"

"She wasn't up for a full spectrum analysis. And her physical showed no warning signs to suggest she needed it. The test results that were performed were not enough to pick up on early stage degeneration, Cliff."

"But you would have seen something! You would have known!"

The doctor shook his head, "The leukemia cells are spreading at a considerably faster rate than what we've seen in her case before. I don't even know if we can stop it this time."

Cliff froze in his place. His chest caved. No words. No thoughts. Though, he was sure it would all come crashing out, once it all sank in. *Why did Dr. Lee question their ability to stop the spreading disease? They'd never made that comment before.*

Kimmi was tugging harder on his arm now. Her entire body leaning out to get Cliff to leave the clinic with her. "Please, let's just go. We can deal with it later."

Cliff just stood glued to the floor, not budging. Then numbly, he reached out placing his hand on his sister's face, feeling the warmth in her cheeks. Kimmi stilled only slightly as Cliff walked his fingers down to the soft gullet of skin just under one ear and watched as she winced when he pressed into the lymph node.

"We don't have to do anything now. Let's just go, please?" Kimmi whispered.

"I'm afraid she doesn't have that kind of time, Cliff." Dr. Lee interrupted, "We need to start her on heavy chemo right away. I've gone ahead and scheduled her to start day after tomorrow." He paused a moment, then pulled a bottle from his white coat and held it out for Cliff. "She needs to go ahead and start taking these now." He handed over the treatment pills used for her leukemia type. "You'll need to bring her in early and we'll hold her over the weekend on full treatment. Then depending on how she's doing, we might be able to let her go home for the holiday. Start yourself on a protein-rich diet. I'd like to go ahead and start pulling stem cell blood from you. So, I'll get you scheduled for Monday as well."

Dr. Lee studied the young man's face. Rigid and tight like a tension coil that was bound to snap any second. But, at this very moment, Cliff wasn't even fazed by his sister's attempts to pull him away.

Kimmi had always somehow been a ray of hope, not only for her own conditions, but for others, too. Dr. Lee had been treating Kimmi since she was twelve, when he took Dr. Karenth's place here at the CTC. If any patient of his— and as far as he was concerned they all deserved one— but, these two, most certainly deserved a break. Just not the kind he feared was coming too quickly. "I'm sorry, Cliff."

He watched the two as acceptance seeped into the siblings, feeling a deep rotting pit of emotions inside himself. The ray of hope, that often followed the girl like an aura, wasn't there this time.

Cliff suddenly wrenched his arm, breaking out of Kimmi's relentless tugging, grabbed her, and pulled her into him. His arms wrapped around her with a tight squeeze. He buried her head against his chest and laid his head over the top of hers. He was angry and numb at the same time. It wasn't fair— wasn't fair at all. And he could feel the deep pool of pain threatening to consume him. So, right now, he fed the anger.

"Would you like me to call one of the volunteers to give you a ride home?" Dr. Lee offered behind him.

"No." Cliff didn't move but chewed at his lips a moment. "I think I'm gonna need the walk," he murmured into the top of Kimmi's knit cap.

"Keep her wrapped up tight then. She can't afford to get sick at this point."

Cliff turned with Kimmi in his arms and marched, or rather barreled, forward, through people and doors until they reached the outside when the cold October air hit them. It still wasn't enough to cool the heat Cliff felt raging inside him. His arms locked around his sister's shoulder, clutching her so tight and close, he knew it was making it hard on her to walk normal. But, he couldn't bring himself to let go. He'd never let go of her.

His phone was ringing by the time they'd traveled four blocks. He didn't want to look. Didn't want to answer. More likely either Diesel or Pyotr calling. Cliff couldn't even look at his phone; that meant talking, and if he did that, the churning of emotions bottled up inside would explode. He wasn't ready for that; he wasn't ready to have Pyotr take it away from him. Without his anger, Cliff wasn't sure he could survive this again, watching his baby sis wither away before his eyes. The endless highway of tubes pumping drugs and toxins into her system to kill the very thing that tried, time and time again, to kill her.

His arm tightened around her again, but not a whimper came from her. Even when his phone rang again, tucked away in his coat pocket; Kimmi didn't withdraw from him or protest his strangling hold.

Pyotr thumbed his phone closed when, for the fifth time, Cliff didn't answer. It wasn't like his lover to not answer his calls. Even on his shifts at work, Cliff always managed to take a moment to respond by text at least. But that wasn't where Pyotr's lover was.

When Dr. Lee called with the news from Kimmi's test runs, Pyotr felt Cliff's raging emotions building to the point of breaking as the doctor shared the details that Kimmi's leukemia had surfaced again. Only this time the prognosis wasn't even remotely hopeful.

Nevertheless, what was important right now was figuring out where the two had disappeared to. That was what Pyotr was concerned with at the moment, finding Cliff before the young man went into a total melt down.

Pyotr grabbed his coat and headed out of his office, letting Mary at the front desk know he had a family emergency, and have his patients reschedule. He took off across town toward the Cambridge Hospital, only to be told the two had taken off on foot.

Driving down street after street, Pyotr called Cliff's phone again, but still no answer. Pyotr sat at the red light, staring down the street, trying to keep his own emotions in line. *Where had they gone?* He scrubbed down his face, fretting over his lover and the turmoil that would be consuming Cliff. A car horn behind him, rudely brought Pyotr back to the present and to the green light staring back at him. Ignoring both, Pyotr opened his phone, and did what he promised never to do. He intervened and called Kimmi.

The phone rang several times until a bright cheery voice answered with automation: *"Hi, this is Kimmi Patterson. Sorry I missed the chance to chat so leave a message so I can hit cha back."*

"Kimmi, please tell me where I can find you." And he hung up. A cacophony of blasting, blaring horns rioted up behind him, so he stomped the gas and took off.

Turning the car toward home, Pyotr made his way along the streets of Manhattan, eyes scanning for any sign of Cliff and Kimmi.

He was about to take the ramp back over to Long Island when his phone beeped with a text message. *It was Kimmi.*

Txt:— Near the boathouse. —Kimmi

Pyotr quickly cut the wheel and kept heading down FDR drive. He felt the weight lift from his chest when he spotted them heading across Macombs Bridge. Cliff marching to the tune emotional rage and Kimmi tucked under her brother's arm, snuggling into his warmth.

The commuter traffic was too heavy by now for Pyotr to even consider stopping on the bridge, though he tapped the brakes a few times seriously thinking about it, but as he passed the two on the side walk, he saw the tension biting down in Cliff's face. The hard marching walk in the cold was what his lover needed; so, Pyotr continued past them, and pulled into the empty lot of the Macombs Dam Park. The very same place he caught up with Cliff and Kimmi after the two had come out to see him rowing. It was the night he and Cliff made love for the first time.

There was some reason Cliff needed to come full circle. But, even with all of Pyotr's knowledge, he wasn't sure what had led his lover to come to this spot. It wasn't along the way home.

He stood at the edge of the park, waiting as Cliff and Kimmi approached, Cliff's face growing tense with every step that brought him closer. The threads, Pyotr knew would have to come undone at some point, were about to snap.

Cliff reached the edge and stopped abruptly, just staring at Pyotr. His jaw clenched, tightening, his brow furrowed with pain barely contained.

"Cliff?"

"No!" Cliff suddenly shouted, "I don't want to be consoled. I don't want to be told we'll get through this! Don't do what they do." Cliff instantly steered to walk around him.

Pyotr side lunged to corral him off. "What is it they do, Cliff?"

Cliff stopped if only to shout at him. "Tell me it's going to be okay. That's what they do." Cliff shook furiously. "Don't tell me that. Because it's not going to be."

"I won't," Pyotr softened his responses. "I just want you to know I'm here for you. I'm here for you both."

Cliff sucked in a breath as if he intended to say something, but the act nearly cost him his control, and his mouth clamped shut. His eyes went to the sky, a winter sky as grey and forlorn as his eyes. They'd always been that way until recently. What worried Pyotr most was Kimmi's, for the first time, matched her brother's. Neither of the two was expecting this round to end well.

Tears pooled in Cliff's eyes, but Pyotr's lover's wiped them away with the back of his coat sleeve before they could fall. "I can't do this, Pyotr." Cliff nearly pleaded for the escape.

"Then we do it together." Pyotr took a step back and to the side, a gesture that both didn't close in on him, but also opened the path for Cliff to follow, and he did. Pyotr knew Cliff needed to expel some energy, walking him through the park would help with that. But, they didn't make it far when Cliff stopped at one of the pavilions and decided to take his rage out on a picnic table.

Kimmi knew where her brother's thoughts were. It wasn't fair; getting sick so many times, to survive not just once but twice, only to get sick again. She watched as Cliff began dismantling a table, then she turned and wandered off toward the water. She sat on the sea wall, still watching her brother rage back and forth, pacing while Pyotr tried to console him. She couldn't stop the tears which made the cold, winter air much worse. Her sniffling nose didn't help either. She was on that cusp of self-pity, but what was worse was that she had ruined her brother's life. Not on purpose, but that didn't change the fact Cliff had given up nearly everything to take care of her. It was only of some comfort that he enjoyed being a paramedic now. And then they found Pyotr. Pyotr was wonderful. Though, she couldn't help worrying that her latest diagnosis might hinder that as well.

She glanced down at the water as it raced by. There was a loud clatter of noise and she snapped around to see one of the park's trashcans go flying across the lawn, then Cliff bolted after to give it another good kick. He liked kicking and throwing when he needed to get the anger out. And then there was Pyotr, watching over him like a guardian angel.

She jumped off the wall and walked along for a moment, taking an occasional glance over her shoulder. By the time she had worked her way down the sea wall to the boat launch, Pyotr had her brother tightly wrapped in his arms, bringing the physical rage to a halt. She stood there just staring for a long pause, then took a deep breath, turned and went down the steps to the boat launch for the kayakers.

She held steady to the rail, careful not to slip on the icy sludge that coated the concrete ramp. She paused, glancing back over her shoulder careening up on her toes to see over the top step, watching Pyotr and Cliff sitting under one of the far pavilions where Pyotr had finally gotten Cliff talking rather than screaming. *Good.* Pyotr had become the perfect solution to her brother. He would love him as he deserved.

She turned back to the water that swirled around, ready to whisk her away, just like a kayak or a canoe. Her thoughts sank into its liquid motion while she still held fast to the rail, staring into the clear water to the silt bottom and slowly without thought kicked off her boots and stepped in.

The icy cold water caught her breath and she gasped several times, feeling the frigid bite in her feet. She took another step until she stood shin deep with both feet side by side in the river's edge.

She glanced down at them; the pale flushed color of her pale pink feet with neon-sunburst-orange toenail polish glared up at her in contrast to the murky bottom. And despite that first rush, she felt completely numb now.

The whole world silently withdrawing from her. Just the sound of her breath in her ears and the slosh of water waiting on her. Nothing else. No cars. No people.

No cancer—

No illness. No pain. Just— *numbness.*

She felt her heart beating in her chest, heard its pulse in her ears. A hard steady pounding. The fever that had bum-rushed her cells, now racing to be extinguished in the frigid waters that swallowed it's heat up around her feet. Calling her to come in. Just her and the expressionless reflection looking up at her. She need only take a few more steps and the river would do the rest.

It was so cold, she'd go numb instantly. *She wouldn't feel a thing.*

Her foot came up—

"KIMMI!"

Her step yawed like someone calling her out of a dream to wake up.

"Kimmi!" Cliff cried out again, just as he came scrambling down the steps behind her. He quickly rushed into the frigid water, and snatched her up in his arms, slinging her away from the water's edge, and carried her back up the stairs. The absence of the numbing cold replaced with an instant attack of a thousand needles prickling her feet.

Pyotr was right there at the top of the steps, his coat off, and he quickly wrapped it around her bare, pink feet, and rubbed at them furiously as they carried her toward the car. She didn't move or make a sound, just silent tears streaming down her face.

Through blurry blues, she could see the tension in her brother's jaw. Cliff wanted to say so many things right then, but he kept them all inside. "Don't." Was all he would allow himself to say at the moment as he squeezed her in his arms and kissed the side of her head.

Pyotr opened the door to the back seat of his car and Cliff scooted in, setting Kimmi across the seat, and then sat next to her, taking her feet into his lap. At that instant, Cliff became her EMT. Her own personal nurse as he had always been. Only, his attentiveness didn't stop there.

"What were you thinking?"

Kimmi's thoughts buckled inside her as she spotted Pyotr's eyes flicker back at her through the rearview mirror as he drove them home. She could see the lines around his face that etched out deep concern for her and for Cliff. The man truly loved her brother and she knew her brother was head over heels for him. She didn't want to be between them. Not like this. Despite her mental struggle to lock herself up inside, her lips began to quiver with the sobbing that threatened to come.

Cliff was occupied with rubbing the blood circulation back into her legs and feet. His scolding hadn't stopped yet. "Just two hours ago the doctor told you to stay warm. You can't risk getting sick if we're to get through this again." He grabbed up her wrist and stilled, checking her pulse. Not satisfied, he moved his fingers to her neck. It wasn't her pulse that was evading him; it was his own racing one that interfered. "I want to know what you were thinking," his voice tightened into a demand.

"I don't want to put you through this again," she whimpered, "It's not fair. Would it not be better for you if I ended this?"

Cliff's face melted into one of sheer horror then melded into rage. "End this!? You think I go through all of this just so you can end this?" Cliff's hands went back to her feet and started rubbing them again. Harder now, as much of his anger came out in his hands that it hurt, causing her to wince. "I don't want you gone! I want you to stay with me. It's you and me, remember? We didn't get this far just so I could be rid of you!"

"I'm sorry," Her sob kicked out with a hiccup.

Cliff fell silent. He was ready for plenty more yelling, but Kimmi's face was now streaked with tears, and he couldn't bear to make more of them. He kept quiet the remainder of the drive, purposely avoiding Pyotr's gaze that occasionally glanced back at him.

When they reached the house, Pyotr took Kimmi, carrying her upstairs to her room. "Grab some towels from the linen and toss them in the dryer for a few minutes. There's an electric blanket in the linen as well." He gave the gentle suggestion to his lover before disappearing into Kimmi's room with his precious load.

When Cliff came back up from the laundry room, Pyotr was waiting for him.

Cliff diverted his eyes, but he knew his lover had something to say, if he allowed him to say it. It was the one thing Pyotr never crossed into without open invitation. "You think I'm handling this wrong, don't you?"

Pyotr stepped up, taking Cliff's arm just below the shoulders. His grip meant to comfort rather than control, "Yes."

Cliff looked at him, all that knowing and experience etched on his face that moment.

"You're angry because she's sick. You're angry at your parents for leaving. You tell her she's not to blame for this, yet you yell at her for it. The action only reinforces her feelings that she is to blame for your despair."

Cliff's face went white and he swallowed hard but kept quiet. What was there for him to say?

"Losing one's parents in a singular instant is devastating to the mind and body. It is not easily forgotten or healed. So for you to feel anger even now is natural. Especially with news of a reoccurrence of her illness. Yelling at her isn't what either of you need. Don't guilt her to live, either." Pyotr leaned in and kissed Cliff on the forehead, lingering there a moment as if to transfer some of his love into the storm that brewed behind grey eyes.

At the sound of the buzzer from the dryer going off, Pyotr let him go to tend to his sister.

It was late when Cliff came down stairs from Kimmi's room.

"I didn't expect you tonight," Pyotr murmured to him, holding the book he'd been reading out of the way, as Cliff slipped over him on the sofa and buried his face into Pyotr's chest without saying a word. Pyotr closed his book and wrapped his arms around his exhausted lover, exchanging glances with his brother, Pavle, who'd been talking with him about what they might be able to do to help Kimmi's treatments, and what would be needed there at the house.

Pyotr had watched many of his own patients slip away from illnesses. Cancer— Gulf-War Syndrome— AIDS— But, this was different. This was closer. And, it tore at him painfully.

It was going to be the third time Kimmi would undergo chemo treatment in her life. And as Pavle had explained, after looking up her medical records from his computer, they were able to see what Cliff had not yet disclosed. Her doctors were calling for an intense attack of chemo and radiation, full on dosages, as much as her body could take. It was all or nothing now. The plan was to shoot her with everything they had, and then receive the bone marrow transplant. Once the new stem cell transfusion took, she would undergo the chemo again. It would be a brutal undertaking. But, the doctors hoped that the hard hit would set her back into remission, perhaps for good this time. Anything less and the chances of recovery were slim this time around.

Pavle turned and glanced at Pyotr with a grim look, "Aside from the prognosis, you do realize we have both just violated a few HIPPA laws?"

Pyotr knew full well they had. But this was his family and he would willingly do it again, "Shall I wake her up to get her permission?" He shot back sardonically.

Pavle shook his head only slightly, not really trying to argue with him, "It's not Kimmi's permission you need. Cliff still has power of attorney. It's him you have to concede with."

Yes, for the second time, Pyotr had intervened, but he wasn't sorry for it. "Just tell me."

Pavle's expression crew shadowed and when he shook his head Pyotr didn't figure it was denial rather it was the answer.

Pyotr felt the timer working its way down. His little family was running out of time and he didn't want to miss any moment of it. He already had it in his head that in the morning he would file for a sabbatical at his practice, with the exception of a few special cases. Then notify all his brothers and the twins, Thanksgiving would be here at the family home. Everyone in the Laszkovi family was required to come, with or without their families. He would not be denied this moment.

CHAPTER ELEVEN

Pyotr made it easy for everyone to join him. He didn't care what day their family Thanksgiving came on, what was important was having everyone together and to prevent competition with in-laws, he set the gathering for the entire weekend just in case a few couldn't make it for Thursday. As it turned out, they all came— and just in time for a Thanksgiving Thursday.

Kimmi too.

The first to arrive had been Pavle's ex-wife, Maggie along with their two boys, having come in the night before offering to help out with the food preparations. Maggie and Pavle, though divorced were still close friends. They'd had a good life together, but after the boys had reached their teens years, they came to realize they weren't right for each other anymore and called it quits before the grudge could affect them. And of course, there was the underlying part that Pavle had been gay from the beginning. But, family was family and the holidays were spent together.

Thursday morning, Artyom, his wife Mira, and their six kids arrived, bringing with them the first rays of sunshine. And as the day warmed up, under the late fall sun that morning, the rest of the family began to arrive one by one.

Next in were Sasha and his twin lovers, Isaac and Isaiah. Shortly after was Trofim flying solo followed by the twins, Varvara and Andjela.

Darko came in, he too was single, but he had a date scheduled to arrive for the weekend with hopes of striking a deeper relationship with the man he'd rescued on the side of the road a few weeks back. Theirs was an interesting tale to tell. Maxum had gotten a flat. His new car, for all of four hours, and he didn't have a clue as to where his spare tire was. Darko had pulled over on his chopper and fixed the man up. However when Darko's gaydar went off, he claimed a rather bold reward, and pulled the man in for a deep kiss right there on the side of the highway. Darko's grime covered hands ended up ruining the poor man's suit. The penance was offered, welcoming him to come over for a dinner date, bring the ruined suit, and Darko promised to pay to have it dry cleaned should he come by for a nightcap, or— stand him up and the man was on his own for the cleaning charges. Maxum showed up, sans the suit, nonetheless he did deliver something else. And Darko had since been driven to have more of it in his life.

Shortly after noon, Jovan made it in with his two kids minus an ex-wife who hated him along with the rest of the world. And then Rury and his flaming beau, Liam.

Stanislav and his wife were the last to arrive. He looked exhausted as if he had physically dragged her and the car himself just to get there. The chances were good that Pyotr's perception wasn't too far off, given Stanislav's wife, Frannie and her disposition on the sinful ways of *gays*, as she referred to them.

Frannie had just reached the top of the stairs along with Stanislav when she came to an abrupt stop at the sight of Darko enjoying a playful kiss with his new handsome beau. Her face twisted in an expression of disgust at them and cast it on the other men in the room, who seemed too accepting of the act by her judgment. Frannie took one look around the room and at the soiree of obviously gay men gathered.

Pavle got off without an indictment in lieu of Maggie's presence. But, at that point, what was one more fag in the room? Frannie turned tail and bolted out leaving a trail of curses and Hail-Mary's, tales of brimstone, and a few other biblical things no one else seemed able to interpret. Stanislav, of course, followed after her. He hadn't driven all the way from upstate just to turn around and go back. He hadn't seen his brother Pyotr in a over a year.

The visit was long overdue and frankly Pyotr just needed him to be here with his big brother. Stanislav, the eldest of the babies, had been their mother's little angel. He had always been the sweet little boy in the pack and the most forgiving. Something his wife took full advantage of.

Pyotr followed, going after them. He wasn't about to let Frannie ruin the weekend for the rest of the family. It had never been a secret that several of them were gay, so it was absurd that she would arrive only to throw a tantrum in their presence. Pyotr had also already taken full notice of the grave need in his baby brother's face and he wasn't about to let that go unattended either.

Stanislav managed to catch his wife's arm and pull her to a stop in the courtyard, under the trees. "Fran, wait. This is family. Can't you give it a rest? Just for one day?" he pleaded with a tired argument. One they'd had too many times over the three years of their marriage. The fact that she'd had Pyotr and the others physically removed from their wedding ceremony should have been grounds enough to call the arrangement off. But, he forgave her on the spot, because he had not told her. He just never thought it was something that had to be brought up. He grew up with gay brothers— he thought everyone did— until that day.

"Frannie, please. It's a holiday for family. Won't you reconsider and come in to join us?" Pyotr called out to her with the most controlled self-induced hospitality he could properly manage within himself, having borrowed from years gone by when he had to do so for teachers and caseworkers scrutinizing his guardianship of minor siblings.

Frannie spun around to snap at Pyotr, jabbing a finger up at his overbearing height. "You'll burn in Hell for your sins."

Pyotr had never forgotten the hateful stunt she'd pulled at the wedding. Even when Pyotr and the rest of the family had left the chapel, Frannie didn't let bygones be bygones. She made it near impossible for Stanislav to come visit and she stood fast on her religious beliefs. Frannie's family's open, first-class-fascist-insults, with both their religious and political catcalling were not the only values the family tagged into the charge of impostordom. It also wreaked of disturbing logic that fell less then short of mad men.

That was all fine and dandy, except the part that Pyotr should burn in hell for his sexual preferences, and he'd since lost his patience for the argument with Frannie. "Then we might as well learn to get along, since we'll be keeping each other company down there. Won't we?" his voice tightened.

"Wh- What?" Her mouth popped open in a morbid *o* shape. "Ah! How dare you." Frannie's anger went from hot to volcanic at that instance.

"What, Frannie?" Pyotr tilted, "Did you really think you could carry on with so much hate in your passing down judgment, and not have to repent for it?"

Frannie's mouth gaped open again. She wasn't used to Pyotr sassing back at her. He usually threw some psychological jargon at her about unhealthy emotions or about her misplaced religious zealots to support her own fragile trust in the world. But, for him to dare suggest that she would go to Hell with him, was obviously not boding well, nor did she come prepared with a quick come back for his argument. After a long moment of brooding thought, Frannie drew her hand back with every intention of slapping Pyotr.

(•ω•)

Stanislav had had enough and suddenly, he took a firm grip on his wife's arm. Not only stopping the physical assault, he called for her to silence any further verbal retort. "Stop now!"

Stanislav's exhausted mind drifted from the burden he could no longer bare; his eyes going up to the large picture window of the great room and his brothers, all lined up, looking down at him. Darko's hand went up against the glass, in a gesture to reach out to him. It ripped at his heart. He hadn't seen any of them, only Pyotr, in the last three years, and that was only once last year. He loved Frannie when it was just the two of them. But, when others were around, it wasn't the bliss he had hoped, and he missed having his family. Now, with Pyotr having adopted Kimmi and having a lover, with Trofim back in the States, and his brothers' rowing team taking championship— so many things Stanislav didn't want to lose out on. Without even a thought, his hand went up as if he could touch Darko's, still on the glass, and then Pavle, Trofim, and then Rury and his two sisters— they all reached out for him. Only Sasha and Jovan were missing.

"Dinner is almost ready, perhaps we can all settle down for a peaceful evening in the dining room, so we can give thanks for the things we do have." Pyotr's voice switched to something warm and more welcoming. The gentle tone meant to change the mood and turn it into one, a shade more cooperative.

Stanislav let Frannie jerk her arm from his grip, pulling his attention away from his family. He knew it was coming, he raised a hand out to beg her to keep silent, but the hateful words were already coming out, and he was helpless to stop them. "I will not sit with a bunch of Hell bound homosexuals, and pretend to give thanks, and neither will Stan."

"If Hell be damned then we are both going. I'll keep a seat warm for you." Pyotr's warm attempt turned tight against Frannie's less than cordial words,

"Nevertheless, as of now, your seat here at my house has gone cold. I do not want you here. However, Stanislav stays. I have precious little time left with my family. My brother will remain and honor me with his presence, while Kimmi still lives."

"She dies because her brother is a homo like the rest of you!" Frannie's seething words respected no boundaries at that point. Words that would seal her fate within the family with permanent severance.

Pyotr's face turned red, his whole body clenched, his fists curling at his side so tight his knuckles turned white. "If you were one of my brothers, I would surely throw you over my knee and tan your hide right now. As it is, I want you off my property— NOW!"

Stanislav saw the raging pain in his brother's face, and his heart clutched at the sight of the tear that streamed down Pyotr's cheek. The strain so great, he looked like it had taken twenty mental bulldozers to prevent the explosive retaliation from happening.

Stanislav took hold of Frannie's arm and lead his wife out to the car, and forcibly placed her in the driver's seat.

Frannie looked at the steering wheel then to him— still standing outside the car, "You're not leaving with me?" she dared to sound surprised.

"Frannie, do you love your parents?"

"What? Mom and Daddy? Of course, I do— you do, too."

"Thing is, honey—" His lips rolled into a tight grimace. "I hate your parents. And I hate being around them. But, I've put up with them for three years of holidays and family visits because I love *you*. This time I am going to stay here with my family and frankly I don't want you with me, right now. I'll be home in the morning."

"Your bags will be waiting at the door," she told him through pursed lips. Not one word hesitated as they came out, as if she had rehearsed the line for some time.

Stanislav sighed, "Hopefully, that's not true. But, if it is, I'll deal with that tomorrow. It will not change anything about today." He straightened, letting out a long, painful sigh. He did love her. Yet, living with her judgments on the world had taken its toll on him. He'd lived with it for a long time, only he was no longer willing to give up his family as the price to stay with her. He couldn't do it to Pyotr. And if she was right and God was turning his back on his family because they were gay— *well then shame on Him.*

Stanislav took another deep breath and did his best to let the love he felt show on his face, but he wasn't sure she was looking for it. "Go home, Frannie."

He turned as his car drove away, nearly walking into his brother, Jovan. Stanislav stilled, meeting his brother's eyes.

"You'd throw your life away for Pyotr just like that?"

Stanislav's brows bunched up with anguish, showing Jovan he clearly thought the question in itself was unacceptable. "He did it for us." And he brushed past him not wanting to get into another discussion about the rights or wrongs of Pyotr.

☙∞❧

Jovan stared after Stanislav, watching him head back inside. Stanislav had been too young to understand when they were forced to leave their home to come here to the States. If Pyotr sacrificed, he had it coming to him. It was his fault they had to leave in the first place. Papa had said nothing when he came back the night the soldiers drug him out of their home. But, Jovan was certain it had something to do with Pyotr and his secret lover. Bad enough his brother chose to sleep with men, but to sleep with an Albanian at the time, which was far worse where they came from.

Jovan had learned to live with it, but he had never forgiven Pyotr. The others had been young enough they were able to adjust. However, he had been just a month away from graduating and he had a scholarship to join the university just as Pyotr had. All that gone. He couldn't even pick up where he left off when they arrived to the United States, all because he didn't speak English. He practically had to start all over in school and he blamed Pyotr for that, too.

As the family had arrived, most of the brothers remained gathered in the living room, catching up on news with each other, and occasional trips to the kitchen to steal a tid-bit morsel of anything that was left unattended while the Macy's Thanksgiving Day Parade showed on the television in the background.

Cliff kept glancing about the room from one brother to the next always settling back to Sasha.

"What has you puzzled, *dragi*?" Pyotr tugged at Cliff.

"Sasha does. All your brothers look the same except Sasha."

Several of the guys broke out in laughter that quickly spread from brother to brother like a wild fire. Giving the obvious notion that it wasn't the first time the difference had been mentioned.

"Sasha was our mother's milkman baby," Darko called from across the room.

Sasha, who was sitting within reach of his brother, punched him in the arm with little effect. "I was not."

With a laugh, Darko jumped up, grabbing Sasha, and dragging him to the floor in an instant game of rough-housing with Darko clearly at the advantage.

"Was he really?" Cliff glanced at Pyotr, not expecting any further comments from the other brother.

"Shut up, Cliff!" Sasha was cursing in Cliff's direction. But, it was about all Sasha could do, being pinned mercilessly under Darko's hold.

Pyotr let out a chuckle. "No, but that didn't stop anyone from teasing our papa about it."

"Did he ever think, he wasn't?" Kimmi suddenly appeared next to them, returning with her tea before they ate.

"Not a chance." Jovan spoke up then, "Mama was a demanding woman. So, there wasn't a night that went by that papa wasn't expected to perform in their bed. However, there was a time when she openly threatened to give him a red-headed bastard next time, if he didn't start putting out some *double x* chromosomes."

"So then what happened?" Kimmi looked back to Pyotr.

Pyotr gave a warm smile. "He gave her two."

"That's us!" Two female voices called out in chorus from the kitchen to back up the claim and then the dark-haired, blue-eyed twins stepped into sight with identical smiles. "Supper is ready."

Later at the dinner table, the family and friends had all pretty much stuffed themselves and no one was in any hurry to leave their very comfy seats, and the talk and jokes were still going strong. Though a few had fallen quiet, especially Jovan, who'd somehow, worked his way into an obvious brooding mood. The five or so vodkas likely played a part in the stoking of his inner embers. But, it was holiday, so Pyotr wasn't pushing to be the family doctor today, though he would make himself available for his brother if Jovan asked it of him.

Kimmi was letting the food settle in her stomach, the constant laughter not helping in her case. Cliff was taking advantage of her paused status and was stealing nibbles from her blueberry pie.

"Here, *dragi* ." Pyotr's arm pulled Cliff into him and slid his own pie plate over in front of him in offering to salvage what was left of Kimmi's favorite desert. "Don't be such a *shejtan*."

"No, you did not!" the objected shouted over the table.

All eyes turned to the brooding brother at the end of the table. They'd all gone stark in their silence as Jovan stood ther, red in the face, glaring at Pyotr.

"Come, sit back down," Pavle, who was closest, whispered to Jovan, placing a gentle hand on his brother's arm.

TALON PS

Jovan jerked his arm away from Pavle. "You did not just use an Albanian pet name for him."

Pyotr nudged Cliff to sit up and he leaned forward but said nothing. His physical position only stating he was prepared for any physical challenge Jovan was known for in their younger days.

The physical part didn't come, but the Serbian words of pent up rage and animosity did. Pyotr came to his feet and the two went at it across the table. Pavle and Darko, the next two oldest, trying to find some room to call a truce went unheard.

Cliff was mortified by the heated argument, and with so many of them, some adding to the feud, others seemed to be attempting to settle it calmly. A few he wasn't sure since he didn't speak Serbian, and by the look on Sasha's and the sisters' faces, they weren't able to keep up with the argument either. But, then Jovan said something, the one thing they all understood right along with the glass he tossed.

"It's because you were fucking that Albanian monkey we had to leave home in the first place!" The glass was a bad aim glancing off the table in front of Pyotr and zinged off in another direction. Cliff saw it pass in front of his face. In a split-second, instant reaction, Cliff swung at the glass, knocking it out of the air, just inches from hitting Kimmi in the face, sending it shattering against the wall.

Pyotr had watched the glass fly like he was seeing it in slow motion. The near hit on his daughter had Pyotr raging in a flash. He jumped around the table in a flash, taking Jovan by the shirt, slung him around and into the wall.

"You son of a bitch! You've been carrying that around all this time? Why do you say this?" Pyotr growled into his brother's face.

Jovan tried to wrangle free, but Pyotr's fists were curled tight into his shirt and jacket together. There was no getting free from the brother who'd kept them all safe and protected. Not to mention, refereed all the fights between the siblings as they grew up.

"It had to be you. Why else would Papa make us flee the country?"

"Because Papa ran an underground paper printing, posting warnings of raids and sources for aid. He spoke out against Milošević. The night the police took him, he bartered for our lives. He promised to lead them to the hidden print press in exchange for his release."

"Wh-?" the stuttered word was shared by most of the Laszkovi family.

"Why did you never tell us this?" Javon stammered. His eyes white with objected horror. His voice tainted with painful betrayal.

"Because it wasn't your responsibility to know this!" Pyotr shoved into him one last time then tossed himself back. Turning, his hands raked through his hair and he bowed his head stepping away.

"Pyotr?" Pavle called their eldest brother.

Pyotr said nothing.

Pavle drew close. His expression ran deep that he had always suspected there was more to the story, but trusted Pyotr kept it to himself for a reason. "Pyotr, what happened to them?"

Pyotr glanced over his shoulder, finding a dozen set of eyes staring at him widely, their surprise no more than his pain, clearly evident on his face. He had not only sacrificed, he had carried the heaviest of burdens. "There was a raid a few days later. Word came out that several martyrs were executed on a firing line for disobeying the news blackouts, and for ridiculing Milošević directly."

"They were shot?"

"I don't know for sure, but yes, most likely."

"And you didn't think to tell us." Pavle was deeply hurt. That never in all this time had Pyotr told them what happened to their parents. Letting them assume they had died during the NATO raids months later.

"Tell you what?" Pyotr's face screwed up with the question, "That Papa not only gave up the location of the press, but the names of those involved as well?" Pyotr turned away again, his head hung low, and he leaned against the wall a moment as if needing it to steady himself. "They gave him twenty four hours. He was supposed to call everyone in the group to meet so they could be arrested. He warned as many of them as he could. Said they would be found no matter what and to use the time they had to get their families out."

"The others on the truck?" Jovan gasped, his brows pinching back with the recalled pain of leaving their lives and parents behind.

"Yes. They all sent their children away." Pyotr glanced over his shoulder, finding Jovan standing behind him.

Jovan threw himself into Pyotr's arms, his own wrapping around the man he blamed all these years for his loss, "I'm sorry. *Žao mi je.* I thought it was something else."

Pavle was there next, then the others. All gathered, one by one, piling into the hug.

(◕ᴗ◕)

Cliff was still at the table completely awe struck and moved his arm, pulling Kimmi into him, and hugged her as he watched Pyotr with his family. All ten of them, gathered around the one man that had managed to keep them together through hell and high water.

Cliff glanced at the other added family members at the table like him, seeing the same compassion, and a few teary eyes, and Cliff felt pretty damn warm and fuzzy inside right then.

The pile of Laszkovians stirred and began to break up. Pyotr's hand darting out from the thick of bodies to pat each one of his siblings, "Come on, let's move to the great room for a drink. And if there isn't enough to go around, we'll just have to wait for Jovan to go take a piss."

The family laughed, while Pyotr came back around the table, one hand out, touching Cliff's face to reassure himself then he squatted between his lover and his daughter. "You okay?" Pyotr quizzed Kimmi.

"Oh my god, is this what families do on Thanksgiving?" Kimmi asked under her breath. She had heard of family holiday horror stories before but had never been ringside for one. She didn't hold back that she found the whole thing a little more than overwhelming.

Pyotr smiled. "There's eleven of us, plus a few wives and a gaggle of nieces and nephews now. A disagreement is bound to come up. It's how we land on our feet that counts. Arguing is part of life, as long as we make sure our love for each other wins out in the end."

"So well said, Pyotr," Maggie swooned from across the table. She was one of the ones wearing tears. "Thank you, Pyotr."

Pyotr sent Maggie a warm smile and planted a kiss on Kimmi's forehead, then turned to Cliff. "And you."

Cliff raised a brow at him.

"You, I could really use a kiss from." The older Laszkovi sighed to him. Letting it show that he really did need some reassurance from Cliff that love was with him.

Cliff smiled and leaned in. Nothing pleased him more than knowing Pyotr needed him as much as he needed Pyotr.

They gathered in the great room and right away the tv was on with the football game and several of the guys were sucked into the excitement as a means to burn off the tension. The ladies gathered, putting together a game plan for shopping in the morning.

Pyotr stretched out on the sofa and Cliff took up homebase between his legs and laying back on him so he could snuggle with him.

"So what are you boys going to be doing while we're out spending the paychecks?" Maggie glanced at Pyotr while she strummed through the newspaper flyers for the best Black-Friday bargains.

Rury's boyfriend, Liam, was instantly ecstatic, "Oh, I am so going with the girls." He turned to Rury. "Hon, dear, where's the credit card?" Liam tossed a broken-wrist wave, Rury's way that got the girls laughing hard.

Rury rolled his eyes, but even that didn't stop the grin on his face as he fished out his wallet and passed over a card.

"You know how I love to shop," Liam cooed.

"God thing I can afford to let you."

"Bonus kisses." Liam blew a few over for fun.

"Just no fur coats."

"I know you like it smooth and hairless." Liam teased with a wiggle of his hips, before reaching for one of the flyers on the floor.

Kimmi hid her face behind her hands, blushing at the open banter.

"Well, Pyotr?" Maggie had not forgotten her question.

Cliff shifted to look up at him. Pyotr was in his zone, but he gave her a sleepy like smile.

"We're going out on the river."

"The river?" Maggie straightened. "Are you insane? It's freezing outside."

"You know better than that. Some men play football Thanksgiving weekend. Laskovians go sculling." Pyotr defend their exalted plans.

The room of brothers chanted out loud in response, "Real athletes row. Everyone else just plays with balls!"

"Is there room for everyone?" Jovan paused from the game to look over his shoulder.

"I have the two quads and I got the keys for the boathouse if we want to switch up for any one of the longs. You coming?"

"For a chance to row with the Greenwich Queen Champions? Wouldn't miss it for all the tea in Serbia." Jovan regaled to his brother.

Despite the outbreak earlier, Cliff knew the banter wouldn't be taken wrong. They were all really proud of the team and they deserved the notoriety that went with their new championship.

"So can I go shopping with the girls?" Kimmi looked hopeful at her brother.

Cliff felt the nudge from Pyotr before he could answer. Just a bit of encouragement to let her live it up. She would be in good hands. But his response didn't come near quickly enough when Pyotr sent another elbow nudge his way to answer.

"Okay, she can go." He chewed at the inside of his cheek, bottling up the mirth to keep her locked inside, away from the germs, and cold. And most of all, too far from his watchful eyes.

"You can give Maggie the 101 care package before they go and we'll all have our cells on us if there's a problem." Pyotr's reassurance was purely for Cliff. He didn't usually try to steer Cliff when it came to Kimmi, but he knew it would be good for her to be out and about with the girls and have a little bit of freedom from her brother. A few last new experiences.

Cliff only frowned back at him, bordering on pouting over the release he'd just granted.

"So, I really can go?" Kimmi's eyes lit up despite the weariness that had begun to set in after a long day with a house full of guests.

Pyotr didn't make a sound, nor did he nudge Cliff again. He'd given the encouragement, but as he had always said within their relationship, Kimmi was forever Cliff's responsibility.

Cliff could see she really did want to go. Nevertheless, he still wasn't all too sure of how good of an idea it was. Kimmi had already undergone three days of high elevations of chemo and radiation. Then monitored for another three. She'd only come home yesterday and was expected to return again the following Monday. He glanced at Maggie. That woman had the sweetest face he'd ever seen. And the pressed smile and the look in her eyes spoke to him. *It's okay, dear, you can make this decision.*

"You know, I can send for a wheelchair for her." Pavle pulled away from the game to make the offer, "Maggie can keep her in it, so she doesn't wear out. I know that's a concern in her condition. We could even set up for a nurse to be with her for the day."

Cliff took in a deep sigh, "No, that won't be necessary, but I think a chair would be best. But not one of the department store ones. She has to have her own."

"Done." Pavle turned to his ex-wife, "I'll make the arrangements, Mag. You'll just have to swing by my office at the hospital to pick it up."

Maggie gave Kimmi and Cliff both a warm look. She understood the concerns that had underlined the conversation, but she was glad the young man could let go a little for Kimmi's emotional benefit. Life without living, just didn't count.

Pyotr reached out taking Kimmi's chin in his fingers and pulled her around so he could see her face better.

Cliff saw the day's wager on his sister's face but knew full well she wouldn't go to bed. Not with so many people still up. "You're looking tired right now. Wanna curl up here with us?" Cliff asked. Kimmi nodded, and he and Pyotr were instantly shifting on the sofa to make room for her as she saddled over their legs and tucked herself under Pyotr's arm and wedged in between their warm bodies and the sofa. It wasn't long before the bundled family of three was sound asleep in a typical post turkey-day nap.

Pyotr woke to a flash of bright light, startling him from his slumber. He blinked his eyes open, finding an overly teary-eyed, happy Maggie beaming over him with a camera in her hand. She didn't say a word as he looked up at her, just that million-dollar-smile that likely made angels jealous— she was that warm and sweet.

His eyes went to the camera in her hands and reached a long arm for it. She hit a button then turned it around for him to see the viewer. Pyotr glanced at the image on the LCD screen of himself with Cliff out cold on his chest while Kimmi was still curled up under his arm. They'd all been sound asleep in each other's arms.

Pyotr grinned in a way he couldn't explain and handed it back. "I want a copy of that," he whispered.

"You bet'cha." Maggie's smile refreshed before tip-toeing away.

CHAPTER TWELVE

The gang of men arrived at the boat house just as the sky began to glow a greyish yellow with the coming sun. The morning air was bitter cold, and several of them bounced on their toes, huffing cloudy breaths onto their fingers as they stood on the dock and watched the team rowers get the boats ready.

"So ever row before?" Pavle was quizzing Darko's date, Maxum, for any experience. Sculling was a big thing with them, but it wasn't a huge sport with most men.

"Can't say I have," Maxum answered, his eyes glued to the bent over frame of Darko.

"Put him in the coxswain seat then," Pyotr called out, directed the others as he assigned positions. "Then Darko can take the stroke position in front of him. This way Maxum gets an up-close and personal show of his man in action."

Darko was instantly grinning to himself, happy to get the favoritism from Pyotr. It never failed to impress the man you were fucking when he was watched you row.

Pyotr, Darko, and Pavle loaded up in the eight slider scull first. Darko taking the first seat on the rudder end as Pyotr had suggested, while Pyotr himself took the first position at the bow, while Pavle took one of the center seats. The rest of the guys squatted at the edge of the dock waiting for the call to load up. Pyotr gave out a call like someone calling hut for a football pass, and he, Pavle, and Darko, in unison, leaned out away from the dock to counter the boat's listing due the loading of the rest of the crew. Rury was positioned immediately behind Darko, then Jovan. Behind Pavle sat Stanislav, Trofim, Cliff, and last was Pyotr. All held the dock's edge and Pyotr gave the okay to Darko who then helped Maxum into the coxswain seat, facing his lover.

Another call from Pyotr and they all shoved off the dock and away they went. The chant called out by Darko, Pavle, and Pyotr that set the rowing cadence for everyone else, to fall into and set the rhythm but soon changed over into conversation as they headed up stream.

"So tell me again— why is Sasha not out here with us? He is still on the team, is he not?" Jovan called out to anyone willing to answer.

"He wasn't going to risk the boys going out unsupervised," Cliff answered.

"He sure is overly possessive of them, isn't he?"

"Needs to be," Pyotr offered up the details, "Isaiah had another setback not too long ago. So Sasha's had to keep the twins under tight supervision. Taking them shopping with the girls was a way to reward them with some time out for them."

"You gotta hand it to him, though; it's a lot of responsibility having just one partner with a mental illness, but he has two, and Sasha takes good care of them. Isaac and Isaiah live a far better life with him than they would with anyone else," Darko called back.

"Yeah, I'll definitely give him that," Rury chiming in as he shook his head, "I just don't know if I could handle having two husbands."

"So, what's it feel like to be champions now?" Stanislav changed the subject.

"Feels mighty good," Trofim responded to his little brother, sitting in front of him.

"I wish I could have come down to see it." His voice trailed off and a frown came over his face that no one could see but was certain it was felt. "I've missed too many things. Sasha's wedding— the races— Pavle's divorce." They all laughed.

"So how is it you came up with the name?" Maxum asked aloud.

"That part's pretty obvious, we're all gay," Darko answered with a wry grin as they pulled at the oars in unison.

"Hey, hey, speak for yourself," Jovan retorted.

Darko laughed over his shoulder, "I meant, everyone on the team. A few even live in Greenwich Village. So that made it legit. But it started off as a goading to get another team from Greenwich Connecticut to accept a diamond challenge. That got us in the competition circuit. We kept it because once word was out, there was an all-gay male sculling team, we had guys from all over coming out to cheer us on. Girls too, actually."

"We have one of the largest fan bases outside of a collegiate team in the entire New England district," Pyotr added proudly of his team and their fans. "So the name Greenwich Queens stuck. It's legit yet rhetorical at the same time," he added in mid stroke.

"Damn, I'm sweatin' my ass off— I'm ready to lose a layer," Darko called ahead for the oars to still so he could strip off his jacket.

"Well, you got the cox'n in front of you. Put him to work," one of his brothers called back to him.

Darko let out a slight chuckle. "That'd be you." He popped his brows at Maxum.

"What am I supposed to do?" Maxum glanced around as much, or little as the case may be, in the small space he was squashed into, without disturbing the rudder handle.

"Call them to, *let it run.*"

"Let it run?"

"Yeah, only louder. So we can all hear it," Darko pressed.

Maxum straightened. "Let it run!" he called out with a perplexed expression, not knowing what it meant or what to expect, and right then all eight rowers stopped rowing, lifting their oars from the water. Darko peeled his sweater off his freshly pumped arms, bulging under the thinner thermal protection of the body armor shirt. The unhindered view earned a lip licking expression from Maxum, while several of the others followed suit.

Pyotr took advantage of the moment and slipped an arm around Cliff and pulled him back for a kiss. "Mmmm, you look incredibly sexy rowing in front of me." He kissed him once more and paired it with a nip to his cheek, "I may end up jumping you in the shower."

A call from the coxswain had Pyotr returning to position, setting his oars in line and followed in sync as the chant and swing of oars went back into play.

Pyotr watched the muscles of his lover's arms and shoulders roll with each stroke. Though, Cliff had never had a lot of muscle, he had enough to satisfy Pyotr's own preferences, and just under the strain of the oars had them pumped up like a tantalizing party favor.

But his daydream fantasizing was interrupted when some form of chaos at the tail of the boat had everyone's oars tangled like match sticks, followed by an outburst from Rury about Darko's lover pulling his cock out to tease him.

Pyotr joined in the laughter, at least, he wasn't the only pervert onboard, and Pyotr couldn't help but feel happy for his brother. Darko was more like him than any of the others and would one day make a fine possessive husband.

Cliff shot a glance over his shoulder to him; the playful dare from his blond-headed brat glinting in those grey eyes had Pyotr's own member swelling in his gym pants. "If you do, the others are going in the water," he dared him.

CHAPTER THIRTEEN

They got the 911 call that afternoon; a junky too high and the girlfriend made the call. On the ride in, the info came in, that no first responder enjoyed hearing.

Cliff was trying to get the IV in the guy's arm, but their doped-out patient was less than cooperative, and in a sudden jerk of his arm to retaliate, Cliff's hand slipped and the needle came out of the patients arm and pricked his own finger, piercing through the nitrile gloves.

Cliff sat back in his seat, staring at the droplet of blood forming on his blue latex finger then at the man. Heat and rage building in Cliff like a fast burning fuse.

Sasha stared at him with equal shock. But Sasha's brain quickly started to process the need for action, "Hurry, start pumping the blood back out to make it drain."

But their patient wasn't through with his act of insubordination. "Fuckers. You're like pigs, you think I don't know what you're thinking? Well here!" The man hawked up a mass of snot in his throat and spit it into Cliff's face.

Cliff recoiled, but there was no place to go in the small space of the ambulance. He froze with his arms out and he glared at the mucus the man had cast at him, "Stop the truck!"

"What's going on back there?" Ozzy, their driver, called back to them.

"STOP the fucking truck!"

Cliff jumped out the back before it could even come to a complete stop. A bottle of sterile saline in his hands, Cliff quickly began to squirt it over his face, keeping his eyes and mouth squeezed shut as tight as he could hold them. His mind was racing, he couldn't hold still. He could hear the car horns blaring at them, coupled with the typical New York road-rage curses. But the only thing registering in Cliff's mind was the echoing words of the call from the radio—

~~*"Be advised, subject is registered HIV positive."*~~

Oh god— Kimmi. Cliff reeled around, splashing more of the saline over his body until the bottle was empty. Still, he kept his eyes closed, he stumbled— he was off balance. Rage and anger and hate— yes, hate— "DO YOU HAVE ANY IDEA WHAT YOU'VE JUST FUCKING DONE!?" Cliff screamed at the top of his lungs.

Hands grabbed him, pulling him just as he heard a car's horn blasting too close for his own good. The hands and a voice tried to calm him. Sasha's voice— Sasha's hands— Cliff knew it was him. Sasha's hands felt like his brothers. Then Cliff smelled the sterile solution and bleach. It didn't really matter; there was still the pin prick in his finger. But, in their situation they did it anyways.

Sasha shoved a towel in Cliff's face and wiped at his eyes to dry them so Cliff could open them and see finally. When he did, they burned with pure hate for the man inside the truck.

"Fuckin' bag him!" Cliff cursed.

"Stay here! Don't move," Sasha ordered, and then jumped into the truck. Ozzy was already coming around from the driver's side, reaching back taking the ends of the sheet as Sasha handed them over and they stretched the crisp white linen sheet out over the man strapped down on the gurney and tied the corners down tight, essentially *bagging him*. It was a humane way to keep the unruly patient from spitting on them any further so they could complete the transfer to the hospital. Once there, their patient would become the problem of the emergency room, as well be arrested. Not that any of that was going to make Cliff feel any better right now.

Sasha jumped back out, corralled Cliff into the front seat of the ambulance, and they continued on.

"Fuck!" Cliff cursed from up front.

"It was just a prick. You had two sets of gloves on for precautions. So, it's a good chance it wasn't enough. You'll probably be okay," Sasha tried to console him from the back. "You didn't get the needle in his vein yet."

Cliff growled. "It was in his arm." He banged his head back against the seat several times, the anger and rage boiling in his skin. He wanted to beat the hell out of the patient. Tear his limbs off. The only thing stopping him was that Sasha was right there and there was still a good chance he would not be infected. But if he bludgeoned the man, that chance would get slim, fast. Rage soon turned to sickness as Kimmi's face flashed before Cliff's eyes. He was her donor. Her *only* donor—now, he would have to undergo AIDS testing.

"You'll have to wait fourteen days before we can run an accurate test," Kimmi's doctor talked with him when he was called down after the news of what had happened.

"Kimmi is scheduled for a bone marrow transplant in just five days!"

"Not until your tests come back negative, Cliff. I'm sorry, I know that's not what you want to hear—"

"What about the stem cells we harvested last week?"

"It's not enough. It'll buy her some time, but—"

Cliff held up his hand, he didn't need Dr. Lee telling him what he already knew. Even if they stopped the chemo treatment now, they had already destroyed too many blood cells for her to go without a full transfusion for long. He only hoped she could hold out long enough for him to get the test.

Pyotr rushed to the hospital as soon as he got the call from Sasha. He found Cliff pacing the ambulance bay, just outside the ER. But the second Cliff saw him coming, he backed into a corner, ordering Pyotr to stay back, and right then was the moment Cliff proceeded to come unraveled.

"No! Don't come near me!" Cliff cried out, backing away along the wall. "Oh god, I can't."

Pyotr stopped his pursuit, hovering just a few feet from his distraught lover. "Come here, Cliff."

"No." Cliff swatted Pyotr's hand away when he reached for him. "I can't!" His head kicked back and the trapped emotions broke out with a wail, "*Oh god, no*— I'm gonna lose you both."

Cliff crumbled to the ground. It was only then Pyotr was able to reach him without getting slapped away. He scooped his young man up in his arms, forcefully hugging him against his chest, and held tight.

"No! Goddamn you, stop! You can't touch me right now. We can't risk it."

Cliff tried to fight him off, but Pyotr caught him in his arms pulling Cliff in tighter. His arms clutching at his young lover, tightened even further as Cliff tried continuously to fight him off.

"Don't," Cliff whimpered in the trap of Pyotr's body.

Pyotr ignored Cliff's struggles and brought his head down, crushing his lips against Cliff's mouth in a forceful kiss. His tongue steeling its way inside his troubled lover's mouth before Cliff could clamp his lips tight and shut him out.

Cliff pressed hard and only barely managed to wrench his lips from him, "You can't do this," he cried and pleaded. Wanting to be in Pyotr's arms more then he wanted to be any other place in the world, but he didn't dare risk his lover's life for the sake of simple comfort.

"I can and I will. You belong to me and I shall do with you as I wish." And Pyotr came over him again, bringing their lips together to prove to his young lover that he intended to keep kissing him as he saw fit. "*Shhh, dragi* . You can't infect me with anything just by me holding you."

Thirteen days were counted out; none spent in idle waiting. Cliff had convinced Pavle to run a blood test on nearly all of them. The cancer center searched for possible alternative donors only to be turned down because of her high rate or reoccurrence. Even Diesel Gentry looked to his brothers and a few friends for a possible donor. But from the hospital's perspective, those candidates were littered with questionable lifestyles that came with automatic denials.

Cliff laid curled up next to his sister, foreheads touching as they talked in whispers like they used to when they were little kids, hiding under the sheets made into a tent while their parents argued over how they were going to pay for everything. "Tomorrow they can run the test. They said it only takes a few hours and then we'll know for sure and then I'll go straight into the sterile room for the extraction."

Tears welled up in her eyes and Kimmi shook her head.

"What do you mean no? Sure— Doc Lee says we can get started right away."

"I don't want you to do it. I mean, get the test, but do it for yourself—" Her head shook again like a short rattle, struggling just to move at all. "But not for me."

"What are you talking about?" Cliff stiffened.

"I'm saying, I don't want you to go in for the bone marrow extraction." The wells in her eyes suddenly broke in a slow stream, then dribbled down her cheek.

"Kimmi, we've done this before. It's no big deal. At least now, I have someone who's willing to kiss my ass and make my booboos better afterwards," he joked with her, hoping it would raise her spirits some. Only Kimmi didn't laugh.

"I don't want another marrow transplant," the words came out in a barely audible whisper.

Cliff stilled a moment. Even the fingers he was caressing her arm with came to a complete stop. "What are you saying?"

She smiled— soft, loving, and pained, but he could see she had already made the tough decision. "I'm saying, I want you to let me go." It was so soft, the words barely spoken, only her lips moving, "I've taken up enough of your life, now it's time for me to go."

Cliff's head was shaking, refusing what she wanted him to hear. "No. Don't say that. You're not taking up my life; you're a part of it. I can't just let you die."

"You're not. You're going to set me free." She forced a smile for him. "Please, Cliff; I already had them bring up the papers. They said I could even go home. I don't want to be sick anymore." More tears streamed down, and yet she smiled at him.

"It means nothing. I didn't authorize any papers to be signed."

"I'm nineteen. I can sign them myself." Through all the rain that glossed her eyes, there was still the sunshine he'd always seen there.

"Please, do this for me."

Cliff couldn't stop his own tears from coming, nor could he say yes to her. He just couldn't bring himself to surrender the word and for the first time since Kimmi had first started getting sick, *she* held *him*. And he buried his face under her chin and sobbed.

KIMMI'S FAREWELL PARTY

Christmas had come and gone. As did New Year's Eve, and finally Kimmi was allowed to go home for the little time she had left. However, with her blood cells completely destroyed, Kimmi only had days.

The day after they brought her home, Pyotr had the whole family over, along with friends, for a cook out in the back yard. The house transformed into a display of faux spring, decked out with a huge array of party favors and colors. Lots of streamers, tea lights, lanterns, and the smell of barbeque filled the rooms as the guys took turns watching the grill out back.

Kimmi's hospital bed had been moved out into the family room, against the French paned doors that looked out over the backyard. Several chairs had been dragged over circling around her as friends and family took turns visiting and sharing memories.

Among the friends and guests was Trenton Leos, whose hand never let go of Katianna, and with him were his brothers: Diesel, Marcus, Dane, and even Harper had arrived with them. There were even more friends from the cancer center, wearing the all too familiar teary eyed smiles, as they said goodbyes to one more friend.

(ᵔωᵔ)

   "Hey, you awake?" Cliff tiptoed up to his sister's bed.

Kimmi opened her eyes with a deep breath and managed a smile.

"There's someone here to see you."

She forced on a smile that managed to find its way through the sullen graying of her skin. "There's a house full of people."

"Yeah, but this one came special just for you." Cliff smiled at her. The deep love he felt was tearing in his eyes and he stepped away making room for Diesel.

Kimmi looked up at the rather large, muscular man who had about as many tattoos as her window had sun catchers. It wasn't until she saw the flowers in his hand with all the bright neon colors did, she realize who he was and then her smile was unstoppable. "You're my guardian angel," she beamed up at Diesel Gentry. "You came!" Her arms shot up in anticipation of a hug she would not be denied from him.

Cliff watched from across the room. His heart swelling so much it hurt and he couldn't stop the tears from flowing. Diesel had done so much for them over the last eight months and never once asked for anything back. Diesel would have gone on anonymously had it not been one of Kimmi's parting wishes to see him. Cliff almost lost it when Kimmi's arms shot up to demand a hug from Diesel, who carefully lowered to the edge of her bed and pulled her up into his, while his sister delivered a *Kimmi-hug*.

Kimmi hugged like there was no tomorrow. Perhaps because for her, she knew there would be so few. But *Kimmi-hugs* weren't sorrowful embraces, they were always happy ones, the *full of love-n-life* kind of hugs. She gave the best hugs on Earth, like snuggling up in a favorite, warm furry blanket. And they were nothing, if not brief.

Most people began to fidget in her arms after a while, but not Diesel— Cliff glanced at his watch. "Kimmi must be going for a world record. Six minutes and still going," he commented aloud when Pyotr slipped in behind him, wrapping his arms around Cliff's waist.

Later, Cliff had resumed his place at his sister's side, joining in with the conversations with her and Diesel, the three occasionally breaking out in laughter.

"So what do you think they're talking about?" Dane Masters motioned in Diesel's direction, talking with Trenton and Pyotr, while keeping a possessive arm around his androgynous brother, Vince. Occasionally using his wine glass to tease with a threat of dripping some of the contents on the blousy-like shirt his brother wore. Who, up until recently, had been known to all as Vida, but a new transition was at hand, and Vince was coming out.

"I bet he's telling stories about Walter and Ed," Trenton answered chuckling at the two.

Dane laughed almost nervously. "Yep, those stories are always entertaining."

Vida glanced up at his brother. "Who are Ed and Walter?"

Dane chuckled lightly, "A couple of WWII geezers that like to hang out at Diesel's gun shop. The shit those two pull—" he shook his head just thinking about it. "They make John and Max from that film *Grumpy Old Men* look tame. I swear, if Diesel hadn't sponsored the dorm they live in, they probably would have been thrown out a long time ago."

Pavle stepped up to join them as they all chatted leisurely, his gaze relaxing on the man with Dane considerably. "Hi, Pavle." Pavle held his hand out toward him more specifically.

Dane twisted his brother and reached out taking Pavle's hand in a firm handshake. "Dane Masters." He nodded his head to Trenton and Katianna, "This is Trenton Leos and his slave, Katianna Dumas." But Dane stopped right there with the introductions.

Pavle caught the hint but was finding it hard to take his eyes off the man he'd nt be given an introduction to. His soft blond hair fell well past his shoulders and brushed smooth. His shirt was feminine yet he left the top couple of buttons open revealing a flat chest. Pouty lips and high cheek bones gave a sweetness to his slightly squared, masculine jaw and an Adams apple. "And you?" he blurted out, disregarding Dane's attentive block.

"Vida Masters."

"Vince Masters," Dane corrected the response with a slight slur.

Vida playfully swatted at him with disregard but grinned forgivingly when the man hanging on him rolled his eyes and forced himself to glance away while he and Pavle shook hands with a soft, lingering grasp.

The matching surname didn't slip Pavle's attention and to cover his intent to flirt, he struck up the dull conversation of *them*. "So, how long have you two been together?"

"Oh—" Vida tried to straighten away from Dane's arms "We're not—"

"All our lives." Dane interrupted, his arm pulling Vida back in, and planted a big kiss on the top of his platinum blond head, loosening the hug-hold only enough to allow his brother to stand straight.

"You two seem rather— close." Pavle searched for a word that he hoped wouldn't offend, not sure which answer from them was the right one. Were they together? They almost looked like siblings. Soul mates perhaps? Certainly, looked happy like they were— the way the androgenous one's eyes glistened as he looked up at the taller Masters, holding him possessively.

Vida or Vince, another issue Pavle wasn't clear on, cleared his throat before addressing the question properly. "We're brother-sister."

"Brothers," Dane corrected with a static tone.

Brothers— brother-sister— *okay, maybe he'd had too many beers*, Pavle thought to himself, glancing down at the bottle of dark ale in his hand then back to the one who had captured his attention. But, *ah* hell, the very glow of the beautiful face standing before him had caught his attention the second the androgynous creature strolled into the house and Pavle didn't have a clue as to how to act upon his attraction.

Dane's arm only tightened further, seeing the attention Vida-Vince was getting, and that made the man's face glow. But for Pavle, it stirred something in him, despite the unusual closeness between the two in front of him, *Vida-Vince* made his dick hard. And that was something he hadn't felt for another in such a long time. And he decided it was worth a rather forward inquiry. "Are you two always this close?" And almost instantly cleared his throat nervously when not only did Dane and Vida look at him oddly, but so did Pyotr.

Dane pivoted, "You see those two over there?" He pointed with an outstretched arm toward Cliff and his sister snuggled into each other's arms, laughing and cuddling, despite the rest of the world then he looked at Pavle. "Would you ask the same of them?"

Pavle swallowed hard, knowing where he had made the fatal flaw. Pyotr would smack him on the back of his head were he still a young lad right now. "No."

"No amount of affection is too much for my brother," Dane planted another kiss on Vida's temple.

Vida took the proffered affection willingly, even if he felt a little silly under his brother's overzealous show. But Vida knew something about his brother and that was that Dane was hurting inside. Something no one else, but his brothers-in-arms, would be aware of. Dane didn't see a dying girl, he saw a young man losing the sister he had always tended after, and Dane felt a kinship to the events that were about to happen all the way into his own heart.

Within the Dominion of Brothers, they all knew Dane would not fare well if anything happened to him. So, Vida stayed right where he was, smothered by his big brother's arms, even if it meant missing out on the possible interest of the handsome man.

The day was winding down, while some had gone home, Trenton and Diesel still remained as did most of Pyotr's brothers that lived in the area.

They were gathered in the living room, nursing harder tonics than the beers from earlier. Katianna was sitting with Kimmi reading what could have only been an excerpt from one of her erotica romances, made clear by the bright red blush on the young girl's face, and the double-handed hiding as Kimmi gasped in youthful innocence.

Pyotr watched as his friend, Trenton, still watched his Unicorn like a hawk watched its prey. The kidnapping of Katianna was still showing its teeth in his friend's actions and Pyotr wondered how this affected their lifestyle of D/s. "Trenton, we're good friends, but I worry over the effects from the kidnapping on you and Katianna's relationship. Does this concern you? Has it caused doubts for the two of you and your arrangement?"

Trenton shook his head and a deep rooted expression of contentment came over his face. "If anything, it has enforced our bond."

"And how about the rest? How has she recovered from her trauma?"

Trenton took in a long breath, glancing back over at her. Clearly it had been one of the hardest, most painful things the man had ever endured. War and battle are one thing, but coming so close to losing the one you love, especially when their bond was still so new, was quite another, and could have grave consequences on a man's soul.

"The nightmares are few and far between." Trenton began to explain, "I can soothe her without ever waking her up now." He looked back at Pyotr, attempting a confident expression, "She never steps from mine or Diesel's sight anymore."

Pyotr only nodded, but he did so with assurance. Such nightmares were not expected to vanish overnight, and that Trenton had managed her therapy on his own was impressive. It also further revealed the man's knowledge and deep caring for his woman.

CHAPTER FOURTEEN

Kimmi's hospital bed remained in the family room, now transformed into her bedroom. She slept in front of the French doors, which let her enjoy the outdoors whenever she wanted and never be separated from the rest of the family. Nearly all the glass panes of the door within reach had been painted over by her.

The friends and guests not only came to say farewell to her but helped her to see them finished.

The next day, Kimmi's passing came.

Cliff had been curled up at her side, Pavle attended to her comfort, having exchanged out the empty bottle of morphine for a full one that morning, enough to hold her over for a couple of days and keep her comfortable.

Kimmi was mumbling, describing to Cliff about her next world adventure, using the things she had discovered over the internet to paint her fantasy as she traveled first class on the back of a whale to Hawaii to see the volcano eruptions from the water, then for a hike through the rainforest and pick exotic flowers to weave together into a crown for her head. Her evening stop finished off with a luau with food and dancing— and she kissed a pretty boy. At first light, she was back on her whale heading for her next destination.

Kimmi's entire life had been fabrications of her imagination. Only, now, her imaginary trips had grown more elaborate and exotic, ever since Pyotr had come into their lives. She'd never gotten to finish school because she was always so sick, so at her request, Pyotr taught her new things. He let her pick the topic then he filled her head with as much as he could until she was ready for the next topic. She got to know all the animals of the sea and all kinds of places around the globe.

Pyotr stayed at Cliff's side the whole time, like the mother hen he was. He listened to her story as she tried to share it, half dazed from the morphine given to keep her comfortable. There were frequent long pauses between the details as she drifted in and out of sleep. Each time, somehow, she managed to pick up right where she left off, before dozing off again.

Pyotr recalled when he was teaching her about Tibet and the Tibetan beliefs. She was completely enraptured with it when she learned they believed in reincarnation and she decided she wanted to go there, so she could make a wish that she would come back and be a healthy girl. That way she could grow up and be a dancer or maybe she'd still be an artist, only she wanted to create the stained glass windows found in the large chapels. In her new life, she'd get married, have lots of babies, and take vacations to different countries. However, it was hardly a month ago when she confessed to Pyotr she wanted to change her wish. She didn't want to come back if it meant her life would be any different than what it was. She didn't want to live without her brother; she didn't want to risk having a life with one less ounce of time or love the two of them shared together. So, the only wish she had now was that after she was gone, Cliff would find peace, and go on living, and be happy.

Curled into her brother's chest, their fingers stitched together in a seamless hold, Pyotr kissed the top of his daughter's head over and over as she wove her magical journey for them.

It was right about the time when her story had her arriving in Tibet, to climb the steps to the Labrang Monastery so she could spin all the colorful prayer wheels, that her narration stopped—

A half hour later, Kimmi Patterson slipped away, and the silence in the room soon broke with the muffled wails of her brother.

CHAPTER FIFTEEN

Weeks had gone by and Pyotr, as promised, stayed at Cliff's side, together they mourned and comforted each other. However, Cliff also put their sexual relationship on hold, clinging to his fears that he would infect Pyotr and lose him, too.

Cliff had just gotten out of the shower when Pyotr barged in on him completely naked and beautifully hard.

Pyotr was instantly grabbing Cliff, lifting and setting him on the counter. Pyotr tore the towel from Cliff's waist and lifted his legs in his arms, trapping him in his hold.

"No, don't do this." It was hardly the protest Cliff meant, but he loved Pyotr's body and even more, loved feeling it against his own. He was starved, yearning to be subdued, and possessed by him, and his resistance was breaking down.

"You've had two tests run. Both came back negative., I won't let you push me away any longer," Pyotr growled intent to keep Cliff in his arms.

Cliff's hand went up, slapping against Pyotr's chest while the other went stiff behind him, holding his body up. "How do you know about the tests?"

"I had Pavle check your file."

"That's cheating."

"Yes, it's cheating. But you can't keep pulling away from me— I love you too much to let you go." Pyotr's very confession floored Cliff and his hand softened against Pyotr's demands.

Pyotr lifted Cliff's legs higher and spread them, positioning himself between them until the head of his cock rested against Cliff's tight, little hole. "If there is any reason that would make this rape, say it now."

He almost called out a color, but it was too soon, so stick per his bad habits, Cliff said nothing. Pyotr took it as he willed and Cliff felt the slick slide of his lover's cock, and he almost had to let loose a bratty smile that Pyotr would go to such lengths to pre-prep for a spontaneous invasion, and not a moment passed between him when he felt his lover's cock slowly fill him.

Pyotr pressed over him, taking Cliff's mouth in the same motion. They both moaned, while Pyotr took on a more growling type as his hips began rocking back and forth against Cliff's body, the hard shaft stretching with a mind boggling mix of pleasure and pain from being so tight.

Their tongues tangled in a deep kiss then released each other so they could catch their breaths. Cliff's back slammed against the mirror, bending his head in a near unbearable position as Pyotr's rhythm grew aggressive, plowing against his inner walls. Cliff's scrotum caught in the tight friction.

"Put your arms around me." Pyotr growled and when Cliff did, Pyotr's arms flexed under his legs and lifted, carrying his younger lover out and into the bedroom, each step sending Pyotr's cock into Cliff's ass further.

He felt Pyotr's thigh against his ass as his knee went up on the bed and then down, they went. Cliff felt the bed hit his back and Pyotr came down over him, bringing his legs up in the cradle of Pyotr's arms, essentially lifting Cliff's ass off the bed for easy drilling.

His lover kissed and licked his lips between gasps as Pyotr drove every carnal inch of his hard rod into Cliff's tight shaft, sending them both toward a fast release. His own cock slapping against his belly, engorged to an impossible purplish-red and dripping pre-cum onto his belly.

"Dammit, *dragi*, I'm going to cum too soon. You've made me hold out for so long." Pyotr nipped Cliff's lips and chin repeated between growling breaths, "You're so tight, I don't think I'll be able to hold out for you."

Cliff reached up wrapping his hands around the back of Pyotr's neck, pulling him down for a deep kiss, tasting the hunger and need there. "Then cum inside me. I don't deserve to cum with my *Glavar* after making you wait." Cliff made his first attempt to talk dirty for his lover, which earned him a gruff smile from Pyotr.

"Oh, you'll cum tonight. I'm not done with you yet." And just then Pyotr's head kicked back as he roared out.

Cliff felt the pulsing in his ass and he willed his muscles to tighten around the thick cock, winning another ragged expression from the man.

Pyotr released Cliff's legs and lowered until Cliff was pinned under the dead weight of his lover. He caressed the domineering man's head and kissed him, enjoying the exhausted after quakes that shook against him, smiling because they all belonged to him.

The rest of their night was spent fulfilling their desires for each other's bodies and when sated exhaustion claimed them, Cliff drifted to sleep wrapped in Pyotr's arms and legs. The man Cliff loved more than he thought he ever would, whispered in his ear, "I got you."

EPILOGUE

It was early summer, Cliff stood on the deck of the whale watching tour boat with his forever lover, Pyotr, at his side. A gentle arm placed around his shoulders as he held the stained-glass Tiffany box, which just moments ago, had held Kimmi's ashes until they could make the trip so she could be with the whales. Now, the box he hugged to his chest was empty and yet full at the same time.

Cliff leaned back against Pyotr as they stared out on the ocean, watching the whales drift back into the distance as the boat came about to head back into port. Pyotr's strong arms wrapped around him gently, like they belonged there and nowhere else.

Letting his sister go was the hardest thing he had ever done in his life. But, he didn't have to go through it alone. Pyotr was with him and would continue to be with him for however long that was going to be, and if he had anything to say about it, it was going to be forever, and then some. His reached up to grasp the arm that hugged across his chest and Cliff let out a deep sigh.

"*Dragi*?"

Cliff let out another long sigh, "I'm going to always miss her."

Pyotr nuzzled against the dark blond hair of his lover. "We both will."

"You think maybe one day we can go to the place in Tibet just for her?"

"If you like. Yes, we can plan for it. However, this year we've been invited down to the Island Resort with Diesel and Trenton."

Cliff bent his head to the side and looked up at Pyotr over his shoulder. "He's going after that guy, Paris, isn't he?"

Pyotr nodded softly. "Yes, I believe that is his plan."

Cliff felt a slight mischievous smile coming on as he thought about all the things he had heard about the adults-only resort, "I hear you can have sex anywhere you want on the island. And they have employed subs to serve the guests."

"*You* would be my only *robovati* while we were there." Pyotr's lips nudged against Cliff's head.

Cliff's gaze drifted back out to the water and the life he had been a part of drifting on the horizon's deep navy blue surface. Heartache still lingered, but he didn't expect it to ever fade or dispel any new day-dreaming. A gift he learned from Kimmi. "What does *robovati* mean?"

Pyotr pulled Cliff's head back to look in his eyes. "*My* slave."

Cliff turned in Pyotr's arms to face him and leaned in, pressing against the hard body that wrapped around him possessively. Cliff recalled one afternoon coming home from work and dragging Pyotr on top of him in a playful display right there in front of his sister, as if it had been the most natural thing to do, and it was.

Cliff tilted his head to look up at blue eyes already awaiting him. He rocked his hips forward to reveal an extra detail that grew hard against Pyotr's body in a display of his rapidly developing acquiescence to their mutual growing fondness for exhibitionism. "Maybe we should practice a little before we go—" he gave Pyotr a bratty grin. "Just in case, *Glavar?*"

Pyotr let out a lusty growl of approval and hugged him tight, "Just in case, *dragi .*"

TO BE CONTINUED—

ABOUT THE AUTHOR

We Came— We Saw— and then we made it sexy.

And that's pretty much how the Twins came to write Erotic Romances and Dark Fantasies. Both Talon and Tarian have been writing together since they were kids, challenging and competing with each other, and always each other's biggest supporters.

Writing has always been an affair creating fictions of Dark Apocalyptic Fantasy and Film Scripts in Action/Drama and Sci-Fi. It wasn't until they began an Ancient History Fantasy together that the works turned to the Erotic Genre and they've been hooked ever since. However, the final product comes out as richly detailed as we believe all stories should be created: holographic worlds of love, pain, frustration, and challenges beyond the every day. We believe a good story should take you on an emotional ride, pluck your heart strings, and zing you about until you're dizzy. All for readers to submerse themselves into and escape from their day when they need or desire, and to whet your appetite for more.

So, make sure to reserve plenty of private time, pour a glass of wine, and find a cozy spot, because as Talon always says—

" I'm about to make you wet

Talon ps.

ROUGH ATTRACTION

THE DOMINION OF BROTHERS SERIES: BOOK 4

MM-Romance / Billionaire Romance / Smoking Hot Bad Boy with a Besotted Heart / Erotic-Romance / When You're the Affair / Raw / Sexy Car Collection / Family Bonds / Sexy Men Row / Smouldering & Scolding Burn Right Out the Gate / Extreme Heat / Explicit Language

Like brimstone and caramel. When two men come together with a Rough Attraction that burns as fast as Nitro-fuel in their veins, it's hard to find the cruise control and trust that they can make this last for the long run.

Life and relationships aren't always neat and clean, or come in perfect little packages. Maxum St. Laurents knows this all too well. After being in a four-year relationship that does everything but bring him pleasure and fulfillment, he finds himself struggling to keep working at it. It doesn't help matters that the man who satisfies every need and want he could have is the man he is having an affair with. And for Maxum, affairs don't translate into long term relationships.

Darko Laszkovi just couldn't help himself when he spotted the handsome man ranting over a flat tire on the side of the road. Moreover, he couldn't be happier when the reward turned into an insatiable lover he hoped to keep for the long run. But, despite the rough attraction that holds them to each other like power-magnets, when Maxum struggles to let go of a relationship that doesn't work, Darko's patience and understanding that we aren't always where we want to be, gets tested to the max.

5-Stars! ~ "Often-times when stumbling around looking for a new book, I find myself blindly groping the shelves between the spaces of my previous purchases, hoping to find the rare gem to fill the void left by my previous literary adventure. But not this time. What started as a curiosity has latched on to the Dominion of Brothers' series with a passion that won't let go!" ~ Author Nick Hasse

EXCERPT FROM CHAPTER ONE

Darko cruised along the highway, keeping to the right lane. It was morning traffic time and he was not in such a hurry to put him and his chopper into the death race 2000 against New York's finest. At least that's what it typically felt like when trying to dodge the all too many *gotta get there first* zigzag drivers of a typical New York morning commute. Let them have it. As for him, he'd get to work when he got there and that's all it ever was for him.

The morning was just like any other. That is until he spotted the striking mancandy stranded on the side of the road, cursing at a new model Mercedes. Even the feuding expression on the man's face as he passed, had Darko licking his lips and his cock itching to reach out and touch someone. *Dayyum* Both convinced him instantaneously the man was worth a day's good deed and he quickly pulled off into the emergency lane, turned his bike around and rode back down the shoulder to the car and his beau-in-distress.

He kicked the motorcycle into idle in front of the Mercedes, swung a leg over, and strolled up to the side of the car with a gait that spoke more about cocky seduction than mechanical know-how. Pulling the gauntlet glove free from one hand, Darko let his fingers drift lightly over the glossy paint, as if to caress her curves. The car was so new, he could smell it, even on the highway of rushing traffic and its acrid stench of exhaust fumes.

He glanced down to inspect the rear tire— flat as a twink's chest, however, the *man* was anything but. Tall, perhaps just breaching six feet, this would put the man, eye to eye with him— sun-streaked, golden-brown hair and completely out of place with the polished exterior of this man. Maybe he groomed it back nice and smooth this morning, or maybe not. Regardless it was now disheveled in his aggravation.

The hint of tan to the man's face and hands marked him for an outdoors man in favorable weather, and the stark muscles hiding under the expensive looking, light grey suit and crisp, white shirt, said he was in good enough shape for some serious sheet rumbles. Of course, as far as Darko's assessment went, it wasn't hurting matters at all, that the man was packing a sweet looking ass inside the tailored slacks either.

Darko bit back the impulse to lick his lips, but the view of eye candy the man exuded was worth the stop already.

"Looks like you got a flat?"

The man spun around. "Obvious is it?" Not at all amused, nor gathering too quickly he was about to be rescued.

Oh, and he's got some fire to boot, Darko thought to himself and now his cock was more than itching for a scratch or two from this brisling man. Getting to romp around with Paris on more than one or two occasions had certainly cranked up his appetite putting him on the manhunt for a new playmate. But back to the rescue at hand— "You need some help?" Darko turned sincere in the offer.

"I can change my own tire, if I could just find the fucking tool kit to do it with." The disgruntled man spun on his heels, throwing his hands up in the air in a shouted gesture towards the car, more frustrated with himself than anything else it would seem. The hands lowered, landing at his hips, and he turned back to the offer of assistance. "I've had the car all of half a day and already it's got a flat and I can't find anything." All that fire, in a blink, leveled off to an admission of defeat. *Control at its finest in this one.*

A few of the golden highlights of hair now hung misplaced around his face, touching smooth round cheeks that softened a hard stare. A pair of lips, despite tightening into a grimace presently, were absolute kiss-candy as far as Darko was concerned. Just then the man's eyes caught the light of the late morning rising sun. Brown would not be the color Darko'd use to describe them, because when the man looked at him, they lit up like coins tempered with a mix of copper and bronze. The coloration reminded him of Tiger's-Eye stone. He liked how they shimmered, glancing at him. Moreover, Darko liked how his eyes dropped to check him out just as his own gaze was drifting down for another appraisal of the frame underneath the handsome face that just caught his breath, mm-hmm— *dayyum.* Darko soaked up the sight and then finally offered a smirk of understanding, "My brother had one of these."

"It's my first. Will certainly be my last as well," Mister-knight-in-shining-armor threw out a few vows of retribution.

Darko stepped up, helping himself, where he opened the door, reached behind the headrest of the driver's seat, and pressed the hidden concealed button. There was a soft click under the rear seat and when he lifted it, it exposed the hidden compartment there. Inside, he fetched a black bag that would make the job of rescuing his rough tempered, knight-in-*shiny*-armor all the easier.

He strolled back around toward the rear of the car but not passing up on the chance to brush against the man's backside as he passed in order to steal a frisk with the same fingertips, he used to feel up the car. It almost seems like a game of *tag your it*, when his beau-in-distress followed right behind him and might have chanced a touch of his own when he stepped in close to watch.

Darko began assembling the extended crank bar. "You see, the snobs that designed the car decided they didn't want to see the tools or the spare tire. They thought the sight of them marred the rich physic of the car's design." He lined the extension bar through an indention just above the bumper and pushed in until it caught and he began to crank it around.

His beau-in-distress bent over and could see the dark object lowering down from the under carriage. His spare tire.

Darko dropped down, reached under, unfastened the caddy and tugged the tire out from under the car.

Another twenty minutes later and Darko had the car good as new. Nor did he miss to notice the man was eyeing him now about as hot and heavily as he had him.

"You don't know how much I appreciate this." His rescued-man glanced at the watch that might have cost more than the car. "I might actually make my meeting after all." He watched as Darko placed the flattened tired into the trunk along with the bag of tools. Those glinting eyes tracking more so on the cords of Darko's arms as they flexed with the movement than on the tire being placed in his car. "I'm not sure how to repay you—" he pulled a business card from his lapel pocket. "But if there's anything you could—"

Darko twisted, grabbing the knight by his suit coat and yanked their bodies to collide together. His mouth instantly crashing over the other man's, in an avaricious kiss. Darko licked over his lips, soliciting entry and with barely a note of hesitation, his knight gave it to him. The feisty and richly dressed businessman tasted like one of those fancy coffees and a hint of fruit jam on toast, but it was his tongue that had Darko swelling in his pants. Because the man consciously kissed back; the caress of his tongue was powerful, hungry, and completely pliable against his own, as if this man was made to fit him, like a pair of rich leather gloves. He could just imagine the man fucking with a pair on and that visual put a finality to his impending hard-on.

Darko released the suit coat, gliding down the man's arm until he clasped around his knight's hand, and moved it to grope the established erection in Darko's jeans. And for a tasty treat, Darko gave him a sample of his plaid hips, rocking forward, to grind the hard bulge of his cock into the man's palm.

Darko let out a groan and an embarrassed smile broke over his face. *Grrrhhh*— that had just been too damn good, striking when the man was least expecting it. He was about to move in for another kiss when Darko realized what he'd done to knight's suit. He leaned back, glancing down, making a slight clicking noise through his lips and then stepped back. The suitcoat and white shirt were now ruined with black smudges of tire soot from Darko's hands.

The man's eyes, burnishing with the same heat Darko'd just felt himself, dropped in response, discovering the same exact condition in which the kiss had precisely left him in.

Quickly, Darko snatched the business card still in his knight's hand and pulled the fancy pen from the man's shirt pocket, leaving more smudges. "Looks like I messed up your pretty clothes." Making no actual apology, Darko scribbled over the backside of the card then tucked it back into the man's shirt pocket, along with the pen. His hand lingering just long enough to let his fingers feel the firm body behind the shirt and tweak over the hard nipple hidden there. Yet again, leaving further evidence of Darko's touch in a hand-print of grime. "That's my address. Be there for dinner. Tonight. Bring the suit— and I'll pay for the dry cleaning. Stand me up, and the suit is your problem." He grinned; a rather self-satisfied smile that held no hint that he might actually feel bad for messing up the man's expensive clothes.

As storm brewed on that face— still shocked and smoldering from the kiss held back any horror or rage that it was at the price of his threads.

Darko turned, heading back for his ride.

He sat on his chopper, closing up his leather jacket and pulling his gloves back on, all while he watched the reflection of the man behind him through his rearview mirror. His knight wore the expression of a well kissed man and Darko was feeling all his bets on it would be enough to bring him calling.

DISCOVER THESE OTHER TITLES BY TALON PS & TARIAN PS

DOMINION OF BROTHERS SERIES
Becoming His Slave
Domming the Heiress
A Place for Cliff
Rough Attraction
Taking Over Trofim
Right One 4 Diesel
Touching Vida~Vince

(ᵔᵜᵔ)

LA SERIE DES FRERES DU DOMINION - {French Edition}
Devenir Son Esclave - Partie 1 & 2
Dominer l'Heritiere
Un Havre pour Cliff
Attirance Brutale

(ᵔᵜᵔ)

QUANTUM MATES:
Pt 1~ What Torin Wants

(ᵔᵜᵔ)

DEAR SOLDIER SERIES:
Dear Soldier, With Love
Dear Soldier, With Love II: A Lost Soldier Named Grey

(ᵔᵜᵔ)

LYCOTHARIAN COLLECTION:
Bond of the Lycaon Concubine

(ᵔᵜᵔ)

TALON's KEEP COLLECTION:
Feral Dream by Talon ps
Danny's Dom by Nick Hasse

(ᵔᵜᵔ)

That's My Ethan

(ᵔᵜᵔ)

Muse Me Only
Inspire Moi Seulement {French Edition}

THE TEDDY BEAR COLLECTION:
Their Plane from Nowhere
Big Spoon & Teddy Bear
Ivan vs Ivan
TIME: Wounds All Heal
Shaggin' the Dead

THE SADOU ORDER – A Dark Taboo Series
Perfect Boy / Perfect Son

TARIAN ALSO WRITES UNDER THE FOLLOWING
PEN NAMES FOR SEPARATE GENRES:

STEPHAN KNOX ~ *Historical Fantasy And Post Apocalyptic Sci Fi*

Anáil Dhragain (Dragon's Breath)

Keeping With Destiny

ROCK HARDING ~ *Adult Coloring Books*

The Adventures of Hugh Jorgan

CONNECT AND FOLLOW THE TWINS:

WWW.Talon-ps.com

Milton Keynes UK
Ingram Content Group UK Ltd.
UKHW020128070524
442290UK00014BC/619